The Voyage of Promise

"Kay has a way with language and shows such passion through her writing that you feel as though you are right there with Grace."
—Robin's Nest Reviews

The Voyage of Promise

Promise

Book 2 of The Grace in Africa series

Kay Marshall Strom

Abingdon Press fiction
a novel approach to faith

Nashville, Tennessee

The Voyage of Promise

Copyright © 2010 by Kay Marshall Strom

ISBN-13: 978-1-4267-0212-9

Published by Abingdon Press, P.O. Box 801, Nashville, TN 37202

www.abingdonpress.com

Published in association with the Books & Such Literary Agency,
Janet Kobobel Grant, 5926 Sunhawk Drive, Santa Rosa, CA 95409,
www.booksandsuch.biz.

Cover design by Anderson Design Group, Nashville, TN

Library of Congress Cataloging-in-Publication Data

Strom, Kay Marshall, 1943–
    The voyage of promise / Kay Marshall Strom.
        p. cm. — (The Grace in Africa series ; bk. 2)
    ISBN 978-1-4267-0212-9 (trade pbk. : alk. paper)
    1. Women slaves—Fiction. 2. Slave trade—Fiction. 3. Africa—Fiction.
I. Title.
    PS3619.T773V69 2010
    813'.6—dc22

                            2010023705

Scripture quotations are taken from the King James or Authorized Version of the Bible.

Excerpts appear from John Newton's "Thoughts upon the African Slave Trade" from *The Posthumous Works of the Late Rev. John Newton*, vol. 2 (Philadelphia: W. W. Woodward, 1809).

Text excerpts noted by italics in chapter 15 are taken from *The Parliamentary History of England: From the Norman Conquest in 1066 to the Year 1803*, 36 vol., William Cobbitt, ed. (London: T. Curson Hansard, 1806-1820) and Malachy Postlethwayt's *The Advantages of the Slave Trade* (London, 1746; updated edition 1772). Speakers for each quotation are identified in the text. Spelling and punctuation have been edited for ease of reading.

Printed in the United States of America

1 2 3 4 5 6 7 8 9 10 / 15 14 13 12 11 10

Please join me in prayer and action for the 12 million people who today still live as slaves— fully three times as many as in 1792.

Acknowledgments

So many people contribute to the writing of a book, from the advisors (agent Janet Grant) and wonderful editors (Barbara Scott) to patient family members who never quit encouraging (Lisa, Jo Jeanne, Mom) to faceless people I only know through the Internet who lend their expertise in specific areas (Dale, the expert sailmaker).

Thank you, thank you, to every one of you!

I want to specifically thank Kathy Force, whose endless patience and encouragement, as well as keen eye for detail and willingness to point out the places that "just don't work," have meant so much to me. Kathy knows Grace almost as well as I do!

Thank you to my husband, Dan Kline, my chief encourager, main editor and critic, and my best friend.

1

West Africa

1792

The African sky sizzled a deep orange as the blistering sun sank across the wall. All day long one *griot* after another had stood before the village, each storyteller taking his turn at weaving together a piece of the tale of how a few African captives had outsmarted and outfought the powerful white slave man in his own slave fortress and won freedom for many. Each storyteller did his best to make his piece of the story the most dramatic, the most spectacular, the most breathtaking of all. Each one decorated his tale with songs and poems and gorgeously crafted words, so that when the entire story-tapestry was complete, his part would shine more brightly than all the others. And each storyteller's efforts were rewarded with energetic chants and cheers from the crowd.

Grace, settled comfortably between Mama Muco and Safya, grabbed at her little son who was once again doing his best to wriggle away from her. "Stay close, Kwate," she warned. Grace tried to be stern with the little one, but even as she scolded, a smile tugged at the edges of her voice. Never in her life had she been as happy as she was at that moment.

As the sun pitched low on the stifling evening, as the feast goats crackled in the roasting pit, as children threw beetles into the fire to toast and then dig out and pop in their mouths, drums beat the celebration into a fever pitch. People had poured in from villages far and near to join the celebration and bring offerings for the ancestors, for the great rebellion was a part of their lives too. Their *griots* came along and jostled for a chance to stand before the people and weave in their own village's piece of the story. And because it is in the nature of a storyteller to be a gossip, each one tried to outdo the others in passing along the latest news about the restoration of the slave fortress, Zulina. A new white man ran it now, one announced. He was called by the name of Hathaway, and he was a harder man than Joseph Winslow ever was.

Grace caught her breath. *Jasper Hathaway? The man her parents had tried to force her to marry?*

Another storyteller jumped to his feet. "The beautiful Princess Lingongo," he said, "even now she sits on the royal chair of her people beside her brother. I heard it from one who saw it with his own eyes."

Grace gripped Mama Muco's arm. "Mother is alive!" she gasped. "How can it be?"

Mama Muco kept her attention fixed on the *griot*.

Thinking Mama Muco had not heard her, Grace shook Mama's arm and said, "Did you hear that? Did you?"

Mama Muco refused to look her way. Only then did Grace understand; this news came as no surprise to Mama.

"Does Cabeto know?" Grace asked. When Mama Muco still did not answer, Grace demanded, "What other secrets are being kept from me?"

"We cannot control what happens around us any more than we can change what happened to us in the past," Mama Muco said to Grace. "All we can do is decide how we will live our own lives. Our life here in this village is good. Let us be happy and give thanks to God for this day."

Far down along the village's stone wall beside the wide-open rusty gate, sixteen-year-old Hola shuffled impatiently, his musket propped against the wall. "I want to hear the stories too," he complained to Tetteh, who stood guard with him. "And I want a fistful of that goat meat before the good part is all gone!"

"You have heard those same stories every year for the last five years," said Tetteh, who was two years older and half a head taller.

"But every year the *griots* have more tasty bits to tell us," Hola insisted. "Besides, every one of the last five years I have had to stand guard, even though no one has ever tried to do us harm. So what would it hurt for you and me to take turns at the gate tonight? I'll go listen to the stories for a while, then I'll come back and you can go listen."

Tetteh shrugged. "We should not disobey our elders. But if you are not gone too long, I suppose . . ."

Hola was out of sight before Tetteh could finish.

But even as Hola slid noiselessly in behind a clutch of other young men, the last storyteller finished weaving his tale and the drums pounded out *durbar*! Celebrate!

Mama Muco, full of wisdom and years, stood up and danced her way over to the fire. Safya, with her gentle ways and the look of sleep forever on her eyes, got up and joined Mama, clapping her hands and shuffling in time to the drums. Ama, who had only recently come to the village with her two brothers, followed. Then, one by one, other women shuffled up and joined the growing dance line.

"Come on, Grace!" Mama called out.

But Grace, grinning self-consciously, hugged little Kwate to herself and shook her head. She was glad to have an excuse to stay out of the dance. She enjoyed watching, but the fact was, even after five years she didn't understand African dances. Whenever she tried to participate, she looked every bit as awkward and out of place as she felt. *There is no African in your hands or feet, Grace,* her mother used to tell her. *They are all English.* Evidently her mother was right.

Tawnia, who was almost twelve, leapt to her feet and pranced toward the end of the line, but Mama caught the girl by the shoulder and gave her a gentle shove back.

"Child, you are not yet a woman," Mama scolded. Yet as Tawnia stomped away, Mama chuckled.

The men sat together in small groups and watched the women dance. Suddenly Cabeto jumped up. As Grace tossed back her auburn-splashed raven hair and laughed out loud and little Kwate clapped his plump hands, Cabeto waved his arms and danced with an awkward limping gait toward another group of men who had just helped themselves to roasted goat meat. He tore the shirt off his back and threw it down in front of an older man with graying hair and a sturdy round face.

"You, Tuke!" Cabeto called, his handsome face glowing in the firelight. "Will you be brave enough to dance?"

Tuke jumped to his feet. His arms flying wildly, he kept right on chewing as he danced over to a group of young men and threw his shirt down in front of them. Cabeto roared with laughter, and everyone else joined in as Hola, the youngest of them all, answered the challenge. He jumped up, tore off his shirt, and danced more outrageously than anyone.

"Dance, Hola!" Tawnia yelled, and everyone else took up the chant.

Tetteh, alone at the gate, struggled to see what was going on. Why was everyone calling Hola's name? Tetteh had to admit that Hola was right when he said that standing guard was the same as doing nothing at all. There had never been a threat to the village. Maybe Tetteh would also go and watch the celebration. Just for a few minutes, perhaps . . .

When the dancing finally stopped, Chief Ikem, his walking stick grasped tightly in his wizened arm, stepped forward. He stood directly in front of the fire. Shadows of dancing flames reflected on his midnight-black face. They seemed to bring to life the intricate tattoos etched across his forehead and down both his cheeks, the markings that had so terrified Grace when she first saw them in the dim light of the dungeon.

The chief raised his staff over his head, and the drums silenced. Flames roared upward, sending a shower of sparks soaring into the sky.

"Five years past, in this season when all sweet potatoes be dug, we be a small band of survivors from the rebellion," Chief Ikem said. "No hope be left in us."

Instinctively, Grace hugged her son close. How well she remembered. Back then, they were newly released from their chains in Zulina slave fortress. She and Cabeto and the others whose talk she could understand, and Ikem and his old wife who spoke a strange tongue and held to different ways. Ikem, who pleaded for peace but fought so valiantly for freedom. When the band of survivors founded a new village, they looked to him, the elder man of proven wisdom, to be their chief.

"Five years past, when all sweet potatoes be dug, we work together to raise a village out of the ashes left by the slave trader and the killer lioness. But now, those years lie with the ancestors. Tonight, with all sweet potatoes dug, we celebrate a happy village of peace and love."

Had the dream of peace and love not come so persuasively from the wise lips of Chief Ikem, someone might have noticed an owl soar through the firelight and perch in the highest branches of the ghariti tree that brings life to the people, and so recognized the harbinger of calamity. Had Hola and Tetteh lived enough years to understand that just because something had not yet happened, it didn't mean it never would happen, they might have closed the gate in the wall, slipped the bolt into place, and stood fast at their post. Had the fire not roared so brightly that it blinded the villagers' eyes to everything else, at least one person in the crowd might have noticed that not all the trees were motionless, as trees should be on a breath-lessly still night.

But none of that was to be. It was a night of *durbar*. A night of celebration. The fire crackled, the drums called for festivity, and everyone laughed out loud and clapped their hands and rejoiced together in the happy village of peace and love.

2

In the simmering glow of early dawn, Grace sighed rest-lessly in her sleep. Little Kwate squirmed on the mat next to her and nestled his fluffy head further into the crook of her arm. Mama Muco, freshly awake, stretched out her morning aches. She paused for an extra moment to take in Cabeto's rhythmic breathing, then she silently hefted herself from her sleeping mat of banana leaves and padded her way outside the thatched-roof mud hut that the family shared. She would start the morning fire, just like she did every other morning.

Only this morning wasn't like every other. This morning slavers lay in wait. They pounced quickly, but not quickly enough to keep Mama from bellowing out a call of alarm.

Cabeto lunged for his musket, but before he could ready it, two Africans rushed into the hut and threw a net over him. He kicked and fought, but his struggles only entangled him more.

"Run, Grace!" Cabeto yelled. "Take the boy and run!"

But it was too late for Grace. It was too late for all of them.

Clutching her screaming son, Grace grabbed for Cabeto as the slave catchers dragged him from the hut. But rough arms snatched her away and shoved her outside.

I must do something! Grace thought in desperation. *But what?*

Outside, pure horror greeted Grace. In the stifling shards of first light she could see the village's strong young men—those whose responsibility it was to stand guard at the gate—and they were all bound together with strong rope. Hola and Tetteh struggled against their bonds, but Tawnia, who was tied with them, did not. She stood perfectly still, her young face etched with horror.

In a great feat of strength, Cabeto's brother Sunba ripped free of his bonds. He snatched up a fallen tree branch and cracked it against the skull of an attacker, then he hit a second one. But before he could raise his makeshift club a third time, a blow from the butt end of a musket knocked him cold.

"Do no damage to him," ordered one of the African attackers to the one who hit Sunba. "He will bring us a good price."

But the second attacker wrinkled his face and scowled at Sunba's scarred back. "Not this one. He bears the marks of a troublemaker. His price will not be like theirs." Here he motioned toward Hola and Tetteh, and Ama's two brothers.

The young men still blinked in confusion. What had happened? They had stretched out on their sleeping mats just as they did every night, except that this time their bellies were filled with roasted goat and their heads swam with memories of Tawnia giggling and doing her best to dance like a woman. They lay down brimming over with celebration, and the next thing they knew, strangers yanked them out of their dreams, pulled them outside, and tied them up so tightly that the ropes cut into their flesh.

Suddenly the African attackers on either side of Sunba fell to the ground, first one and then the other. Ikem's arrows protruded from their chests. Another attacker fell, then another. But as skilled and courageous a fighter as Ikem was, his weapons could not stand up against the slave catchers' firepower. Before he could pull out another arrow, a muzzle-loaded lead ball exploded into the old man's shoulder.

So many attackers! And hidden everywhere! They poured out from the papaya grove and they ran from inside the storage huts. They came from the goat pens and appeared from behind the ghariti trees. First they grabbed the men, forced them to the ground and bound their wrists. Then they secured them with rope tied around their necks. "Struggle and it will cut your breath away," they warned.

"I will not be a slave again!" Tuke yelled. He wrested himself free and leapt away. The first musket shot missed him and so did the second, but the third hit him in the back and he fell.

"Cabeto!" Grace screamed. She clutched her crying son and frantically fought her way through the confusion. But immediately an attacker grabbed her, then a second one jabbed her with a musket.

"Are you the one they call Grace?" the attacker with the musket demanded.

"Please, my son!" Grace pleaded.

"She is the one," the other answered. Then, before Grace had time to think, he snatched the child from her arms. He grabbed Kwate by his tiny ankles, then, with all his strength, the attacker slammed the little boy against the rocks. Little Kwate never uttered a cry.

Grace's screams sliced into the morning and joined Cabeto's agonized howls. Grace fell to the ground and knew no more.

By the time the sun added its stifling heat to the horror of the day, the villagers stood lashed together in a single line, numb with terror.

"Walk to the gate!" came the command. "Then on to the fortress!"

At first when she awoke Grace couldn't understand, couldn't remember. But then she saw Cabeto in the line, his hands bound and a rope around his neck, and everything came rushing back.

Mama sat alone among the rocks cradling the limp, broken body of little Kwate. Grace could not bear to look at her son. If she didn't see him, perhaps the horror would not be so.

The line started to move.

"Wait!" Grace yelled. She jumped to her feet and rushed forward. "Take me too! You already took my child. If you take my husband, take me too!"

The attacker who had dashed her son on the rocks pushed Grace away. "Not you," he said. "You are not to go with the others. Not now."

"Why not?" Grace demanded. "Who gave such an order?"

But the line of people—Grace's friends and family—was already on its way toward the gate. Despair blazed with the rising sun.

As the line disappeared through the gate, as two Africans with muskets at the ready barred her from Cabeto, as her happy village of peace and love lay shattered around her, Grace fell to her knees beside Mama Muco and lifted little Kwate from Mama's arms. A cry tore from deep within her, wild and uncontrollable.

Mama Muco pulled Grace to her and enveloped her in her arms, rocking her just as she had when Grace was a little girl. "Ikem has gone to the ancestors," Mama whispered in a voice husky with grief.

"Kwate . . ." Grace sobbed. "My baby . . ."

"He is in the arms of Jesus, child. Let him go."

Grace shook her head and sobbed. "This is the end," she wept. "The end of everything."

As Mama Muco caressed Grace and whispered soothing words into her ear, she wished with all her heart that it was the end. But she knew it was not. She knew this day of awful destruction was only the beginning.

3

$\mathcal{D}$espite Jasper Hathaway's hatred of bone-jarring wagon travel, his fleshy jowls stretched into a self-satisfied grin as he did his best to brace himself on the bouncing seat. *I really am quite the genius,* he thought as he lurched along the rough trail. *And soon everyone who matters will realize as much.*

"Slow down!" Mister Hathaway ordered the African driver beside him. Hathaway gestured to the boundary rocks up ahead that marked the beginning of the land of the local Gold Coast chiefdom. "Have you no respect for the ancestors?"

Jasper Hathaway pulled his handkerchief from the pocket of his waistcoat and mopped at the perspiration that rolled over the folds of his face and down into his collar. *Respect the ancestors! Hah!* Well, playing the part was a small enough price to pay for all that now lay within his grasp. Respect for the ancestors on one side of the world and indulgence of the aristocracy on the other. Which was the more insufferable—or the more ineffective—he truly could not say.

When Mister Hathaway's wagon entered the village, it was at a respectful pace. At his further command, the driver slowed even more, then just outside the royal enclave, pulled the horses to a stop. It was not at all what Jasper Hathaway would call a palace, but this was Africa, after all, so he must make allowances. Carefully, laboriously, Mister Hathaway climbed down. He pushed back a wild shock of thinning brown hair, freed by the jostling journey from the cord that tied it in back, and made an attempt to reassemble his disheveled clothes.

Men walking along the road, women with baskets of fruit or fish balanced on their heads, girls on their way to collect drinking water, boys herding small black and white goats—people going about their everyday business—stopped to stare at the fat white man bundled up in such an excess of clothing. Wheezing and panting, Jasper Hathaway stood beside the wagon and waited. The unrelenting sun broiled his face and withered his patience. His linen shirt soaked through with sweat and his coat sagged, yet he continued to wait. Although he spoke not a word, a fierce anger flared up in his eyes.

Finally the king's *okyeame* approached Jasper Hathaway. "King Obei awaits you," he said. "I will speak to him on your behalf."

Mister Hathaway bowed his head and followed the man into the sacred territory. He would much prefer to talk directly to the king, but he was well aware of the wisdom of following custom. And in this kingdom, custom meant speaking through an *okyeame*, a speaker skilled at cleansing words of unintended nuances, at shaping them into just the right positions and decorating them with rhymes and rhythms, of weaving them together so that they would cause no undue offense.

Inside the royal hut, King Obei sat on a carved wooden chair encased in pounded gold. More importantly, his feet rested on the *sika'gua*—the wooden stool that contained the soul of the ancestors and bestowed on him his authority and power. Even as Jasper Hathaway bent low in honor, his eyes greedily swept the room. So much gold! Thick and rich and hand-tooled! A king's fortune in this so-called king's palace.

"Tell the king that I bring him my gratitude for sending the *slattees* to gather up fresh slaves from the village squatting next to Zulina fortress," Mister Hathaway said once he managed to regain himself. "No life of any importance was lost, I am pleased to report. And I did capture the one I particularly desired. As we agreed, I have brought you a wagonload of gifts—cloth and muskets and gunpowder. I also included rum for the king's pleasure. My slave awaits your command to unload the wagon."

The *okyeame* started to speak Hathaway's words, but the king waved him away. "If we can do business together, we can most certainly talk together," King Obei said. Again Jasper Hathaway bowed. The king did not respond to the gesture, nor did he ask the flushed white man if he would care to sit down.

"I do business with you for the sake of my father who has gone to the ancestors," said King Obei. "You signed an agreement with him, and he would not be pleased to see it broken. I also do business with you for the benefit of my sister, Lingongo. It is not my personal will to be a friend of any white man."

"Is it your will that your chiefdom continue to be the most powerful and respected kingdom on the coast?" Jasper Hathaway asked. "Is it your will to have a continuing supply of firearms and gunpowder so that you may remain the exalted king of such a kingdom?"

"Crisis makes opportunity," the king replied coolly. "Since we talk, let us talk with honesty. It was crisis that made you lord of Zulina fortress, and it was crisis that made me king. And so here we are, united by crisis."

Jasper Hathaway should have let the king have the last word. He should have bowed low, then gone outside the royal hut to where the air was fresh and he could breathe more freely. He should have lowered his bulk under the canopy of shade trees and dozed until his slave unloaded the cloth and muskets and gunpowder and rum, then he should have gone back to his house to wait out the heat of the day with fans and cool drinks. But he did not. The heat made him irritable, and he was tired of affording aristocratic courtesy to this self-righteous African who had dared to side with rebel slaves and fight against the white slave traders, a black man who now acted as though it was the responsibility of white businessmen to keep him in power.

So Jasper Hathaway bared his teeth just the least little bit and said in a tone faintly glazed with rancor, "Why is your sister not here to speak in your stead, o king? Was it not Lingongo who created an opportunity for you out of the crisis?"

If a royal upbringing had taught Obei anything, it was never to flinch at an attack, not from a weapon and not from a word, no matter how offensive, painful, or insulting it might be. For several moments he sat perfectly still. Then, with the same even tone to his voice, he countered, "Why is your rich Englishman not in *my* presence to speak in *your* stead? Is there any decision you alone can make without first seeking his approval?"

Before today, Mister Hathaway would have been tempted to slink away at such a blow. But not now. Because now there most certainly was such a decision, and he had just made it.

Ever since Grace Winslow had chosen to cast her lot with the rebellious slaves at Zulina fortress rather than fulfill her parents' promise that she would be his wife, Jasper Hathaway had been forced to endure the humiliation of snickering whispers and outright laughter, all at his expense. For five years he had borne the pain of knowing Grace preferred to live in a mud hut thatched with banana leaves than in his well-appointed house with him. That she found it preferable to subsist on roots and wild-growing fruits than to dine with him in his impeccably furnished dining room, though a finer table than his was not to be found in all of Africa. Grace, with her satin-smooth bronze skin, had thrown him aside and chosen to become the wife of a runaway African slave! The very idea infuriated Hathaway beyond words.

It was not that he was unable to get another wife—although precious few young women measured up to the standards necessarily set by a gentleman of his standing. But he could not . . . he *would* not . . . allow such a humiliating set of personal insults to go unchallenged.

Yes, Jasper Hathaway definitely *had* made a decision without the approval, or even the knowledge, of his financial backer. Indeed, he had made a most momentous decision. And, he mused with glee, Lord Reginald Witherham would learn of it soon enough with his own eyes.

"Crisis does indeed make opportunity," Jasper Hathaway replied. And though he willed himself to keep his eyes fixed on the king, the call of gold was powerfully strong. "Zulina slave fortress is now in business once more." His glance strayed in spite of himself. Quickly looking back to the king, he said, "I shall look forward to further negotiations on our business agreement. I shall also look forward to greeting Lingongo once again. Shall we say tomorrow then?"

"I do not embrace the ideas of my father," said King Obei. "But I do possess his magical powers. I also enjoy favor from the spirits, as did my father. And I warn you, Mister Hathaway, it would be most unwise of you to rouse their anger."

"Until tomorrow then," said Jasper Hathaway.

4

$\mathscr{S}$creams pierced the morning air and the pungent smell of burning flesh wafted through the open window. With an irritated sigh, Jasper Hathaway pulled himself away from the looking glass and crossed to the widest of the three windows in Zulina's corner room.

Down below was a courtyard where the breeze blew comfortable and cool off the water. There a clutch of men and women from Grace's village huddled together, their clothes stripped from them and their hands bound tight. Tawnia, Ama, and Safya wept together on the far side of the courtyard. Between the three women and the other captives, a fire glowed white-hot. A trustee grabbed Tetteh and dragged him to the fire. Tom Davis, Hathaway's assistant, pulled a glowing-hot metal rod from the embers and seared it into the young man's shoulder. As Tetteh howled, Davis thrust the rod back into the fire and shoved Tetteh toward the women. Already the trustee was dragging Ama's brother, Oku, to the fire.

With a sigh of disgust, Hathaway slammed the shutter closed. "Noisy beggars!" he muttered. Well, he would not allow them to distract him. Not today. For five years he had anticipated this moment, and nothing was going to ruin it for him, especially not the whining of slaves.

As soon as Jasper Hathaway turned back to the looking glass, the scowl on his face smoothed into a look of satisfied approval. He had brushed his hair back slick and smooth and tied it at his neck with a fresh ribbon. New silk stockings and buckled shoes perfectly set off the fine cut of his breeches. Carefully Mister Hathaway adjusted the lavishly embroidered jabots at his neck, making certain that each ruffle was perfectly positioned so as to display it elegantly through the opening of his new silk waistcoat—a handsome garment indeed. How unfortunate that unsightly bulges caused the pocket flaps to protrude in such a distracting way. Well, never mind, he reassured himself. His new "smart coat" would cover up all those tell-tale results of his dining room indiscretions.

He struck a casual pose and stared hard at his reflection. No, it was not quite the look he desired. He picked up a carved walking stick and, with one foot slightly crossed over the other, jauntily leaned against it. No, no, that gave him the look of a lame man. After a moment's hesitation, he reached into his desk drawer and took out a discreetly hidden pot of ceruse makeup power. He dabbed it on his cheeks, gagging only slightly at the foul odor. Then he stepped back to consider the matte-white results. Perfect! Ten pounds, twenty-two shillings it had cost him for the new suit of clothes, but it was worth every last farthing. For what Jasper Hathaway saw reflected back at him in the looking glass was an ideal English gentleman of impeccable taste.

"I'll pay yer price fer the young ones," Captain Hudson was saying to Tom Davis down in the courtyard. "But not fer them two." He motioned toward Sunba, then knocked Cabeto to the ground and kicked him. "Lame, he be. Is you trying to trick me now?"

"He's a strong buck," Davis argued. "A plantation owner could work him hard for more than a year before he'd drop. Maybe two years—three even. Fully worth two iron bars, he is."

"Two bars!" Hudson said with a sneer. "I only buys what I can sell, and it ain't him! And that one . . ." he motioned to Sunba. "Look at his back. He be a troublemaker, that's fer sure!"

In the end, Captain Richard Hudson bought the whole lot, though he paid just half the going rate for Sunba and Safya, and only a third for Cabeto. The captain smiled to himself, but so did the trader. Each was certain he had gotten the best of the other.

When Tom Davis saw Mister Hathaway descend the steps, he paid no attention to the striking silk clothing that bedecked his boss. Instead, he launched directly into a recitation of the slave sale. But Mister Hathaway pushed him aside.

"Where is she?" he demanded.

"She . . . who?" Tom stammered.

"Grace, of course!" Mister Hathaway said.

After Grace had spurned his marriage proposal, when her father blamed Jasper publicly for enabling her to escape her parents' grasp, when the whispers and jokes began to circulate through the white population all up and down the Gold Coast, he started to lay his plan. Five years is a long time to wait, but now at last he was ready to claim both his revenge and his prize.

When Tom brought Grace before Hathaway, she was washed and perfumed, and dressed up in a yellow and green silk frock with a filmy skirt that rustled when she walked. Jasper Hathaway had rehearsed this moment many times in his mind: when Grace entered, he intended to cast her the briefest of glances, and to maintain an air of disinterested disdain. But now, with her standing before him, he could only gape at her willowy beauty. He had forgotten the loveliness of this daughter of an English sea captain and his royal African wife. The splash of fire in her hair, the golden hue of her skin, the intense flash in her eyes—Jasper Hathaway reached out an unsteady plump hand and ran his shaky fingers along the charming pleats of her fitted bodice.

Grace cringed and pulled away. "I will not marry you, Mister Hathaway," she said.

Jasper Hathaway shook himself back to his senses.

"Marry me?" he exclaimed, his eyebrows arched in mock surprise. "My, but you do think highly of yourself! I have not the slightest intention of taking you as my wife. You, Grace Winslow, are my slave. My personal slave. I shall take you with me to London and put you on display for all to see. You shall do my bidding—at all times, in all ways. And should you be so foolish as to try anything daring, I shall clamp a metal collar around your tender neck and fasten you to the wall."

As he had promised, Jasper Hathaway returned to the Gold Coast kingdom, only this time it was not bouncing uncomfortably on the seat of an open wagon in the heat of the day, certainly not perched next to his slave and drenched with sweat. This time he did not make a show of speaking about respect for ancestors. Ancestors concerned him not in the least. This time Mister Hathaway came as an English gentleman—a master of African slaves—seated in a comfortable English carriage with a beautiful slave girl positioned beside him. This time he came victorious and with his head held proud and high.

Jasper Hathaway did not put out his hand to help Grace from the carriage, nor did he offer his arm as they walked through the sacred territory toward the royal hut. "King Obei is expecting me," he announced brusquely as he waved away the king's *okyeame* who had rushed forward to intercept him. "And Princess Lingongo as well. She also expects me."

Bowing, the *okyeame* stepped aside.

Inside the royal hut, King Obei was seated on his gold-encased royal chair just as if he had not moved a hair since Mister Hathaway walked out the day before. Only this time a second royal chair sat alongside the king, one even more beautiful and elegant than the king's own chair. But Grace didn't look at them, nor did she acknowledge her uncle, the king. All she saw was her mother, Lingongo.

"Mother, I thought perhaps . . . that is, with the fire and all that happened . . ." Grace stammered.

Lingongo ignored her daughter completely. It was as though Grace were not even in the room. Instead, Lingongo fixed her eyes on Mister Hathaway, and it was to him alone that she spoke.

"Did you sell the slaves, Mister Hathaway!" This was a demand rather than a question.

"Yes," he answered. "Every one of them to Richard Hudson, captain of the *Golden Hawk*. I have insisted he sail for the Indies tomorrow to coincide with my sailing for London on the *Willow*. Excuse me, I should say when *Grace and I* sail for London." He flashed Grace a victory grin.

Mister Hathaway paused, hoping for a reaction. He got none. So, with a vicious edge to his voice, he added, "I do thank you, Lingongo, for persuading me to reconsider entering into a marriage with so headstrong a half-breed as your daughter. How much preferable it is to be sailing with her as my own personal slave. As a slave trader yourself, you do agree, do you not?"

King Obei's feet stiffened where they rested on the *sika'gua*, but Mister Hathaway failed to notice. Nor did he see the twitch in the king's tightened jaw. He was much too busy bathing himself in congratulatory praise.

"The next time we do business, the price will be double the number of muskets," Lingongo announced in a searing voice. "And never again will you try to cheat us by filling space in your wagon with cheap cloth and watered-down alcohol."

"I will be spending my time in London with one Lord Reginald Witherham," Hathaway continued. "Lord Witherham is a renowned financier and the owner of a magnificent and extremely influential shipping empire—which, as it happens, now owns Zulina slave fortress."

"Your presence here causes disturbances in the land," Lingongo said. "Do not return to our kingdom unless your presence is requested. And because your talk causes the king unrest, you are not to speak to him again unless it is through me."

Jasper Hathaway had intended to end their time together by striking a powerful pose, then pronouncing some sort of an ultimatum or threat. But considering the current direction circumstances had taken, he thought better of it. Instead, he took hold of Grace's arm and pulled her toward the door. But Grace jerked free and turned back to face Lingongo.

"Please, Mother!" Grace wept. "They killed my son . . . your grandbaby! My husband they carried away. Please! Do not let this happen to me!"

Lingongo's eyes, hard and dark, never left Jasper Hathaway's fleshy face. "Leave now!" she ordered. "This kingdom is for the sons and daughters of Africa, and none other."

5

"I am not an expert on ships, but I must say, the *Willow* seems to be a particularly small vessel," Jasper Hathaway groused to the impeccably dressed and exquisitely mannered captain, Clayton Ross. Mister Hathaway gazed up a bit uneasily at the twin masts. "It does not even approach the size of a schooner, I dare say. Nothing like our sturdy sister ship, to be sure." Here he gestured with pride toward the *Golden Hawk*, a slave ship anchored alongside the *Willow*.

For almost two weeks the *Golden Hawk* had lain at anchor in the harbor. Already packed with slaves and fully stocked with provisions, it only awaited the order to set sail for the Middle Passage and the slave markets of the New World. Now, at last, it looked as if the ship was being readied for departure.

Captain Ross turned his back on the slave ship and cringed ever so slightly at the moans of misery that carried over from it.

"Aye, but this brigantine is swifter than a schooner," he said with the lilt of a Scottish burr. "And easier to maneuver she be, as well. If the winds stay fair, she will give you a smooth sail all the way to London. We should dock in two months and a half, God willing."

"Humph!" replied Mister Hathaway. "That is too long for my taste. Is my suite of rooms prepared for me and fully stocked according to my orders?"

"Certainly, sir," said the captain with a polite bow. "But whilst we shall do everything in our power to see you safely and comfortably to England, I do ask you to keep in mind that this is a ship, and as such, it does have its limits. There is only so much—"

"See here, if I am to be cooped up in this hulk for nigh unto three months, I shall expect your crew to see to my comfort," Mister Hathaway replied in a most disagreeable tone.

"That we shall," Captain Ross hastily agreed. "I only meant to say that the limitations of sea travel . . ."

Four crewmen struggled across the deck lugging an over-stuffed trunk, then two more followed with lidded crates.

"There now, already I am displeased!" Mister Hathaway huffed. "I specifically instructed that my quarters be set up a minimum of twenty-four hours before I was due aboard the ship. Now, less than a day before we sail, it still is not done. I am in the midst of overseeing the loading of a slave ship, sir. Suppose I should find it necessary to take my rest in the heat of the day only to discover that my suite is not ready for me? Lord Witherham shall hear about this. He shall indeed!"

Captain Ross was spared the obligation of conjuring up a polite response because just at that minute Lukas Fisher's frustrated voice rang across from the deck of the *Golden Hawk*. "This ship already be packed full!" the first mate called out. "There ain't room fer no more slaves!"

"These are to go on that ship," Tom Davis yelled back. "Mister Hathaway's orders!"

"Well, then, Mister Hathaway can jist come on over and find a corner to fit them in," Lukas shot back. "This ship been loaded and supplied and ready to sail fer a week, and Capt'n Hudson says they's no more waitin'. An they's no space for them slaves of yours, neither."

"I've got no more than thirty Africans here, all told," Tom said. "And all good men and women they be too. No children, no old ones. All prime slaves . . . or very nearly so."

"They . . . be . . . no . . . *room!*" Lukas repeated, his frustration rising. "I 'as to tell ye no, no, *no!*"

"Mister Hathaway says they go," Tom insisted. "And he speaks for Lord Witherham, and Lord Witherham owns the ship. So tight-pack your slaves and make ready, because these others are coming on board, whether you like it or not!"

"We'll run out of provisions," Lukas said.

"Then choose now who you will toss into the sea, because the new slaves are ready at the gate."

Although he was not a man given to compliments, Jasper Hathaway did admire the persistence of Tom Davis in getting the slave ship packed profitably. Mister Hathaway usually insisted on having his own hand in such transactions, but it was not something about which he cared to bother himself this day. As soon as he set foot on board the *Willow*, he insisted that the captain release the first mate—young Jonas Brandt—from his duties long enough to dispatch the lad to Zulina to collect Grace and see her to the ship. She would not be bringing any of her African belongings with her, he instructed. That would never do. Mister Hathaway had already assembled a nice supply of English frocks, each with a hat and a pair of fine shoes to match. Grace was to be seen with him. She must impress herself so deeply upon the minds of all who cast eyes upon her that when they saw she belonged to Jasper Hathaway, they would burn with envy.

Mister Hathaway loosened his waistcoat and sank into the armchair beside the desk in his so-called suite. His accommodations disappointed him immensely. It could not rightfully be called a suite at all. Two small cabins, each opening onto the main deck; that was all. Each room had a bunk bed—although Mister Hathaway had already demanded that his be replaced with a feather bed. His room had a small desk and a rather uncomfortable desk chair, as well as an armchair pushed up against the tiny wardrobe. That armchair proved to be surprisingly comfortable. The other cabin—Grace's cabin—had even less room, furnished only with a small table next to the bunk and a straight-back chair against the far wall. Plenty luxurious for a slave, in his opinion. And unlike the larger room, the only bolt on Grace's door was on the outside—a feature Hathaway found most appealing.

Hathaway's thoughts were interrupted by a tap at the open door.

With a formal bow, Jonas Brandt said, "I present Miss Grace Winslow," and ushered her through.

It both angered and pleased Jasper to note the unwilling spark in the eager eye of young Jonas.

"She is a slave, my good man," Mister Hathaway said brusquely. "My slave. You would do well to remember that."

"Yes, sir." A deep flush burned to the top of Brandt's head. "That she is, sir. Good day, sir."

Mister Hathaway waved the young man away. So this was how the voyage was going to be, was it?

And yet, not an altogether bad herald of things to come.

"Hurry!" Tom Davis's voice echoed across from the *Golden Hawk*. "Move forward now!"

"Why, I do believe my man is preparing your friends for their sea voyage," Mister Hathaway said to Grace. "I hope their accommodations are as comfortable as our own. Come, let us stroll out on the deck and bid them fair travels."

"Force him onto the ship!" Tom shouted to a white man in the back of a longboat packed with all the captives from Grace's village. They had been rowed out to the *Golden Hawk* and, with the help of African trustees, Tom and the other man prodded and coaxed them to climb aboard. But Oku, who was at the front of the boat, refused to move.

"Your musket! Use it!" Tom ordered.

A tall trustee with a blank face pointed a gun at Oku's head. "Move, slave," he said.

Oku moved. He jumped over the side of the boat and sank into the dank water of the harbor.

Hathaway leaned over the ship's railing and yelled, "Tom, you fool! Do not lose the choicest among them before you even set sail! Get those slaves loaded now!"

Ama, sobbing, screamed for Oku. Her other brother, Kome, bellowed in rage. In a flash, the trustee pointed his musket at Ama, but it was to Kome that he spoke. "Move to the deck," he ordered.

Kome, rooted in place, blinked in confusion—from Tom to Ama, to the water where his brother had disappeared, then back to Ama.

"Now!" the trustee insisted.

"Go," Cabeto urged Kome. "Go or we all die here."

As Jasper Hathaway chuckled in satisfaction from the deck of the *Willow*, Kome climbed aboard the slave ship the *Golden Hawk*, followed by Safya, Hola, Tetteh, and last, Tawnia, who stumbled and fell.

Tears filled Grace's eyes and ran down her cheeks and onto the front of her yellow and green silk dress. Her legs trembled and she grasped the railing to keep from falling.

"Ah, the good smell of sea air," Jasper Hathaway announced jovially. "A perfect day to do business, do you not agree, my dear?"

Grace didn't want to watch, but she couldn't help herself. She looked back as Cabeto climbed up from the boat and onto the ship's deck. She choked back a sob, then leaned forward and cried out, "Cabeto! I will see you again!"

Cabeto turned toward her, but immediately a white man knocked him forward and forced him toward an opening in the deck.

"I *will* see you again!" Grace yelled again. This time it was a defiant promise.

A slave on her way to England vowing to meet again with a broken slave bound for the plantations of the New World? Ridiculously impossible! Foolish beyond belief! Jasper Hathaway wanted to laugh in Grace's face. He longed to position himself on the ship's deck and mock her long and loud for everyone to hear. But the strength of her defiance had so unsettled him that he staggered and grasped the railing. Like a blow to the stomach, it knocked his breath away. He had no choice but to hold his tongue.

Mister Hathaway grabbed Grace by the arm and forced her back to the rooms.

"It would have been best had your used your last moments to say a final farewell," he hissed through clenched teeth. "Because you will not see any one of them again. Upon my life, you will not see *him*!"

6

*E*ven before the final agreement was reached, Henrietta Stevens had strutted about crowing like a rooster over the high society marriage she had single-handedly arranged for her daughter.

"A *Lord!*" she exclaimed to everyone who would listen— and to many who would not. "My daughter will be *Lady Charlotte Witherham!*"

She kept up the boisterous talk until her own family threatened to tie a cloth over her mouth.

"Jealous is what they are," Henrietta gushed to Charlotte. "Imagine, my daughter, what life will be like with a true aristocrat for a husband! You, my darling, will divide your time between his lavish estate in Northamptonshire and a sumptuous house in London! Oh, Charlotte, I am absolutely *ecstatic* with anticipation over the life we shall lead!"

Henrietta caught herself, but not soon enough. The "we" was already out of her mouth. And she could see from Charlotte's face that her daughter had not missed the slip.

But in fact, the "we" never came about. After all her plotting and planning, after all her lavish promises and reluctant compromises, Henrietta Stevens had the frightful misfortune to fall victim to consumption. She tried every remedy suggested to her. Eliza Hauley swore by snails boiled in milk—a quarter of a pint of milk to an ounce of snails. So desperate was Henrietta that she doubled this vile treatment. The Methodist leader John Wesley recommended cold baths for the ailment, so she shivered through that therapy as well. But all to no avail.

When her only child officially became the wife of Lord Reginald Jacob Langdon Witherham IV, Henrietta Stevens lay locked away in an isolated sickroom. After the wedding, Lord Reginald sent her away to the country where, he assured Lady Charlotte, her mother would receive the best of care. No expense would be spared. He added an injunction that his wife was to have as little contact with her mother as possible. "For your own good, my dear," he said. When Charlotte opened her mouth to respond, he said firmly, "I have spoken."

Lord Reginald took it upon himself to speak equally firmly to Charlotte on a number of issues concerning his expectations of her. "You have the potential to become a lady of great charm and beauty," he began most gallantly. "Your silken skin is as fresh as an April morning. Never mind your hair. With the assistance of a good hairdresser and a darkening agent, you can very nearly become a first-class beauty. You need none of that awful ceruse on your face, my dear, for you come by the comely look of fragile porcelain quite naturally."

Here his affability failed him and his smile faded. "Your carriage is another matter entirely. It does pain me to be forced into so unpleasant a discussion, but here it is: I am most distressed to see you walking about like a chambermaid. I do not want to be indelicate, Charlotte, but must you move from place to place with great heavy horse steps? Look about you and you will see that to glide to and fro without the jolt of noticeably lifting one's feet is a far more appropriate approach to movement in your new station of life."

Charlotte looked down at her tiny feet covered in finely woven white silk stockings and petunia-pink brocade silk slippers, but all she saw was clumsy horse hooves. She blotted her eyes and vowed to do better.

Benjamin Stevens, Charlotte's father, had not been invited to any of the wedding parties, nor even to the wedding ceremony. Reginald declared that it would be "most awkward for all involved"—which, simply put, meant Benjamin Stevens failed to measure up to his standards. He embarrassed Reginald, so Reginald forbade his inclusion.

"Your father has been in Africa for so many years, my dear Charlotte, that I fear he has all but become one of . . . one of *them*. I am, as you well know, a charitable man, so I am willing to overlook your questionable upbringing. But as you are to be a member of the greatly respected Witherham household, you absolutely must conduct yourself in a manner worthy of that name and standing."

"Why, it does sound as though you are about to offer me a position as a parlor maid!" Charlotte allowed herself to exclaim.

"Nonsense!" Lord Reginald sniffed with an irritated wave of his hand. "I am simply making it clear that whilst I am willing to make allowances for your background, I cannot allow a slave trader to mix freely with my social acquaintances and business associates. And as we are on the subject, I must insist that you never speak to anyone of your connections to Africa."

"Really, Reginald, I—"

"I have already thoroughly discussed this matter with your mother. She understands my position completely. I assure you, my dear, you will be much happier if you put all that past out of your head and simply enjoy your new position as a Witherham."

Position! Charlotte actually shuddered on her wedding day.

The Witherham Larkspur Estate in London truly was breathtaking—fireplaces of jade marble; walls covered with silk damask; a grand room, trimmed in gold and hung with a fortune in artwork, large enough for a party of three hundred people to move about and enjoy one another without feeling squeezed or crowded together.

Certainly, parties had always been a part of Charlotte's social life. No one enjoyed seeing and being seen more than her mother, and wherever Henrietta Stevens went, Henrietta made certain her daughter went along. But never had Charlotte experienced parties on so grand a scale. At a Witherham party, it was not just the perfunctory dancing and feasting, but gambling tables in the parlor and even exotic fireworks displays in the gardens. "We must never have it said that anyone gives a better party than we," Reginald cautioned his new wife. Charlotte was certain the danger of anyone murmuring such an insult did not exist.

Only in her private chambers did Charlotte dare cling to a touch of her past. There, in a flash of defiance, she ordered that the walls be hung with the silk hand-painted foreign scenes that were all the rage in London. But instead of choosing Indian or Chinese motifs, she selected views of the African countryside—jungles with great cats lurking in the trees, rivers with half-submerged hippos, and here and there, black Africans picking brightly colored flowers. Actually, Charlotte had no idea what Africans did outside her father's slave-trading compound. She knew what went on inside the compound, but she refused to include scenes of miserable black people chained to walls, or lines of captives herded into slave ships. These would not fit in her bucolic landscapes.

All through her growing-up years, every other year Charlotte and her mother had made the long, arduous trip across the ocean to visit her father in Africa. Reginald could forbid her to speak of it, but he could not erase her past from her mind. She would never, ever forget Africa.

More and more, Charlotte chose to close herself away in her private chambers and contemplate the life that stretched out before her. Indeed, that was where she was and what she was doing while her husband paced back and forth in front of the marble fireplace in the parlor and energetically aired his grievances before Simon Johnson and Sir Geoffrey Phillips.

"'Liberty, equality, fraternity' indeed!" Lord Reginald declared in disgust. "The French are fools! Evidently it is not humiliation enough that they lost their most important sugar colony in the West Indies to a slave revolt. It seems their monarchy is determined to lose control of the entire country as well. Even now, mobs of peasants sweep unrestrained through the streets of Paris."

Slender build, femininely delicate features, pale complexion, curling hair. Who would imagine that a man so seemingly fragile as Lord Reginald Witherham could contain so much fiery passion?

"Although it is indeed a blessed wind that blows our way, I should say," Simon Johnson pointed out. "For we no longer need seek protection from cheap French sugar." He crossed his stubby, silk-stockinged legs, one over the other, and, with a firm grasp on his clay pipe, folded his hands over his paunch of a belly that obviously had no more need of sugar, cheap or otherwise.

"That is not at all the point, Mister Johnson," Lord Reginald replied in a voice strained with exasperation.

"I should say not," agreed Sir Geoffrey in his ever-affable manner. "The argument is actually against the right of the monarchy to rule the people, is it not?"

"First the American colonies, and now the French," said Lord Reginald. "And it is we, society's finest and best, who in the end must pay the price for such ill-conceived rebellions."

"And pay we certainly do," conceded Sir Geoffrey. "A triumph over privilege—that is their boast."

"Over *privilege!*" sneered Mister Johnson. "Such sentiments constitute a direct attack on *us*, the aristocracy. And more than that, an attack on our place in society. Indeed, on our entire way of life!"

"Absolutely! Most certainly!" Lord Reginald agreed. Each time he turned on his heel and retraced his steps, his agitation grew. "Making a declaration of equality is but one step away from wrenching our birthrights directly out of our hands—along with our profits, by the way—which is precisely why the masses must be kept in their rightful place. They are what they are, just as surely as we are what we are. The aristocracy has a most time-honored purpose for maintaining its exalted position in society—"

"For maintaining its *God-given* position in society!" Simon Johnson interjected, punctuating each word with a thrust of his long-stemmed pipe.

"Indeed!" said Lord Reginald. "For maintaining the position afforded us by the Almighty God himself for the purpose of maintaining a civilized and honorable society in this fair country, and establishing a wise and profitable order abroad."

"Hear, hear!" called Sir Geoffrey Philips. "Well said, sir! Well said indeed."

Not everyone in London saluted society's status quo, however. Englishmen such as Thomas Paine and Jonas Blake, who insisted the situation in France was the first step back to a state of human perfection, did not. Nor did Granville Sharp and Thomas Clarkson, who formed an Abolition Committee and swore their allegiance to fight for an end to the slave trade. Certainly not those who belonged to the Society of Friends—the Quakers—who had long faced persecution for their belief that everyone, including Africans, was equal in the sight of God.

Even as Lord Witherham ranted in his parlor about God-given rights, a clutch of Quakers stood together on the London docks—two women and four men, crushed together in the bustle of the world's busiest port. For eleven miles, a continuous succession of hectic wharves stretched out along the mighty Thames River. The dockside—noisy, filthy, and rife with thieves—was a most unpleasant place to make a stand for the abolition of slavery. Yet the Quakers chose it precisely because it was so appropriate, considering the preeminence of British ships in the slave trade. Standing shoulder-to-shoulder, they held their pamphlets close to their noses so they could read from them in the heavy fog, then in an impassioned chant they raised their voices together:

> *Forced from home and all its pleasures*
> *Afric's coast I left forlorn,*
> *To increase a stranger's treasures*
> *O'er the raging billows borne.*
> *Men from England bought and sold me,*
> *Paid my price in paltry gold;*
> *But, though slave they have enrolled me,*
> *Minds are never to be sold . . .*

Peddlers halted their pushcarts, sailors ceased repeating their sea tales, officers paused in their patrols to gawk at the well-dressed gentlefolk who dared brave the docks for no reason other than to plead the case of faraway Africans.

"What can the plight of them slaves possibly matter to ye?" called a woman selling mackerel from a cart.

"If ye wants a black slave, git yerse'f one!" shouted another. "If ye don't want one, leave 'im be."

Several grunted their agreement.

The Quakers, undaunted, continued with the verses of William Cowper's poem, only now they heightened it with emphasized pathos. More people drifted over to see what was going on as the group chanted:

> . . . Is there, as ye sometimes tell us,
>   Is there One who reigns on high?
> Has He bid you buy and sell us,
>   Speaking from his throne, the sky?
> Ask him, if your knotted scourges,
>   Matches, blood-extorting screws,
> Are the means that duty urges
>   Agents of his will to use?

"Now, that be too much!" a man yelled out. "How dare ye have the gall to speak fer the Almighty hisself? Why, I shan't wonder if He should strike ever' last one of us dead on the spot!"

"The Almighty ain't about to trouble hisself with no African slaves, that's fer beastly sure!" another chimed in.

Not that everyone objected to the Quakers. Quite the opposite was true. A sizable crowd had assembled and most people actually paid thoughtful attention to the words of the poet. The chant continued:

> *. . . By our blood in Afric' wasted*
> > *Ere our necks received the chain;*
> *By the miseries that we tasted,*
> > *Crossing in your barks the main;*
> *By our sufferings, since ye brought us*
> > *To the man-degrading mart,*
> *All sustained by patience, taught us*
> > *Only by a broken heart . . .*

"If ye loves 'em Africans, why don't ye jist git on a boat an' sail to Africa yerself!" a man snapped as he stomped off.

"Have any of you actually *been* to Africa?" a woman asked the chanting men and women—not with animosity, but as a sincere question. "Which is true, that the Africans suffer on the voyage or that they are pleased to be rescued from their heathen life?"

"I 'as been there," answered a gnarled sailor with a gravel voice. "An' I kin say this much: I won't never go back agin. Them captives suffers, awright. 'Tis the lucky ones wot dies on the way to civilization."

> *. . . Slaves of gold, whose sordid dealings*
> > *Tarnish all your boasted powers,*
> *Prove that you have human feelings,*
> > *Ere you proudly question ours!*

A rock hurtled through the air and struck a stocky man at the end of the abolitionist group squarely in the chest. Gasping, he stumbled and fell backward. The woman next to him screamed and dropped her pamphlet, and for several minutes all was confusion. But a lanky man who seemed to be the leader of the Quaker group helped his comrade back to his feet. With the stocky man standing shakily beside him, the leader called out, "No harm done! No harm at all!"

Before the crowd had a chance to shake away the excitement and drift on about their business, the other two men grabbed up the dropped pamphlet and nailed it to the side of a warehouse.

"The lives of innocent men, women, and children are in our hands!" the leader called out. "But do not allow us to decide on which side of this issue you stand! Do not allow anyone to decide for you. Read the words of those who have personally experienced this most disgraceful and un-Christian of horrors that is right now being thrust upon unfortunate Africans. Then and only then, we ask you—decide for yourselves what a civilized nation should do!"

A disheveled man with filthy red hair and a ruddy face blotchy with drink stumbled from the edge of the crowd, grabbed up a good-sized chunk of broken brick, and swung his arm back. But before he could heave it at the Quaker leader, a sailor grabbed him from behind and yanked the brick out of his hand.

"Yer hicksius-doxius with gin," the sailor scolded. "Git away with ye."

"Wot do ye know 'bout Africans?" Joseph Winslow spat bitterly. "Wot do the lot of ye know 'bout anythin' on that cursed shore?"

7

As he did every morning after Grace cleared away the remains of his breakfast egg and his tea with sweet cream, Jasper Hathaway said, "Put a smile on your face, Grace. I insist that you look pleasant and fetching as we stroll along the deck."

And as she did every morning, Grace made absolutely certain not the slightest beam of pleasure brightened her countenance. Yet the melancholy wilt of her mouth, and the sorrow that glistened in her eyes, served only to make her more alluring to the seamen on board the *Willow*.

As was the custom of the sea, the crew of the *Willow* served in two four-hour "watches," or shifts of duty, with the men alternating shifts under the command of whichever officer was on watch duty. But whether on duty or not, the seamen sought out excuses to be on the main deck during the early forenoon watch.

Precisely at the sound of one bell—half past eight in the morning—Jasper Hathaway donned his coat and grasped Grace firmly by her arm. He did not offer his arm as a gentleman would to a lady, but rather he gripped her arm as though he were clamping it in a manacle.

"Pleasant and fetching," he hissed as he propelled her toward the main deck.

As always, the main deck bustled with activity—sailors in work smocks busy at the messy chores of scrubbing down the ship and undertaking its ever-needed repair, others at work on the sails, wearing jackets cut short enough to keep from getting caught when they climbed up into the rigging. The seamen shouted back and forth to each other as they worked, adding to the constant noise of labor mixed with the cackling of chickens packed into the stacks of crates.

"Please, sir," Captain Ross implored Mister Hathaway yet again. "I beseech you to avail yourself of the quarter deck for your daily constitutional. It being reserved for myself and the officers, a stroll there is ever so much more in agreement with a gentleman such as yourself who desires to properly escort a lass." Captain Ross turned to Nathaniel Greenway, the ship's navigator, who walked beside him, and pleaded, "Do you not agree, sir?"

"I remind you once again, Captain," Mister Hathaway snapped brusquely, "the *lass* is nothing but a slave. And being such, the main deck is entirely sufficient for her—the opinion of yourself and your fellow officer notwithstanding."

"And may I remind you, sir, that it is not possible for her to be 'nothing but a slave,'" the captain replied, his voice turning icy. "This is an English ship. Therefore, whilst you are most welcome to have a personal servant at your side, we do not carry slaves, sir."

"Indeed, Captain, I stand corrected," Mister Hathaway said. He slid his left foot forward and, with his leg perfectly straight, executed a ridiculously exaggerated bow. "Perhaps the African heat has affected my brain. But I must confess that I find the English stand on this subject most confusing. No slaves, you say? And yet I am myself the representative of a major slaving interest in Africa, am I not? Most incomprehensible. Do you not agree?" He walked on, pulling Grace with him. "Once again I assure you, Captain, I prefer to stroll along the main deck," Hathaway called back, "with my *slave!*"

"A most disagreeable fellow!" Captain Ross said to Mister Greenway. "Most disagreeable indeed."

"That he is," Nate Greenway replied. "But I dare say, I should rather have him aboard than her."

"Whatever do you mean?"

"You know the lore of the sea as well as I," Greenway said. "Bring a woman to sea, and trouble is certain to follow."

"Why, Nate!" the captain exclaimed with a hearty laugh. "I would expect as much from the superstitious fools who scrub the deck and wash the pots. But not from the likes of you!"

"I pray to God you are right and I am wrong, sir. But I fear otherwise."

In actual fact, it irritated Jasper Hathaway no end to have to step around buckets of scrubbing water and to dodge scuffling seamen on his morning walks. The peace of the quarter deck, where he could gaze out over the ship's wake, would indeed be more to his taste. But months at sea were boring indeed, and he found no diversion quite as amusing as his ability to tease the men with Grace. He saw their hungry looks as she flowed past them in one of her fetching new silk gowns. Let them watch him grip her arm, then they could draw their own conclusions. They need not know her vicious refusal to allow him to so much as stroke her face.

This particular morning stroll, however, was to be Jasper Hathaway's last.

The following morning, Grace awoke with the promise of dawn, and, as always, she readied herself for another day. But unlike every other morning, Mister Hathaway did not unlock her door.

When the sun grew hot, Grace knocked on the wall and called out, "Mister Hathaway? Are you ready for your breakfast?"

But he did not respond.

By the time the sun reached its zenith, desperation overtook Grace and she pounded on her cabin door. "Please, someone unlock this door! Something must be wrong with Mister Hathaway!"

Grace heard voices outside, followed by arguments in which more and more people seemed to involve themselves. As her calls became more urgent, someone yelled for the captain. Then more noises that Grace couldn't identify, although she was certain they came from Mister Hathaway's room. At long last the bolt slipped into place, and Captain Ross flung the door open.

"Your . . . employer," the captain said. "He has taken quite ill. Sometime during the night, I should think. Doctor Wills is with him now."

"Scurvy." That was the diagnosis the ship's surgeon gave Mister Hathaway. "Plague of the sea. I shall see that you have pickled cabbage with each of your meals. And strong rob to drink, too, along with a portion of vinegar."

"Phoo!" Hathaway spat with disgust. "I shall have none of those barbaric concoctions."

"Please, sir, do not make so hasty a decision," Doctor Wills insisted. "This is the only cure for scurvy. And the consequences for leaving the disease untreated are dire indeed."

"Nonsense," insisted Mister Hathaway. "I am not your usual unlearned man. I shall simply eat plenty of fresh fruits and all will be set to right. In fact, I shall have a plate of fruit right now."

"We have no fresh fruit on board," the doctor explained. "It is quite impossible to carry such things on a ship, but we can—"

"What you can do is leave me in the care of my slave! She shall see to me just fine."

"Sir," Captain Ross interjected. "Both Doctor Wills and myself have attended many a man afflicted by this vile disorder. Please, I beg of you, cooperate with the doctor's treatment, and I am certain that—"

"Good day, Captain!" Mister Hathaway clipped.

"But, sir—" said Doctor Wills.

"Good day to you both!" With that, Jasper Hathaway rolled over and turned his face to the wall.

After Captain Ross and the doctor left, Grace stood for some time staring uncertainly at the bulging back of her tormentor. Finally she asked, "Can I do something for you?"

"Get me a plate of fruit," he snapped.

"But there is no—"

Grace didn't even bother to finish her sentence. She quietly left the cabin, closing the door behind her. Doctor Wills and Captain Ross waited just outside the door.

"One time only," Dr. Wills said. He handed Grace a small, shriveled apple. "But this alone will do him little good. Unless he takes advantage of the remedies we have suggested, Mister Hathaway's prospects of reaching England alive are extremely small indeed."

Grace took the apple and said nothing.

"Care for your master if you feel you must," Captain Ross said. "Or if you can see your way clear, leave his care to the doctor here. Either way, should the man pass from this life, you can consider yourself free."

"I shall care for him as best I can, sir, for that is my duty," Grace said. "But he is not my master. And I am not a slave."

"Let me know if I can be of service to you," the doctor said.

Grace was granted access to the galley cooking fire. For even as the attackers had made ready to march her from her village, Mama Muco had grabbed Grace and thrust a small packet of herbs into her bound hands. "The Creator will guard you, child, and the ancestors' medicines will keep you well," Mama had promised.

Alone in her cabin, Grace untied the cloth and spread out the assortment of roots and leaves and tree bark. She selected the drooping pear-shaped leaves of the pawpaw tree and a stem of bitter neem leaves. Doctor Wills led her into the stuffy galley and instructed the cook to let her use an iron pot. Grace poured in a pitcher full of water and hung the pot on the hook in the fireplace. As the water heated, she dropped in the dried leaves, and let it all come to a slow boil.

"Smells good," said Doctor Wills. "Might I take a taste?"

One taste was more than enough. Grace laughed out loud as the doctor wrinkled his face and choked at the bitterness of her concoction.

"Mix it with a bit of rob," Doctor Wills suggested. In answer to Grace's puzzled look he said, "It is nothing but concentrated fruit juice. We mix it by an old Arab recipe. Excellent treatment for scurvy."

Jasper Hathaway sipped a bit of the herb-laced rob, but he complained bitterly. "Bring me more apples!" he demanded. "And lemons and papayas!"

But there were no apples or lemons or papayas on the ship. What there was—soup made of dried vegetable tablets, pickled cabbage, and draughts of vinegar—Mister Hathaway flatly refused. So he simply lay in his bed, his body and bones deteriorating by the day.

As Jasper Hathaway's mind clouded over and drifted in and out, he alternately blubbered his love for Grace and called down damnation on her soul. Grace bathed his pale, fleshy face with cool water as she whispered soothing words, and three times each day she did her best to coax him to nibble at the healing foods. But he scorned her attempts, pulled his nightcap down over his ears, and turned his face to the wall.

Grace closed the door on Jasper Hathaway's room and moved next door to her own cabin. Since the only lock was on the outside, Grace pushed the table in front of the door and stacked the chair on top of it, then she fell onto her bunk and wept for all that was lost to her: Baby Kwate, the sun of her life. Mama Muco, her loving guide. Cabeto, her heart!

Where is Cabeto now? her heart cried. *What is the path that can take me back to him? And how am I ever to find my way to it?*

One night, Grace was awakened from a restless sleep by the ominous sound of the table scraping across the floor. Someone was pushing her door open! Grace leapt from her bed and threw herself against the table, slamming the door closed. She spent the rest of the night on the floor, the weight of her body pressed against the table that pushed the door closed.

The following morning, as Grace stepped toward Jasper Hathaway's cabin, Sam Cooke, a tall seaman with a craggy face and an exceptionally shaggy beard, loitered outside, smirking. Chester Mundy, his shady-eyed cohort in mischief, hunkered nearby, sporting a foolish grin.

"Mornin', miss," said Sam, doffing his cap to Grace and bowing low.

Grace gave a cursory nod and hurried her steps. But already Chester had stood up and skulked forward, taking up a position between her and Mister Hathaway's cabin door.

"Look ye to the sky tonight and ye'll see that the moon be nine days old," Sam intoned. His smirk dissolved into the deep crevices of his face. He moved in close to Grace and pronounced wickedly, "That man wot be yer master . . . 'e will die this very night."

Fear pounded Grace's chest. Frantically she searched for a way of escape. Certainly not to her left. Chester stood over there, his arms folded, staring at her with fight flashing in his eyes. But maybe to her right . . .

"If'n ye be thinkin' of runnin' over where you be lookin', missy, then ye best ready yersef to run right into Jake's arms," Sam said. "Because 'e be waitin' fer ye jist around the corner."

Sam's hand shot out and grabbed Grace by the wrist. She struggled against his iron grip, but Sam just laughed. "Yer master be right, ye knows," he said in a voice etched with an ugly tone. "Ye do be nothin' but a slave. An' on a ship, a slave girl be open market fer us."

Evidently this idea struck Chester as funny, because he burst out in peals of laughter. "Maybe ye will find yerself a wife at last, Sam!" he chortled. "Maybe ye—"

"Stop it!"

At the sound of Captain Ross's voice, Sam's arms fell limp at his sides and the leering mirth faded from the crannies of his face. Grace, shaking with fear and rage, pulled back to the door of her room and set about adjusting her clothes.

"Capt'n, sir!" Sam stammered. "We be 'elping the lady 'ere to the . . . we be givin' 'er a 'and, sir, and—"

"Yes, I saw the helpful assistance you offered Miss Winslow," Captain Ross said with disgust.

One seaman after another left his work station and eased over to watch the action. The captain motioned to First Mate Brandt and declared, "Six lashes for Seaman Sam Cooke,

Mister Brandt. Four lashes for Chester Mundy and Jake Martin for assisting Seaman Cooke in his plan to attack a passenger."

"Capt'n, no!" Sam argued. "We was jist 'avin' us some fun is all!"

Captain Ross ignored him. "As for the rest of you layabouts, half rations for two days."

"What did we do?" demanded a stout, crusty sailor named Billy. "It ain't fair, you goin' after the likes o' us fer nothin'!"

"I did not rise to the rank of captain by acting the fool," said Captain Ross. "I have made it my business to keep my eyes on all of you. Every one of you knew what Sam Cooke had in mind, and every one of you played a part in his despicable game. I will not have my crew behaving in such a perverse way toward a passenger entrusted to my care on this ship."

"But on a slave ship—" someone called out.

"This is *not* a slave ship!" Captain Ross shot back. "This is a merchant ship that has on board two paying passengers. Have I not said as much repeatedly? My duty is to see both of them safely to the shores of England. And, to the degree that it is in my power, I fully intend to do exactly that."

"But she be a slave!" Sam spat bitterly, motioning to Grace.

"A slave she most certainly is not!" Captain Ross bellowed. "Miss Winslow is bound for England, not America. If you value your skin, you will remember that!"

For several minutes everyone seemed uncertain what would happen next. They all looked awkwardly from one to another. But if the seamen hoped for a reprieve from their punishment, they were to be sorely disappointed.

"Dismissed!" Captain Ross ordered abruptly. "Back to work, every last one of you, watch or no watch!" To Grace he said, "Will you be desiring further assistance, lass?"

"No . . . no," she replied.

The captain bowed low, then turned to go.

"Captain Ross," Grace called after him. When he paused and turned back, she said, "Thank you, sir."

If Captain Ross thought his general scolding and all-around punishment would bring the situation to a close, he underestimated the fury of his crewmen. For that very night, as Billy scraped up the last bits of his half portion of pease porridge from his wooden dinner plank and ate his half a biscuit dry, he growled to anyone who would listen, "'Ere we be goin' hungry whilst the slave sits in her private quarters eatin' like she was the queen. So we knows well where our dear captain's heart be. Ah, yes, we knows that fer sure."

8

*W*hether it was day or night, Cabeto could not tell. All he could make out in the stifling darkness was the sweaty body of the groaning man chained in front of him. Cabeto's left wrist was fettered to the man's right wrist. If Cabeto tugged hard against that chain, and the one that shackled his right wrist to the weeping woman behind him, he could raise himself up on his elbows until his head hit against the wooden platform the ship's carpenter had nailed three feet off the deck to enable Captain Hudson to cram an extra one hundred captives into the hold of the *Golden Hawk*. Even pushed up as high as he could, though, he wasn't able to see much of anything.

"Buried we be," the man in front of him moaned. "Buried alive as sure as if we lay under the dirt."

With his ankles locked into irons and chained to rings bolted to the floor, Cabeto found it impossible to change his position. In the suffocating heat, he gasped for air. The hold was so rancid with human stench that Cabeto could not draw a full breath. He could barely keep a straight thought in his mind. Yet he must think straight. He absolutely must.

Somewhere nearby, a woman screamed as her baby struggled to enter a world of insanity.

"Sunba!" Cabeto called.

"I am here, Brother," Sunba's answer echoed back through the dark.

"Kome," Cabeto called.

"I am here."

"Hola."

"Here I am," answered Hola in a frighteningly weakened voice.

As he regularly did at what he guessed to be daily intervals, Cabeto continued the roll call of his villagers. So far, all still lived, unlike the poor young boy on the other side of the woman next to him. She had awakened to find that sometime during the night the young one had gone to the ancestors. For many hours—days perhaps?—she had lain sobbing in the dark, chained to the dead boy. Finally, two white sailors came down, cloths tied around their faces so they could avoid breathing the deadly air, and they carried the boy away. They piled him on top of the bodies of others who had also died and pushed them all up the stairs. In the hold, Cabeto and the woman next to him listened in silence to the splash . . . splash . . . splash . . . splash . . . of those thrown overboard into the sea.

"Tawnia," Cabeto called.

"I . . . am here, Cabeto," the young girl sobbed.

"Safya."

"Yes, I am here," Safya answered hoarsely.

"Ama."

Silence.

"Ama!" Cabeto demanded. "Answer!"

Silence.

Cabeto forced himself up on his elbows until his head hit against the wooden platform. "Ama!" he bellowed.

Kome echoed his cry, screaming his sister's name: "AMA!" Silence.

The two screams wove into one agonized wail. The only other sound was the slap of the waves against the ship's hull.

"Of all my family, I alone remain," Kome cried. "The white man took every other one."

"The white man took you too," said a voice from out of the dark. "You too are gone."

Except for scattered, ragged naps, Cabeto hardly slept. With each lurch of the ship, the rough boards ripped into his naked skin. His lame leg ached from its cramped position. Hour after hour, he lay crunched between two strangers and listened to the cries of misery that poured out around him in a cacophony of tongues. *How like the cells at Zulina slave fortress*, he thought. It seemed impossible that hope could survive in such a place as this.

Yet hope had survived at Zulina. It had more than survived; hope had actually prospered and grown into possibility.

If only Grace were beside me, Cabeto mourned.

Immediately, he shivered with horror. What was he thinking? How dare he wish such a thing! Wherever Grace was, whatever her circumstances, it could not be worse than this slave ship. Even in the clutches of that white man—

"Brother," the woman behind Cabeto whispered, "do you remember the color of fire in the sky when morning awakens a new day?"

"Yes," Cabeto said, and the ragged edges of a smile traced his cracked lips. "I remember."

"Do you remember the sweet taste of palm tree sap when it touches your tongue?" she asked.

"Yes," Cabeto said. "And also the look of calabashes growing golden in the fields. Do you remember that?"

"Yes. But my memories make me sad because I do not think I will ever see any of those things again."

With all his heart, Cabeto longed to assure the woman whose face he had never seen but whose sweaty body cramped his meager space. But what could he say? Maybe she was right. Ama did not answer when he called her name. By tomorrow, who else would not answer?

The woman asked hesitantly, "Will you do something for me?"

"If it is something I can do while chained to you and locked to the floor, then I will do it," Cabeto said.

"The next time you call out the names, will you also call Odera? That is my name."

"Yes. I will call your name each day, and each day you will answer that you are still here."

Odera's request was far more favorable than the one the man chained in front of Cabeto asked of him. "Brother," that desperate man gasped. "I go to sleep now. Please, do not allow me to awaken. Use your chains to send me to the ancestors. Please, I beg of you!"

This Cabeto would not do. But when the white seamen came around with the twice-daily food ration, the man in front of Cabeto refused to reach out his hand and accept his portion. The men tried to force the food into him, but he clamped his teeth together. Even their lash could not persuade him to open his mouth. Let them whip him to death. He didn't care.

Waves slapped against the ship's hull, one after another in endless succession. They set the chains to clanging an eerie accompaniment to shrieks of misery and groans of the dying, a lament overlaid with unending sobs.

When so much time passed that Cabeto was certain it surely must be another day, he called: "Sunba."

"I am here, Brother."

"Kome."

"I am here."

"Safya."

"Yes. I am here."

One by one, Cabeto called out the names of each villager. Then he called, "Odera."

"Here I am," answered the soft voice behind him. "I am still here."

Rats scurried across the floor, gnawing indiscriminately at ropes or filthy wood or defenseless toes. The living awoke chained to the dead. Men and women went mad, and death followed the *Golden Hawk* like a fiery wind billowing out of hell.

But this day everyone answered Cabeto's call. Hope survived for one more day.

9

*W*ere any crewmen on the *Willow* shirking their duties? Were animals allowed too much freedom to roam the deck at will? Did the watch commanders pay due diligence to the sailors' work schedules? Were the rules of cleanliness rigorously observed? Captain Clayton Ross placed profound trust in his officers, yet he found more and more pressing reasons to return repeatedly to the main deck, starboard center. And because the doors to the guest cabins opened off that very area, now and again Captain Ross reaped the reward of a glimpse of the young African woman with a kiss of copper on her skin and a splash of auburn in her raven hair. Fascinating, that's what she was. Absolutely fascinating!

It was not that Captain Ross had any desire to take over in the fashion of Jasper Hathaway. The captain held nothing but disdain for that man with all his disgusting affectations. If Hathaway failed to survive the trip to England, then as far as Ross was concerned, England would be all the better for it. And Africa as well.

It did pain him to see Grace labor over this man who insisted on referring to himself as her master. All her ministrations were met with naught but rebuke and condemnation while the insufferable lout prattled on, too proud and too stubborn to cooperate with his own treatment. Well, the *Willow* had a capable medical man in John Wills. He could look in on Mister Hathaway and administer whatever treatment was deemed appropriate. That was, after all, the job of the ship's surgeon.

But what really concerned Captain Ross was Grace's safety. He was well aware of the crewmen's desire for her. As a matter of fact, he had taken it upon himself to put quill to paper and write out explicit orders concerning appropriate crew behavior toward her. Since the men could not read, he had read aloud the detailed list of commands as issued, complete with a stated penalty for each trespass, whether real or perceived. Even so, no one was more aware than he that his ship was populated with far more seamen than officers. And then there was Nate Greenway's ominous warning. Many others whispered the same ridiculous superstition about the foolhardiness of bringing a woman to sea, of course. But when it came from Nate—an intelligent officer!—it gave even the straight-thinking captain pause.

All these considerations ran through Captain Ross's mind as he found himself drawn again and again to the main deck, center starboard. But being an honorable and upright man, he kept his mouth closed and his thoughts to himself. Until, that is, the day that shouts from Jasper Hathaway's cabin created such a stir that they silenced even the calls and chants of the crewmen at work.

"You *shall* do as I command you!" Hathaway ordered in a rasping rattle. "No! You shall not offer one more argument! You still belong to me, and you *shall do* . . . *shall do as I* . . . *as I order you!*"

"Please . . . please—" This was Grace's voice.

"I still have my whip, and you are still my slave!" countered Jasper Hathaway, though his waning strength drained some of the menace from his threats. "Do not think that because . . . that due to my compromised condition, I . . . that I shall hesitate to use the lash or . . . or—"

Captain Ross pushed his way into the unlocked room. "Not on my ship, you shan't!"

Jasper Hathaway sagged against his pillows looking ghostly pale and gaping at the intruder. He clutched a cloth and used it to mop at his bleeding mouth.

"As commander of the *Willow*, and hence the one who bears ultimate responsibility for the well-being of my passengers, I order Miss Grace Winslow away from your cabin for the remainder of the journey, Mister Hathaway."

"Now, see here. This is my—"

"No, *you* see here, sir. I am captain of this ship, and therefore in full command! And I believe I have made my position on servitude abundantly clear. I applaud Miss Grace for the care she has provided you thus far. But henceforth I shall insist that Doctor Wills take over your care."

"I demand that I be allowed the services of my . . . my personal servant," Jasper Hathaway responded as indignantly as his wretched condition would allow. "Furthermore, I demand that she supply me with the fresh fruit I know you have hidden away for your own personal use. You have no right to provide for yourself and your officers whilst paying passengers go in need."

Captain Ross, his eyes narrowed and a shadow of disgust darkening his face, pronounced in metered cadence, "I assure you, sir, we have no such store of fruits. The officers, including myself, all adhere to the self-same procedures Doctor Wills prescribes for you. As master of this vessel, I have as my personal responsibility the safety of each passenger. It is I who am now forced to issue a demand."

That was how Grace came to be established in the comfortable cabin situated between that of the captain and the one shared by Brandt and Nate Greenway. On the first morning in her new accommodations, Grace arose early and hurried to the galley to prepare morning tea for the captain.

"Capt'n sent ye, did 'e?" chided the skeptical cook. He was a sturdy stovepipe of a man, thick and squat and plain, never without the cooking spoon he swung around him like a weapon.

"Well, no," Grace said. "But I need to serve him his tea before I see to his breakfast, and I—"

"See to his breakfast, is it? And why is that? The captain cain't walk no more, is that the way it be?"

Grace had no idea how to respond to so outrageous a question.

"If'n 'e wants 'is tea served to 'im, 'e kin ask me fer it same as 'e does ever other day," the cook said with a dismissive wave of his cooking spoon.

The fact was that Captain Ross did *not* want Grace to serve him his tea. In fact, he didn't want anything from her at all. "You are a passenger on my ship," he said with a courteous bow. "My only desire is to see you safely to England, and then to wish you well in a new land."

Grace took to joining Captain Ross and Jonas Brandt for afternoon tea in the captain's office. Often Doctor Wills joined them, and on occasion, Nate Greenway as well. At first Grace was quite uncomfortable with the cadre of proper Englishmen—even a bit fearful of them. But as she listened to them talk and laugh, she grew more at ease. She especially enjoyed the stories of their exploits at sea, and of their adventures in exotic countries—China, Spain, Italy, Portugal.

"You will adore London, Miss Grace," Jonas Brandt said to her. "It is the greatest city in the entire world." That's all it took to launch the men into tales of the wonders of London.

"In one way, it is an entirely new city since the Great Fire," said Doctor Wills.

· "The whole city burned?" Grace asked incredulously.

"It might as well have," said the doctor. "Just over one hundred years ago, it was—in 1666. The fire started in a baker's house. Just an ordinary house fire, it was. That happened often since all the houses were made of wood back then. But that summer, not a drop of rain had fallen, and winds blew with an unnatural might. So when one house burst into flames, another followed, then another, then another, then another, until the fire liked to reduce the city to ashes."

"They couldn't put it out?" Grace gasped.

"They tried, of course. But their buckets of water were useless against such an inferno."

"All the churches had lead roofs back then," Nate Greenway added, "and they say that lead melted and poured into the streets like milk."

"Fifteen thousand homes burned in that fire," said Doctor Wills.

Grace gasped out loud. In her mind, she didn't see London burning. She saw roaring flames swallowing up her parents' house.

"Ach! A great tragedy it was," said the captain. "But great good came out of it too. With so much death and destruction, the king ordered the city rebuilt and new houses and shops to be made of brick, not wood."

". . . beauty for ashes, the oil of joy for mourning, the garment of praise for the spirit of heaviness." Words from Mama Muco's holy book. Words from her Bible.

"Never again will another fire like that burn down London," said the doctor. "Such a horror must not happen twice in the same place."

But it had! They had built their village on the place of the disaster, and just look what had happened! Just see the horror that had happened again!

"Come, now! Why tell tragic tales?" Nate exclaimed. "Tell of the Frost Fairs when the Thames freezes over."

"Oh, yes," Jonas said. "Shops and food stalls and puppet shows . . ."

". . . sledding and skating. That is what I remember from my boyhood days," said Nate. "Ice bowling too."

"Mince pies to eat and hot baked potatoes to keep your hands warm whilst you watch the entertainers," said Doctor Wills.

Captain Ross laughed heartily. "The colder the winter, the thicker the ice. The thicker the ice, the better the fair. It is just as I said: From bad comes good. From the worst comes the best!"

One afternoon when the first mate was standing watch and not in attendance at tea, after Doctor Wills had excused himself to see to his patients, and Mister Greenway to consult his navigational charts, Grace found an excuse to stay behind. "Captain Ross," she said when the others had gone, "did you ever sail on a slave ship, sir?"

Slowly, precisely, Captain Ross lifted his teacup to his lips and sipped. His hand shook so badly that tea splashed down the front of his spotless coat. Clayton Ross sighed deeply and set his cup back down.

"Yes," he answered. "Two times I sailed as mate, one time as captain. But I shall never do so again."

"What was it like?"

"Why do you ask about a slave ship?" Captain Ross snapped. "You are not on so accursed a vessel."

"No," said Grace, "but my heart is."

For several minutes, Captain Ross sat and considered. When he finally spoke, it was with a weary voice. "Under my captain's orders, I packed the hold of that first slave ship tight. We set sail in a ship screaming with agony night and day, until I thought I would go mad. But we sold the slaves on the island of Antigua and I walked away a proud man with a bulging purse. The second trip, I hardly heard the cries, so stopped were my ears with the promise of riches. On the third trip, I sailed from Africa not only deafened by the hope of profit but blinded by the promise of power. It was the worst sailing of all, yet I am pained to admit that I cared nothing about the suffering in the tight-packed hold below me.

"Then somewhere in the blinding black of rough seas, as I lay alone on my bunk, one haunting voice rose out of the agony, a lone lament to a life lost forever. The mournful melody echoed up through the ship's boards and pierced clear through to my heart. That single tormented tune will not leave my soul in peace, not to this very day. I never again sailed another slave ship, nor shall I."

Grace stared at the gentle captain in wide-eyed disbelief.

"You will learn, my dear lassie, that it is not only terrible people who are capable of doing terrible things."

"My village . . . everyone was bound with ropes and taken away," Grace said. "They killed my little son, my innocent Kwate. And they took away Cabeto, the love of my heart. Only Mama Muco is left for me in Africa. Or it may be that she is not. How can I know?"

For many minutes Captain Ross said nothing. He didn't even make a pretense of drinking his tea. When he finally spoke, he said, "The horrors of the slave trade are many. One of the greatest is that it destroys the humanity of those who practice it. It must be so. How else could reasonable, decent Christian men and women bring themselves to act in so beastly a way?"

"What will happen to him?" Grace asked in a voice barely more than a whisper. "What will they do to my Cabeto?"

"Do not ask me such a question," the captain replied. "Thank God that you are here, and then let it go. Give thanks to Almighty God that you, at least, are safe."

"Tell me!" Grace demanded with an edge of desperate ferocity. "What of my husband?"

Captain Ross leaned back and sighed deeply. "They will take him to the islands, Antigua or Saint Kitts," he said. "They will work him chopping sugar cane, and there he will stay for the rest of his life. A strong, able-bodied young man—he could live for five years, maybe six."

"But he isn't able-bodied! Cabeto was badly injured in a fire. He is lame in one leg and badly scarred."

"Oh," Captain Ross said. His voice had an ominous sound.

"What?" Grace demanded.

"Well, in that case, they probably will not keep him in the islands. The work there is too hard for someone in a compromised state. They will likely take him on to the United States and sell him at the slave market at Charleston. He will probably sell cheap . . . to be used for dangerous labor."

"And then what?"

"And then they will work him to death."

Grace jumped to her feet. "I have to get to him first!" she cried. "Please, can you take me there? To the United States? To the slave market in Charleston?"

Carefully, deliberately, Captain Ross replaced his cup on the tea service and laid the tea set aside. He stood up and carefully smoothed the creases out of his coat and trousers. "No, I cannot," he said. "Even if I could, I would not. I realize it causes you pain to hear me say so, Miss Grace, but you are best advised to put this man out of your mind. He will not survive more than a year."

"Then that means I have one year to find him!" Grace declared. "One year to find the good in the bad. One year to find the best in the worst."

10.

The slave be in the capt'n's quarters, same as always," Jake proclaimed to the clusters of sailors who complained together all along the lines, who grumbled while they stacked barrels, and matched grievances over the chicken cages. A particularly angry clutch of seamen hunched over a bucket glowing with red-hot coals.

"Under *'is majesty's* pertection, is wot!" Sam mocked. He plucked up a stick, whittled sharp at one end, and skewered a skinned rat. Then he elbowed his way to the hot coals. "As always—ever' hour of ever' day of ever' week, she be in the capt'n's quarters."

"That's cuz she be the capt'n's woman now," Billy growled. He held his own sizzling tidbit over the coals, turning it with an expert hand to roast both sides. "She be a slave and a curse, yet still she lives like queen o' this ship."

"She be queen whilst *we* be the ones wot gits the lash and chases after rats to feed our starvin' bellies," grumbled Sam.

"If we has to run the risks of a woman on board, then by all wot's fair she should be ours," insisted Billy. "'Specially a *slave* woman. The capt'n has no right to keep 'er locked in 'is cabin all fer 'isself!'"

In actual fact, Grace was seldom with the captain, rarely alone with him, and never in his private cabin. She passed most of her days by herself in her own accommodations where she veered back and forth between despair and hope. In her hours of despair, she lay on her bunk and sobbed. In her hours of hope, she flew into a frantic frenzy, weaving together preposterous plots for finding Cabeto and getting both him and herself back home to Africa.

But the times of hope always ended when weariness overtook her. She drifted into a restless sleep, awash in impossible dreams of walking in the moonlight with her husband at her side, their little son kicking at fallen mangos as Mama Muco scolded him from the doorway . . . then, in her strong, husky voice, beckoned them all home for the night. Happy dreams of her life before Jasper Hathaway ripped it apart and dashed it to pieces.

Late at night, when only the brightest stars pierced the inky black blanket of sky, Grace ventured out to walk along the quarter deck in search of the North Star. Always trustworthy, it always showed steady in the same place in the night sky. Somehow, such unswerving dependability gave her hope. Sailors followed the stars. Perhaps that brightest of all stars would lead her to Cabeto.

Grace felt safe on that isolated back deck, since only she and the few officers were allowed there. She gazed out into the dark and remembered Cabeto's eyes, so deep and searching; his ready smile and deep, rumbling laugh; the funny way his hair grew thick on one side and thin on the other.

One evening, Grace paused in her stroll and stood at the railing. She looked up at the stability of the North Star, then down into the powerful depths of the waves that churned in the ship's wake. A refreshing breeze blew and eased her troubled mind. She didn't even notice Doctor Wills step up behind her.

"Jasper Hathaway is in a desperate state," the doctor said.

Grace didn't answer, nor did she shift her gaze from the sea.

"His old scars and healed wounds have opened up into new sores, a particular complication of scurvy. And his teeth are falling out. His mind is breaking down as well."

Still Grace said nothing.

"Mister Hathaway is a stubborn fool. He turns his back on every remedy I suggest and calls me a charlatan who only desires to preserve the real cure for the ship's officers."

"Yes," Grace said. "Mister Hathaway is a fool."

"He asks to see you," Doctor Wills said.

Grace sighed.

"You owe the man nothing. Yet because he is my patient, I am duty-bound to pass his request along to you. Should you agree to see him, the captain and I shall accompany you to his quarters. But should you decide to decline his request, no one will think the less of you for it."

Grace felt as though her body had turned to stone. See Jasper Hathaway again? Stand beside that despicable man, with the captain and the good doctor looking on, and tell him—what? That all was forgiven? Even though her son lay shattered and gone? Even though this very night her husband sailed to the ends of the earth on a slave ship of death?

The doctor laid a gentle hand on Grace's arm. "I have done my duty by my patient," he said. "I shall not speak of this again. If you decide to answer Mister Hathaway's request, I insist that you let me know. If you decide otherwise, justice is well served."

Grace couldn't trust herself to look at Doctor Wills. Instead, she gazed up at the North Star. If it was in Mama Muco's power, Grace knew she would be looking at that very same star and praying to God that it would guide Grace home. And Cabeto—where was he this night? Was it possible for him to look up and see the guiding star?

Everything that had happened to Grace, all of it circled around Jasper Hathaway. He would have been her husband had her parents had their way, despite his most disagreeable nature. *A snake at your feet.* That's how her mother, Lingongo, had described him, even as she was arranging for her daughter to marry him. *Keep a stick in your hand, Grace,* Lingongo had warned, *you will need it.* It was the thought of marrying Jasper Hathaway that had forced Grace to escape from the London house, and it was the fear of his taking her back that had pushed her to Cabeto. And although everything that had happened had come about because of evil intent, she was grateful for the happy years in the village—her life with Cabeto, baby Kwate, and Mama Muco.

From bad comes good.

And then Jasper Hathaway had forced his way back into her life and destroyed everything all over again.

From the worst comes the best.

How could that be so? All Grace knew for certain was that she did not want to see the man. Certainly not in the presence of Captain Ross and Doctor Wills. What she would have to say to Mister Hathaway, she had no wish for the two of them to hear. They were kind men, but what did they know of straddling two worlds—both foreign, both hostile, both treacherous?

And yet, the thought of leaving the solitude of her cabin for the busy-ness of the main deck did hold its share of attraction. For in truth, Grace was terribly bored. From her cabin, she could hear singing and dancing on the deck, and sometimes raucous laughter and wild cheers. She longed to watch the fun. Not to take part in it, of course; just to stand in the shadows and watch. The captain had forbidden her to do so—"unseemly," he insisted, "not to mention needlessly dangerous." But Grace was no child. She could take care of herself.

If I make my way back at twilight . . . she thought. *If I am careful to stay hidden in the shadows . . .*

And now, after Doctor Wills's words, were the captain to discover her where she was not supposed to be—well, she could simply plead a responsibility to look in on Jasper Hathaway.

The very next evening, when Mister Brandt came along the deck at sunset to light the lanterns, Grace opened the door of her cabin the same as she usually did, and she reached out her candlestick to him to light the wick of the candle. But this evening, strains of a strangely sweet music wafted through her open cabin door on the evening breeze.

"What is it that makes such music, Mister Brandt?" Grace asked.

"A fiddle," Jonas Brandt answered. "Jake Martin plays it rather well for a thief who was almost hanged at the gallows and only just escaped from Newgate Prison, do you not agree?"

Grace did indeed. And as soon as Mister Brandt was out of sight, and her candlestick was safely settled on the table, she slipped out the door. She stole past the officers' berths and, following the music, made her way toward the main deck. In the waning light, under the shadows of the deck lanterns, she spied a cluster of seamen hunkered down and crowded together. Jake's fiddle almost drowned out their voices, but Grace was well acquainted with the sound of men calling out wagers. Still, no one in the group looked to be throwing dice.

Odd, that. Nor could she see any playing cards. Odder still. What were the gamblers doing?

Grace inched forward just a bit, then a bit more, taking care to stay hidden behind a stack of barrels. What she saw was a circle scratched onto the floor. In it was a huge cockroach, along with several smaller ones.

"'As ye a favored one?"

Grace jumped backwards and gasped.

Sam stood behind her, sniggering wickedly. "Ever see a cockroach race afore?" He downed his tot of rum, smacked his lips loudly, then wiped his filthy sleeve across his face. "Ye wants to place a bet on yer favorite, then?"

Icy fear gripped Grace and crept up her back. Frantically she searched for a way of escape.

"Do yer dear capt'n know ye come to visit wi' yer old friends?" Sam asked.

Grace tried to push past him, but Sam would have none of it. His eyes flashed viciously and, in a near growl, he said, "'Ere now. Ye be fergettin' yerself, missy."

The fiddle fell silent, and the race was abandoned— although Chester did grab up the biggest cockroach and slip it into his pocket. Billy strode over and placed his body on one side, blocking her way, while Chester stepped up behind her so she could not turn back. Several other men moved in to fill in the gaps on either side. Every eye was on Grace.

"Ye knows wot the capt'n is doin', don't ye!" This was Billy speaking, and his words were an accusation, not a question. "Fattenin' ye up, 'e is, and glossenin' ye perty fer the slave ships. They be set to come by any day now. The capt'n . . . 'e be plannin' to sell ye, 'e does. 'Eard 'im talkin' about it with me own two ears. Says ye'll fetch 'im a better price than all the silk in China."

Grace tried to push past Billy, but he grabbed her and forced her toward Sam. "'Ere, she be yers," Billy said. "Jist as ye said."

Jonas Brandt's lash brought Sam's triumph to an abrupt end. What happened next, Grace didn't know—didn't *want* to know. She turned and ran all the way back to her cabin, slammed the door shut and pushed the table up against it. Sam and Billy were liars, both of them. She knew it was so because she knew their kind. Yet Billy's words tugged at the edges of her mind. Why *was* Captain Ross being so nice to her? Everyone wants something. Experience had taught her as much. What did Captain Ross want from her?

The next afternoon, Grace did not go to the captain's office for afternoon tea. Nor did she go the next afternoon, nor the afternoon after that. The following morning she was jarred by a light tapping on her door.

"Miss Grace." It was Captain Ross. "Please permit us the honor of your company at breakfast."

Grace sighed. She really was quite hungry. For the past two days, hard biscuits and moldy cheese had been her main fare. So, slowly, Grace opened the door.

"Come," the captain said. "A bowl of hot oatmeal awaits you, topped with sugar and cream."

Grace ate ravenously as Captain Ross, Nathaniel Greenway, Doctor Wills, and Jonas Brandt talked of the uncommonly fair weather. They spoke of the shipwrights' Lenten performance of the story of Noah—they even went so far as to mimic Noah's arguments with his wife—Ross playing the part of Noah and Brandt his wife—which set Grace to laughing in spite of herself. They talked of arriving home in time to enjoy the actual plays, what with the excellent time they were making in the fair winds. They talked of everything except what had happened on the main deck.

But Grace had to know.

"Captain Ross," Grace interrupted, "do you plan to sell me?"

"Sell you!" the captain exclaimed. "Whatever put such a preposterous idea into your head? Nothing on earth—nothing in the heavens above or in the depths of the sea—could force me to sell you."

"Billy said . . ."

"Billy! Ach, then!" Captain Ross spat. "Is it that fool that put such fears into your heart, lassie? I will put him to the lash! I will cut his rations for two weeks! I will—"

"No, no!" Grace implored. "Please, no punishments. Only tell me the truth. Why *are* you so kind to me?"

Clayton Ross fixed his eyes on Grace's troubled face. "Why did you care for Jasper Hathaway who has done nothing but oppress and torment you?" he asked with great tenderness.

Grace said nothing.

"Not everyone acts out of malice or greed, Miss Grace. You, of all people, should know that."

Still Grace said nothing.

"My intention was to protect you, yes," the captain said in a voice so soft Grace had to strain to hear his words. "But I suppose it was true that I thought of myself as well. Making penance, perhaps, for my own guilt-seared conscience. Because in Billy . . . and in Sam . . . in those troubled ruffians, you see, I recognize more of my own past than I ever wish to acknowledge."

Jonas Brandt suddenly took great interest in the design painted on his teacup. Doctor Wills paid uncommon attention to a piece of lint that settled on his breeches. Nate Greenway studied the single leather-bound book on the captain's shelf. But it was possible to avoid looking into Grace's eyes by paying rapt attention to such things for only so long.

"I must check on the watch officer," Mister Brandt suddenly recalled, and he hastily excused himself.

"I must see after my patient," recalled Doctor Wills, and he too rushed off.

"And I, uh . . ." Greenway shrugged and simply left without bothering to make up an excuse.

Only Captain Ross and Grace remained. They sat facing each other in awkward silence.

On the shelf on the far wall of Captain Ross's office, between a huge whale's tooth and a carved ivory elephant from Siam, lay the leather-bound book in which Nate Greenway had feigned such an interest. Grace had seen the book many times before, and longed to look at it. Did it tell of distant ports? London, perhaps? Such a book would while away many a long hour on this endless voyage.

"Captain," Grace said hesitantly, "the book on your shelf . . . would it be possible for me to read it one day? I would treat it with the utmost care and return it to you immediately."

"Read?" Captain Ross exclaimed. He burst out in peals of laughter.

Grace, perplexed at such a response, stared at him.

"Come now! Are you serious?" Captain Ross asked. "Surely you do not expect me to believe that you are actually able to read!"

Grace assured him she most certainly could.

"You must excuse me, my dear, but if that be true, then I do believe that other than the four of us who take tea in this room, you are probably the only person on this ship who can do as much." Captain Ross clicked his tongue and shook his head in astonishment. "Imagine, an African who can read!"

"My mother was African," Grace reminded him. "My father was as English as you are."

"In that case, he was not English at all," Captain Ross said. "For I am a proud Scotsman."

The captain went to the shelf and lifted the book from its place and handed it to Grace. "For you to read until we reach London. And to handle with utmost care."

The book did not tell about London. It did not tell of any distant ports at all. But Grace was not in the least disappointed. It was a book like the one Mama Muco got from the missionary—the Holy Bible. When she returned to her own quarters, Grace brought her candle to the small desk in her cabin and immediately set about reading it,

> In the beginning God created the heaven and the earth.
>
> And the earth was without form, and void; and darkness was upon the face of the deep. And the Spirit of God moved upon the face of the waters.
>
> And God said, Let there be light: and there was light.

Grace could almost hear Mama Muco's strong voice pronouncing each word. She had to rub her eyes and shake her head to be certain Mama was not there in the room with her.

Long into the night, Grace read the book. Then she read all the next day, and the day after that. Day after day, Grace sat in her room reading the book. Only occasionally did she join the others in the captain's office for afternoon tea, and even on those instances she was the first to excuse herself so she could get back to reading the book.

One night Grace's eyes ached so badly from long hours of reading by candlelight that she hesitantly set the book aside and moved out onto the quarter deck to clear her head.

"Nyame," Grace breathed as she looked up at the stars. "Did you send the trickster to me?"

"You spend your days reading the Bible, yet you appeal to the sky god," observed Captain Ross, who had come up behind her. "You are indeed a complex woman."

"I beg your pardon, Captain," Grace said. "I did not hear you coming." When Captain Ross didn't answer, Grace asked, "How do you know Nyame?"

"I know many things. I know that Nyame is the African name of the sky god. But what of this trickster?"

Grace chuckled. "I see there is much of Africa you do not know. Nyame is said to send the Eshu, the wandering trickster spirit, to us. It is he who brings change and quarrels to our lives. I think perhaps that I saw the trickster tonight."

"Did you now? And what did he look like, pray tell?"

"Like a cockroach," Grace said. "I saw the men race him with other cockroaches, but of course he could always win for he was the largest and the fastest of all. Unless he wanted to trick them. Then he might lose."

Captain Ross let out a hearty laugh. "You, my wee one, truly are filled with surprises!"

But Grace was not laughing.

"Who taught you to read?" Captain Ross asked.

"My father hired a tutor. My father couldn't read, although he pretended he could. He really wanted me to be an English lady. I'm afraid I was a great disappointment to him."

"Grace, when you get to England, it would be in your best interest to keep this ability to yourself. Do not let anyone know you know how to read."

"Why should I pretend? If I—"

"And if you ever have the misfortune to find yourself in the United States of America, you must absolutely never let your ability to read be known. Slaves . . . Africans . . . they can be killed for the crime of reading."

"Why, I cannot believe such a thing!" Grace exclaimed. "How can it be wrong to learn?"

"Believe it or not, it still is so," Captain Ross warned. "Please, promise me you will be very, very careful. Not everyone acts out of malice or greed, Grace, but far too many people do. You have already met some of them, and you are sure to meet many more."

11

*W*ith a deep sigh, Lady Charlotte Witherham settled herself in the comfortable reclining seat of a traveling sedan chair, a sort of hand-carried coach. A coachman slipped the hinged roof shut and clicked it into place. Perfect! Then he and three other chair-men lifted the contraption up by the long poles slid through side handles and ran along the footpaths toward Larkspur Estate. Their pace was faster than a horse-drawn coach could ever have clip-clopped on that congested street.

"Carried on a cloud," Charlotte's mother used to say of the sedan chair mode of transportation, and Lady Charlotte had to agree. She detested the noisy clatter of horse hooves. And the knocking about one must endure as a carriage rumbled over the rough cobblestones of the poorer streets—well, it was simply intolerable!

Of course, were Reginald to see her, he would fuss and fume something terrible. He always insisted she use one of the fine carriages that bore the prominent and distinctive Witherham Larkspur monogram. But that certainly would not do to fetch her home from an abolitionist rally! Anyway, Reginald would not be at home for another day, so she was free to do as she pleased, which was fortunate indeed, for should he ever discover the true purpose of her trip to her mother's bedside, *fuss and fume* would take on a terrifying new meaning.

It wasn't that Charlotte wanted to actually *be* an abolitionist. It was that she knew for certain she did *not* want to be identified with her husband's rabid anti-abolitionist circle— grown men prancing about expounding on the wretched state of the souls of Africans, spouting platitudes that proclaimed their own righteous intentions, when all the while the issue came down to nothing but money.

Simon Johnson and his vast sugar cane plantations in the West Indies; Sir Geoffrey Philips with his powerful hold over the indigo market; Augustus Jamison, whose enormous interests lay in molasses and rum production in Jamaica. Every one of them had a hand in the slavery money pot. Her own husband was over his head in it. It was his shipping fortune that provided the funds to rebuild the burned-out Zulina slave trading fortress on Africa's Slave Coast. Even now, Reginald eagerly awaited a firsthand report from his recently appointed overseer, one Jasper Hathaway. Charlotte was acquainted with the man. He was a veteran trader she had been unable to avoid in Africa, and to whom she had forever after referred as "that lump of soggy dough."

"Really, Charlotte, for a girl with so excellent an upbringing, you can play such a fool!" her mother had said earlier in the day during Charlotte's visit with her in the country. In a moment of carelessness, Charlotte had let slip a word of her intention to listen in on the public abolition meeting. In Henrietta Stevens's delicate condition, it was not easy for the woman to rouse the strength to make such a show of emotion. Immediately after her pronouncement, her face flushed a most unhealthy dusky hue. Even so, her admonition was not over.

"After all I sacrificed to make certain you had a perfect life! Now you go and put it all in jeopardy by—by—"

Here Henrietta Stevens was seized by an uncontrollable coughing fit.

"Mother, *please*," Charlotte pleaded. She rushed to get a cup of water. When she returned, she said, "I'm sorry I mentioned that silly old meeting. I shall reconsider. Now, please put it out of your mind and let us talk of more pleasant things."

"Daughter," Henrietta gasped, "you will yet be the death of me!"

Even when Charlotte left her mother's side, she was not certain whether she would head for the shops around Larkspur or listen in on the abolitionist rally. She had seen too much in Africa to rest comfortably at night. And yet, the slavery situation was not her affair. Wiser heads than hers were already debating every possible thought for and against the slave trade. Why should she involve herself in the dispute and cause still more problems for Reginald?

In the end, Lady Charlotte headed for the wrong side of London, to the square where someone always seemed ready to rant about something. She edged in among the assortment of people crowded close to hear the speakers. First the Quakers said their piece, then one Dissenter after another added his— Methodist or Baptist or some other such a one as took exception to the teachings of the Church of England. Each one issued a passionate call for an end to the African slave trade. *An end!* That they would actually dare express such a radical idea in the open amazed Lady Charlotte. But what was most shocking of all was the reaction of the people. Why, they actually cheered the speakers! But when the cheers turned to wild calls for action, Lady Charlotte quailed and edged away.

"Here, madame," a nicely dressed man called out to her. He handed her a crudely printed booklet. "You look to be a lady of intelligence. Learn the horrors of the trade from one who knows them well enough. Just two sixpence, and you take this booklet with you."

Impulsively, Charlotte loosened the strings of her purse and took out two small coins. She accepted the booklet and tucked it inside her cloak.

It had been Lord Reginald's arrangement to have his carriage go to the country and fetch Charlotte home on the following day. But Charlotte wasn't worried about that. With her husband away on business for two days, she would simply concoct some story about a friend of her mother's heading back to London and inviting Charlotte to ride along with her.

Why must everything always be done to please Reginald, anyway?

The hired chair moved swiftly and smoothly through the huddled communities of shabby houses on the city's North End. Nothing but shoddy construction, according to Reginald, who seemed to be well-versed in the matter. Cheap houses had actually been known to collapse and crush entire families asleep in their beds, he told Charlotte in an eerily chipper tone. His dainty hands acted out the grisly scenes of crushing and smothering. Charlotte shuddered at the thought.

Since she was alone in the sedan chair, Lady Charlotte pulled the abolitionist's booklet from the folds of her cloak and held it close to her face. In the hazy light, she struggled to read the first page:

> The nature and effects of that unhappy and disgraceful branch of commerce, which has long been maintained on the Coast of Africa, with the sole, and professed design of purchasing our fellow-creatures, in order to supply our West-India island and the American colonies, when they were ours, with Slaves; is now generally understood. So much

light has been thrown upon the subject, by many able pens; and so many respectable persons have already engaged to use utmost influence, for the suppression of a traffic, which contradicts the feelings of humanity; that it is hoped, this stain of our National character will soon be wiped out.

Lady Charlotte closed the booklet. *Stain of our National character!* What a thing to say! Why, her own father worked with slaves, and a kinder and better man she had never met. She closed her eyes and saw again the long lines of African captives straggling into his slave compound, bound together with ropes around their necks, limping and crying from their long forced march across the sun-baked savanna. She saw, too, the captives her father bought from the African traders. Those captives had screamed and cried and begged so piteously as they clung to one another. Still her kind, gentle father had torn them away from each other and sold them to the waiting slave ships.

Yes, Lady Charlotte decided, she would read the booklet. But not here in this wretched light. No, she would hide it under her mattress and read it in the privacy of her chambers, in the company of the cheery black folks painted across her silk damask wall coverings.

The sedan chair runners turned onto the smoothly paved streets of London's West End. Here were the grand shops with which she was so familiar. Here, too, the formal squares that stood against the aristocracy's city palaces—including the imposing Witherham Larkspur Estate. The coachmen ran her up to the front steps of the house, then they hurried to lift back the hinged roof.

Rustin, the butler, stepped outside to meet the sedan chair. "His Lordship is in his study, my lady," he said almost as though he had been waiting for Charlotte.

"Lord Reginald is at home?" Charlotte asked with a start.

"Yes, my lady," Rustin replied. "He has been asking after you. He eagerly awaits your return."

But Reginald was not due to return for another day! It was not like him to change his plans.

"Send the sedan chair away," Lady Charlotte ordered hurriedly. But before the butler could obey, she quickly added, "And, Rustin, there is no reason to speak of my arrival to anyone. Not to *anyone*!"

She hurried inside. Without even pausing for the maid to take her cloak, Lady Charlotte rushed for the stairs and her private chambers.

"Charlotte!" It was Reginald, and he was on his way down the stairs. "Is that you, my dear?"

Without answering, Charlotte darted across to the parlor. She pulled the booklet out from the folds of her cloak and slid it under the cushion of the closest Queen Anne chair.

"Charlotte!" This time the call was a sharp demand, and it came from right behind her.

Lady Charlotte jumped, and her hand instinctively flew to her throat. She stumbled backward.

"Whatever is the matter with you?" Lord Reginald asked, his voice etched with more irritation than usual. He caught his wife by the arm. "Why, you haven't yet taken off your cloak!" He called out to the maid, "Owens! Come and tend to your mistress! And I do believe she is in need of tea."

Lord Reginald led Charlotte across the room and to the sofa. "My dear, you seem to be terribly unsettled. I have never known an excursion to the country to produce such an effect on you. Did you have a difficult day with your mother?"

"My—? Oh, yes. Mother is not doing well. Not well at all."

"As you are well aware, it was my intention to send one of our carriages to collect you tomorrow. I told you as much. But even as I gave the order for the carriage driver to depart, word came to me that you were already on your way home. Of course, I was at a total loss of what to think—as I am certain you can understand."

"Oh, well, I . . . That is, a friend of Mother's . . ." Lady Charlotte stammered. To her relief, the maid came in bearing the tea setting. "Ah, exactly what I need! Thank you, Owens. Thank you!"

The maid collected Lady Charlotte's cloak and gloves and disappeared. She quickly returned to lay out the tea. All the while Lady Charlotte struggled to regain her composure. But in spite of herself, her glance continued to return to the Queen Anne chair. To her alarm, she could see a corner of the pamphlet protruding from under the cushion.

". . . and although I do not wish to seem insensitive, I do think we must talk of a more permanent situation for your mother," Lord Reginald was saying. "As you will recall, it is my expressed opinion that you would both be better off without the visits. Just see how it upsets you!"

But Lord Reginald was not fooled. With the swift precision of a lion that has caught wind of weakened prey, he fixed his attention on Charlotte's nervous glance toward the chair. His hunting instinct sprung into high gear. With deliberate steps, he strode over, grabbed hold of the exposed booklet corner between his forefinger and thumb, and slowly pulled it from its hiding place. He may as well have inserted a razor-sharp claw into Charlotte's throat.

Too terrified to move, Charlotte watched helplessly as her husband read the first page of the booklet. His face twitched, then paled—his fingers clutched the pages ever more tightly until his knuckles turned white.

Slowly Lord Reginald lowered the book and glared over it at his wife.

"What is that you found . . . dear?" Charlotte asked in a ridiculous attempt at innocence.

"Your voice quakes . . . *dear!*" Reginald replied in a low rumble. "And I have no doubt but that you know perfectly well what I found."

Charlotte gulped and willed her voice not to quail. "Why, no," she said with fake lightness. "You know how dreadfully reading bores me. I much prefer to call on my friends, or to visit the shops that—"

Lord Reginald, his face burning hot and the veins throbbing at his aristocratic temples, turned fiery eyes on his wife. "Stop!" he ordered.

Charlotte ceased her babble mid-sentence.

"Idiocy from some abolitionist fool makes up the sum total of this booklet!" Lord Reginald pronounced. "Although its content must most assuredly be well-known to you, for no one other than you would be brainless and impertinent enough to bring such poisonous nonsense into this fine house." His voice seething with his fury, Reginald wagged a finger in Charlotte's face. "Really, I should not be surprised at this alarming turn of events. The time you spent in Africa has doubtless befouled your mind beyond reason. I warned that you were never to let anyone know of your father's degrading involvement in that heathen land, but apparently you paid me not the least mind, because you—"

Charlotte jumped to her feet. "And what of your involvement, husband?" she charged.

"What?"

"What of your involvement in Africa, Reginald? Your ships, your slave-trading factories, your hired trade managers?

What of Mister Hathaway, of whom you have been speaking nonstop for the past year?"

"Now, see here, I—"

"No, you see here. Night after night, you meet with your colleagues for endless hours, talking over countless ways to protect your business investments in Africa. You may know business, Lord Reginald Witherham, but you do not know everything. The times are changing. And so are the sensibilities of God-fearing Englishmen and women."

"You do not know of what you speak," Lord Reginald said with a dismissive wave of his hand. The blinding rage had faded from him, and in its place Charlotte recognized the smallest seed of concern.

"Perhaps, then, my husband, I would do well to learn more."

In an effort to refocus a conversation that had taken a most distressing turn, Lord Reginald charged, "Nevertheless, you purposely deceived me. You collected from an undisclosed person or persons a pamphlet designed to rouse the rabble of this city; you hid said pamphlet from me; and when I discovered it, you persisted in your claim that it had not come from you. You lied to me, Charlotte!"

Satisfied that he had at least scored the final point, Sir Reginald leaned back against the fireplace mantle to bask in his triumph.

"And so, it is speaking the truth that is most important to you, husband?" Lady Charlotte asked.

"Indeed it is. A man of truth has every reason to expect truth from his wife," Lord Reginald replied in the sanctimonious tone that so frayed Charlotte's endurance. "If I cannot believe the words you speak, then you are unworthy to be called Lady Witherham."

In the brief interval that Charlotte was silent, a self-satisfied smile settled across Lord Reginald's face. Then, in her sweetest voice, Charlotte said, "Perhaps the booklet was left by the black woman with red hair and the green eyes that flash with fire. You know the woman I mean. You insist she come to this house to help in the service as a chambermaid. Ena. That is her name, is it not? I do believe you scheduled her to clean your study this very morning whilst I was away visiting mother and you were out of town. But, no, you were not out of town, after all. You were right here at home, were you not?"

Lord Reginald's face blanched.

"Honesty between us. What a fascinating idea!" Lady Charlotte said. Then, with her laugh echoing around her, she headed for the stairs and the security of her private chambers.

12

"he days drag by too slowly, every one exactly the same as the one before," Jasper Hathaway had continually complained to Grace of their time aboard the ship.

Grace certainly did not find it so. One day the sea would lie so still and clear that when she stood on the deck and looked down it was almost as if she were gazing into an immense looking glass. But the very next day, winds would tear at the sails, and the sea—frothy and wild—would pound the ship with such fury she would wonder how the boards held together. One day the steaming deck would be lined with drying laundry and hammocks airing in the scorching sun, and the next day rain would fall in such torrents that even the rats dared not venture out on deck.

"Thank you, God, for the still seas, and thank you for the blowing wind," Grace prayed. "Thank you for the sun and thank you for the rain. Thank you, God, even for the rats."

It was a sincere prayer, too, for it was due to the plague of rats that Puss was on board the ship. The huge orange-striped cat, with bright green eyes and outsized claws, was so effective that some sailors complained he was depriving them of fresh meat. Cook scolded Grace for feeding scraps to Puss: "Feed 'im fer free an' 'e won't work no more. Not much different than a man in that!" But Grace and Puss were friends, and she treated him as such. By mid-journey, Puss was snoozing off a good bit of his work time on Grace's bunk.

While the days were not the same, they certainly were predictable. Grace appreciated that. Every morning, the cabin boy brought breakfast to her room—oatmeal or bread and hard cheese, now and then a fresh egg, and tea with milk. Her mornings she spent reading Captain Ross's Bible. Afternoons, after the cabin boy brought her a cool drink and hard bread, she waited for Puss to come by, and they both took a rest. If the cat tended to his rat-catching business and left Grace alone, she read right on through the afternoon. At the sound of eight bells in the afternoon watch—precisely four o'clock—tea was brought to the captain's office. Grace was always welcome to join the officers. She generally ate her dinner alone in her cabin, for she never felt truly comfortable with the men.

Sometime after the first watch—eight in the evening—when the air was cool and the deck quiet—Grace strolled along the quarter deck and paused to look out over the rail. She made it a practice to draw in her mind a detailed picture of Cabeto, lest she forget some feature about him. The wrinkles around his laughing eyes, the ripple of muscles in his strong arms when he brought the hoe crashing down on hard ground, the touch of his calloused hands, strong enough to crush a gourd yet tender enough to wipe the tears from Kwate's baby cheeks. Cabeto, a brawny man of peace, a gentle man of action.

Alone with the moon and the stars and her memories, Grace begged Mama Muco's God to take care of Cabeto. "And please show me the way to his side."

One gray day, Grace left her cabin door ajar in hopes that Puss would stop by and cheer her up. She was feeling particularly lonely, not even in the mood to read the holy book. In the early afternoon, an off-key work song drifted over from the main deck as the sailors set a rhythm for pulling the lines. Grace longed to watch them work and listen to them sing, but she knew better.

Eight bells. Tea time. Grace sighed heavily, and stretched out across her bunk. But the crewmen stopped their singing, and Puss still had not come to keep her company. So Grace pulled herself together and brushed the wrinkles from her dress, then went out to join the officers for tea.

"You look a wee bit off your pace, lass," Captain Ross observed. "Are you feeling well? Perhaps Doctor Wills should listen to your lungs."

Grace assured the captain that her lungs were perfectly fine, as was the rest of her. She ended with a terse, "Thank you kindly, sir, but you need not concern yourself." Then, in the awkward silence that followed, Grace blurted out the question that had been plaguing her mind all day: "Are there Africans in London?"

"What a question!" Jonas Brandt said with a laugh. "Of course there are, Miss Grace. Many thousands of them."

"What do they look like?" Grace asked. "I mean, do they dress like English or like Africans?"

"Like English, of course," Mister Brandt answered. "Just as we are dressed—frocks and hats for the women, and for the men, breeches, stockings, coats, and waistcoats."

"Are they slaves and trustees?"

"Not slaves," Jonas said. "They work at regular English jobs—porters and watermen and hawkers and such. As for trusty, I should suppose they are as dependable as any other men in London."

The others broke out in hearty laughter.

"You must forgive Mister Brandt," Captain Ross said to Grace. "He has not had the misfortune to spend time in the slave trade. As it is a trustee's job to keep slaves in line, and as Englishmen do not keep slaves—not officially, at any rate—London has no need for trustees."

Grace shook her head in confusion. "No slavery in England? That I cannot understand," she said. "The Englishmen in Africa—that is to say, men such as Mister Hathaway and my father—well, slaves are their business. And Mister Hathaway is on his way to London to meet with his . . . his . . . with his partners in the slave trade."

Captain Ross sighed and shook his head. "You are not alone in your struggle to understand the contradiction. It is indeed a perplexing situation. It is true that Englishmen are active in the slave trade, yet it is also true that in London almost all Africans are free." After a moment's pause he added, "Of this you can be certain, lass: once you reach England's shores, you will never again need worry about being bought or sold."

When did I first dream of sailing across the sea to England, the land of my father? Grace wondered.

Once when she was very young—no more than six years old, surely—she and her playmate Yao climbed to the highest branches of the gharati tree on the far side of her parents' compound. Gazing over the wall, she had bragged to Yao that she could see the other side of the world. Was that the first time she dreamed of sailing away? Or was it when her father came home from a year at sea and brought a book just for her, with wonderful stories and illustrations all about glorious England? Of a certainty, it was well before she sneaked away from her parents' house, climbed over her father's wall, and forever left her family's English compound on the African savanna. Before her capture and the slave rebellion. Before the first joint of her forefinger was sliced off and sent to her father. Before her first life came to an abrupt end. All that had happened only five years earlier, and the dream had been with her far longer than five years.

"Miss Grace? Miss Grace?" It was the doctor's voice. "I say! Have you left us and gone someplace else entirely?"

"Oh . . . no, sir!" Grace answered quickly. "I do apologize, sir. I was just thinking. Just remembering."

"Of course you were, my dear," said the captain. "Now you have two worlds fighting for you."

"I have always had two worlds, but neither one has ever fought for me," Grace replied in a voice barely more than a whisper. Rather than offer an explanation, she asked another question: "Are there any in London like me? Not really African and not really English? Half and half, and neither and both?"

"Oh, yes," said Captain Ross. "Half and half, and some half again. Many neither and many both."

Grace looked at the teacup in her hand. It was just like the one she had long ago learned to delicately hold. White porcelain, it was, decorated with intricately hand-painted blue forget-me-nots.

"My mother would like this teacup," Grace said to no one in particular. "She hates everything else English, but she loves English teacups."

Uneasy laughter sprinkled across the group, but Grace didn't seem to notice.

"Did you know that my mother, Lingongo, is an African princess? She is, although my father always said that would not count for much in England."

"Unfortunately, he was most likely quite right," mused Doctor Wills. "In my experience, one kingdom seldom has much use for the royalty—or the populace—of another."

Another pensive quiet settled over the group. The waning afternoon had dragged on well past teatime. At the sound of the ship's bell, Doctor Wills heaved a sigh, shook his head, and announced, "Ah, well, as pleasant as this time has been, work calls to me. So with reluctance, I shall bid you adieu."

"Yes, yes, the duties of the ship. They ever await us, do they not?" Mister Brandt said with a laugh. He too stood to go. Captain Ross did not ask either to tarry.

Grace also set her teacup on the table. But when she stood and began to say her farewells, Captain Ross interrupted, insisting, "No, no, Miss Grace. Please, sit a wee bit longer."

A worried look crossed Grace's face.

"It is not a matter for concern," the captain said quickly. "On the contrary. You asked several questions of me. Now I have one to ask of you." Again he urged, "Please . . . sit."

Grace perched uneasily on the edge of her chair.

"Have you managed to read anything in the Bible I lent you?" the captain asked.

"Oh, yes!" Grace said. "And I recognize many of Mama Muco's stories in it. Joseph, the slave who saved his family. Pharaoh of Egypt, so stubborn that God sent Moses to call down plagues that filled the people's houses with frogs and their fields with locusts and their rivers with blood until the Pharaoh finally let the slaves go free. Naomi, who was far from her land and her people, but she went back home again and found a new and happy life."

"Excellent, Miss Grace," the captain said. "I was always partial to the story of Noah, perhaps because he, like myself, was a reluctant man of the sea. How about you? Have you a favorite?"

"Perhaps I would have to say Esther," Grace said thoughtfully. "She was a slave like me—much greater than me, of course, because she became the queen of the entire land, and I know that will never happen to me in England! But it doesn't matter, does it, because being queen wasn't the important thing about her. The important thing was what she did with her power. Captain Ross, did you know that Queen Esther risked her life to save her people?"

"Yes. I have heard the story of Esther many times."

"There was a special reason for her to be a slave in that far-away land," Grace said, "even though Esther didn't know what the reason was. Mordecai told her, 'Who knoweth whether thou art come to the kingdom for such a time as this?'"

What Grace didn't tell the captain was that she had read the story of Esther not once, not twice, but six times. And each time she read it, she wondered: *Could this be my story too? Could I be a slave on my way to England for such a time as this?*

"If I die, I die!" Grace whispered.

"Come, come, my dear lass! I hardly think it will come to that!" Captain Ross said with a nervous laugh.

He set his teacup down on the tray and stood up abruptly. Grace knew what that meant. It was time for her to thank the captain, bid him goodbye, and retire to her own room. That would be the polite thing to do. It was the only proper thing to do. But Grace could not. Something pressed hard on her mind. One more question of extreme importance.

"Captain Ross," Grace ventured. "I am afraid you will think me terribly impudent and improper, yet I must ask you. I must beg you, sir. When you next go back to sea, will you take me with you? Please, Captain, will you take me to the United States in America, to the place where they sell the slaves?"

The captain raised his eyebrows and stared at her in disbelief. "I most certainly will do nothing of the kind!" Then, the hurt showing in his blue eyes, he said, "After all I poured out to you from the depths of my heart, would you still take me for nothing but a slaver?"

"Oh, no, sir, I know you are no slaver. I just mean, in your travels, could you find it in your heart to take me to where my husband is?" Grace's voice trembled and her eyes filled with tears. "I must find him, Captain Ross!" she pleaded. "Please, oh, please! Will you help me?"

"I would never take a girl of your color into a place so crazed with slavery, Miss Grace. It would be the end of you. No! I most definitely will not!"

Grace covered her face and wept.

"If you have any sense, lass, you will commit your husband to the care of the good Lord in heaven," Captain Ross said. Although his voice was not unkind, it was firm. "Then you will get down on your knees and thank God that you are on a civilized ship sailing in another direction. By God's grace, you will never see the United States of America."

13

$\mathcal{S}$et me up another quid!" Joseph Winslow yelled as he pushed toward the cleared circle. But his voice was lost in the roiling din of feverish bets shouted out from all directions, the wagers punctuated by the cheers of winners and curses of losers. Joseph leaned over the pit and fixed his glazed eyes on the battered four of the original thirty-two fighting roosters that still stood on their feet. Vicious metal spurs gleamed bright on their legs, and their beaks, sharpened to razor points, showed flecks of chicken flesh and smears of blood.

"Grant me a wager on the red 'un!" Joseph ordered. He slammed his fist against the side of the pit and motioned in exasperation toward the most intact of the sorely mangled birds.

An elegantly dressed nobleman shoved his way up ahead of Joseph. The nobleman's shoulders, clothed in the sleek satin of an opulent coat, scornfully pushed Joseph's greasy shabbiness away from the pit. "Twenty pounds!" the nobleman called as he reached out a handful of silver coins. Immediately, the pit boss grabbed up the nobleman's bet—and his coins.

"Give a bloke a chance!" Joseph cried in exasperation. "Jist a quid is all me asks!" He ran his hands through his disheveled shock of red hair, then down over his unshaven face. "Jist a quid, mate! Wot's a quid to the likes o' ye?"

In all the uproar, it could well be that the nobleman had no idea Winslow was even beside him. But the pit boss knew. And he heard the shabby man's plea to place a bet despite the fact that the man's hand was empty. He leaned over to Joseph and demanded, "I takes ye fer a waster, is wot. Does ye even gots a quid?"

"I do!" Joseph shot back in indignation. "And I insists ye put me down fer a quid wager!"

Cockfights sometimes lasted for hours, but this one did not. Even as piles of money whipped from hand to hand to hand, and as shouts rose from a rumble to a roar to pandemonium, a mangled white rooster reared back his head, and, slashing with a sudden fury of spurs, ripped the red rooster to shreds. The uproar accelerated into absolute bedlam as the victorious white rooster charged the two remaining contenders. But Joseph Winslow was no longer watching. He had already lost. Slouched low, he shoved his way back toward the door. He didn't get far, though. Two burly dockworkers grabbed him, one on each side; lifted his feet off the floor; and shuffled him back to the pit boss, who was waiting with his hand out.

"Yer quid!" the boss demanded.

"I's good fer it, I is!" Joseph pleaded.

The burly fellows grabbed him up, and although Joseph kicked and argued and fought with all his might, they dragged him over to a basket that hung down from the eaves.

"It only be a quid!" Joseph begged. "Wot's a quid matter to ye?"

The two stuffed Joseph into the basket and clamped the lid down tight, buckling it securely. Joseph was locked inside.

Ignoring his pleas and cries and curses and threats, they tugged at the attached rope until the basket hung directly over the pit where it swung back and forth.

"And there ye'll 'ang til dawn, and maybe longer!" the pit boss called as he shook his fist at the hapless Winslow. "Let ever'one see ye fer the cheat ye be!" Glaring around at the others who surrounded the pit, he called out, "An' let it be a warnin' to the rest of ye who think ye kin make a wager and not pay!"

As the last contender fell and only the mangled white rooster remained standing, the betting frenzy turned to jeering at Joseph Winslow's expense. Mortified, he swung in the basket overhead and contemplated the worthlessness of his life.

But the fights didn't stop. The circle was promptly cleared, and a new round of fighting roosters was prepared for the pit. Their wings were already carefully clipped and their tails trimmed, and all had their beaks filed and sharpened. Now each bird only need be fitted with deadly metal spurs—the champion's gleaming silver spurs—and they were ready to fight. As Joseph hung over the pit, the crowd of men below jostled for positions around the circle beneath him. Gentry in well-coifed and curled powdered wigs and fine clothes of satin and silk crammed shoulder-to-shoulder with dock ruffians on one side, and on the other, poor wretches with not a shilling to risk. Immediately the fresh crop of fighting roosters set to attacking one another. And immediately the least of the birds fell. Once again the uproar of bets and threats was in full swing.

Sir Geoffrey Philips, who looked as though he would be far more comfortable sipping tea in a well-appointed sitting room than pushing his way through the frenzied crowd at a cockfight on London's shabby East End, nevertheless plunged headlong into the wild crowd. He shot a threatening look at

Augustus Jamison, who lagged behind him, hungrily eying the gold and silver as it changed hands. Sir Geoffrey's fingers traced the bulges in his own purse.

"Gus, do come along!" Sir Geoffrey called out to Mister Jamison.

But the admonition did no good whatsoever. Already the spellbinding noise of betting had grabbed Mister Jamison and pulled him in with its fever pitch.

Sir Geoffrey did his best to push past the two burly guards and head directly for the pit boss, but it was an impossible task—until he pulled out a bag of gold guineas and waved it for the boss to see. Then, miraculously, a path opened up before him. He could not help thinking that his would have been a considerably easier task had Gus Jamison been at his side where he belonged, for Gus was an impressive hulk of a man. Unfortunately, however, Mister Jamison had a weakness for a game of chance—any game of chance. It was a struggle for him to keep his mind on the job at hand.

Sir Geoffrey did his best to make the pit boss understand him. He pointed up at Joseph Winslow in the basket, then he tried to pantomime the men letting Winslow down and unlocking the cage to set him free. Immediately the pit boss reached for the coins, but Sir Geoffrey refused to loosen his tight grip on the bag.

"Bring 'im down," the boss ordered.

Only after Joseph Winslow was hauled down and released from the basket did Sir Geoffrey drop the bag into the pit boss's eagerly outstretched hand. And only then, when the negotiations were over and done, did Augustus Jamison amble over and join them.

Joseph Winslow had no idea what was going on, and he didn't really care. He was just glad to be set free from his prison. Sir Geoffrey took one of Joseph's arms and Mister Jamison grabbed the other, and the two set about the task of weaving Winslow back toward the door.

The pit boss took one last opportunity to administer a swift kick to the seat of Joseph Winslow's pants. "And don't ye never darken this door agin!" he called after them. "Swindlers ain't welcome in this establishment!"

When the three reached the walk outside and closed the door on the din of the cockfight, Joseph ran a dirty sleeve over his blotchy face and puffed out his cheeks in relief. "I thanks ye kindly, I does," he said. "Jist a misunderstandin', is all. I was on a winnin' streak, and me—"

"You are Mister Winslow?" Sir Geoffrey Philips asked. "Mister Joseph Winslow?"

"The very one and the same," Joseph said. "Some calls me Admiral, for I be that—"

"Mister Jamison and I are on our way to a coffeehouse one street over. Will you permit us the honor of your company?"

Joseph looked at them warily. "A pint o' ale would do me better," he answered. "An' a bit o' somethin' to ease the grumblin' in me stomach." When neither man responded but merely kept walking, Joseph said, "I 'ppreciates yer 'elp, but I cain't pay ye back right this night. Me creditors owes me, they do."

"It is not a debt, sir," said Augustus Jamison. "Consider it a gift . . . to you from Lingongo."

Joseph could not have been more stricken if the moon had fallen from the sky and landed at his feet. His face blanched and his tongue froze in his mouth. If the two men hadn't caught him, he would surely have fallen on his face.

"Me woman . . . Lingongo . . ." Joseph stammered. "She be in Africa."

"Yes, we know," Sir Geoffrey Philips said.

"She be a wicked, wicked woman. Nothin' wot 'appened there were my fault. I was a 'onest man, I was. A English gentleman, I was. Admiral Joseph Winslow, that's wot they called me there. An' they showed me respect when they said it too. No more they don't, though. They don't do that no more."

Sir Geoffrey, walking stiff and tall with his carved walking stick, and Augustus Jamison, his face blank and unreadable, walked in silence as Joseph prattled on. They took care to steer Joseph around a man who lay dead and unattended on the roadside. Such an occurrence was not uncommon in this part of the city, where the worst off of London's down-and-outers too often departed life with no one to bury them. As did most of the upper class who had occasion to walk the streets of London's gritty East End, Sir Geoffrey and Mister Jamison simply ignored the dead man, just as they ignored the general dirt and grime and the piles of rotting rubbish. It was not like the West End, where remarkably lofty standards stood in stark contrast to these.

Finally even Joseph shut his mouth.

"It is a pitiful thing to be stripped of respect," Augustus Jamison allowed.

"Aye," Joseph agreed. "That it be, sir. That it most assuredly be."

"To be left hanging in a basket for all the world to mock and ridicule." Mister Jamison shook his head sadly at the very thought. "That is indeed a wretchedly low state for a man to sink to—especially one who was once so honorable and respected a gentleman."

"A gentleman and an admiral," Joseph corrected.

"Yes," said Sir Geoffrey. "Of course. A gentleman and an admiral."

"And all this time your woman—your *African* woman—has been free to live in comfort and luxury, and to tell tales at your expense."

"Is that wot she be doin'?" Joseph demanded. "That woman be tellin' tales 'bout me? Still mockin' me even after I be gone?" Rage boiled up in Joseph and he clenched his fists in fury.

"It does not have to be so," suggested Sir Geoffrey.

"Wot do ye mean by that?" Joseph demanded.

"Only this," answered Sir Geoffrey. "Even now, it is possible for you to be the victorious one. It can be you who walks proud, you who wears the fancy new suit of clothes, you who eats fine meals."

"And it can be you with a bag of gold coins in your hand ready to wager on the cockfights," said Mister Jamison, his own eyes glistening. "Or you to test your luck with a roll of the dice. Or you to buy yourself a place in a game of Lanterloo, if that is your preference. It appears to me that, given a fair chance, you might well see your fortunes change."

"Perhaps you will once again be called Admiral and greeted with a salute," Sir Geoffrey suggested.

"Yes, yes! That be true, jist like I always says!" Joseph Winslow insisted—and he fairly slathered at the thought. "But 'ow kin I make it 'appen? Tell me, fair sirs, 'ow kin I git me chance?"

Sir Geoffrey leaned close and whispered in a conspiratorial tone, "Very well, my good man, we shall tell you." He took Joseph by the arm and steered him through the open door of a coffeehouse, then over to a quiet table where they could have privacy, yet still enjoy the welcoming warmth of the fireplace. "Mister Jamison and I have a proposition for you, Mister Winslow. I think you will find it agreeable. Most agreeable, indeed."

14

"Johnny seen 'er in her private cabin pertendin' she could read!" Chester panted in disgust as he toiled alongside the crewmen moving sheets in order to set the sail on the foremast.

Sam, whose job it was to bend the sails to the yardarms, called out in a mocking voice, "Laddies, laddies! Git on yer 'ands and knees and make a cushion fer me wee lassie so's she kin walk acrosst the deck on yer backs. And if'n yer backs ain't soft enough fer 'er tender feet, then ye jist bare yer backs an' ready 'em fer me cat, 'cause a good lashin' is wot ye'll git!"

Sam's imitation of Captain Ross's Scottish brogue met with peals of laughter that quickly turned into sarcastic catcalls.

Standing on the bow of the ship, out of sight of the working crew, Nathaniel Greenway pulled a dingy handkerchief from his pocket and wiped it across the heavy brow of his salt-crusted face. He frowned and lowered the sextant with which he had been measuring the angle of the sun, and he contemplated his options.

As a young lad in Liverpool, the thought of traveling the world had been the height of excitement for him. But Nate had passed his thirty-seventh birthday on the coast of Africa, an age most sailing men never lived to see, and he was feeling his age. A year's voyage aboard a damp, creaking vessel, an endless supply of brittle hardtack biscuits—mostly weevil infested—quarters shared not only with the surgeon but also with rats and more vermin than he cared to consider, bowl after bowl after bowl of pease porridge. And if all that weren't discouraging enough, a voyage cursed by a woman on board, and a captain more concerned about pirouetting for her than about performing his duties.

"If you will allow me to speak freely, sir," Nate Greenway said to Captain Ross with a courteous bow, "rumblings of displeasure amongst the crew are causing me concern."

"Long voyages always produce rumblings of displeasure," Captain Ross replied with a wave of his hand. "Please be assured that I have everything under control. You are free to focus your concern on the position of the ship, and leave the handling of major day-to-day affairs to me."

"Sir, the men openly ridicule you," Nate Greenway persisted. "They feel slighted and cheated by you, and exposed to disaster because of your lack of sensitivity to their fears—which, I might add, are not totally unfounded."

"If you are quite finished—"

"No, sir, I am not. If I may be so bold, I think you would do well to shower less attention on Miss Winslow and spend more time overseeing your crewmen."

Captain Ross's face hardened. "And you have great personal experience as captain of a ship, I assume?" he replied.

The unexpected sharpness of the captain's words slashed Mister Greenway to the quick.

"No, sir. I only mean to say—"

"You have already said more than enough, Mister Greenway. You will do well to tend to your charts and navigational instruments and allow me to tend to the men on my ship. Do I make myself clear?"

"Quite clear," said Mister Greenway. But an impatient darkness passed over his craggy face. He was not yet finished. "I merely wish to share an observation which I trust you will consider, sir."

"Then I should respond that it is an observation best kept to yourself . . . *sir*."

"Because it is a matter that seriously affects every one of us on this ship, including myself, I really must—"

"You have said quite enough!" the captain snapped. "Good day, Mister Greenway."

The fact of the matter was that Captain Ross, in his kindly concern for Grace, was indeed neglecting his crew. His ordered lashings—sometimes as many as ten for a single offense, when that offense involved Grace—were unduly harsh. And on three separate occasions he had cut rations to the entire crew because of the actions of a few. "You all knew what the others were planning and you could have stopped it. Instead, you chose to do nothing. Therefore, you are equally involved," he said in defense of this practice.

Each lash, each cut in rations, each time Grace entered the captain's office for tea—every incident that could possibly be offensive—was duly noted, offense was taken, and the matter was whispered from one seaman to another to another to another. And with each retelling, the captain was depicted as more pandering toward Grace, and more cruel and unfair to the seamen.

Sam and Billy in particular seized upon every possible opportunity to jeer at Grace and blame her for their difficulties. They positioned themselves as close as possible to her cabin door, especially when she left it open a crack for Puss to come in, and between gulps of rum, they belted out their own original mocking songs, such as this one:

> *Sweet with sugar cane,*
> *And strong with the sweat of them wot dies,*
> *Black slaves in the fields,*
> *Lame black Cabeto, dead in the fields.*

✺

While the men's behavior did not seem to faze Captain Ross, the tone of the ship grew consistently more rancorous on the seamen's side. And on the officers' side, it became more defensive and subdued. Doctor Wills and Jonas Brandt both made an effort to tread softly around anything that might possibly erupt into controversy. Nate Greenway's manner, on the other hand, hardened into steely brittleness. As for Grace, she no longer joined the officers for afternoon tea, for she felt increasingly awkward and out of place in their presence.

One day drifted into the next. Late one evening, when Grace made her way out to the quarter deck to trace the image of Cabeto in her mind, she saw to her surprise that the moon shone round and full in the sky. Since the *Willow* had sailed with a full moon, that meant the ship had been at sea for two months.

More than four weeks had passed since Grace started reading Captain Ross's leather-bound Bible. She had finished reading about the beginning of the world, and also about the law and the time of the judges and the record of songs—the book of Psalms. Actually, she had come to a very sad part of the book. Once again, it was a story of slavery. Messengers, called prophets, had tried to warn the people what was coming—Jeremiah and Ezekiel, and others too—but the people refused to listen to them. So many warnings, but so little change.

Grace stood in the moonlight and stared up at the brilliant shimmer of the moon on the still ocean waters. A star flashed bright, then streaked across the sky. What did it mean? Good fortune or foul?

What would she find in London, Grace wondered. Her father? The last time she saw Joseph Winslow, he shook his fist at the heavens and called down a curse on her, his own daughter, who had risked everything to save his life. Charlotte Stevens, perhaps? Hah! In Africa, Charlotte would not so much as acknowledge Grace's existence. Why would she do more in England? Mister Hathaway—were he still alive? No, no! Oh, dear, no. Not him!

The truth was, Grace had no one.

Well, she did still have Cabeto. But the ship on which he was held captive was sailing to the other side of the world, carrying him off to more horror, and then to certain death. Unless . . .

Grace hurried back to her room. Puss was on the floor beside her bunk, so Grace left the door open a crack and lay down fully dressed. It didn't matter. She was in no mood to sleep, anyway.

Deep in the twilight hours of the first dog watch, Puss bolted upright, his ears flattened back and his tail fluffed out.

"What is it?" Grace asked.

The cat bolted from Grace's cabin. Only then did Grace hear the shouts, then the running feet. She jumped up and hurried to the door.

"Mister Brandt!" she called out to the first mate. "What is happening?"

"Our ship is sailing past another that is aflame," he answered.

Grace followed the first mate to the railing. It seemed the entire crew had already gathered there. In the inky black of night, all she could see were flames shooting up into the air. They cast eerie shadows around them and across the sky. A ghostly pall danced over the deck.

"Evil, that's wot it be," someone called out. "Pure evil."

Others muttered their agreement.

"Cursed be the burning ship, cursed like we be too," wailed someone else—a cry that called for still more muttering.

With the buzz of so many voices at once, it was impossible to tell who said what. But Grace didn't care. The murmurings of discontent faded into the background as the ominous smell of smoke relit the awful memory of the fire that had swept through Zulina fortress. With the breath of new fire on her face, Grace once again saw her parents' house swallowed up in flames.

Phantoms leapt dissonantly across the ship's deck, mocking ghosts of her destroyed village . . . of her life . . . of her hope.

Grace covered her face and ran back to her cabin. She slammed the door, then threw herself across her bunk and sobbed out her despair.

As darkness gathered, Jonas Brandt tapped on Grace's door, just as he did every evening at twilight when he made his round lighting the ship's lanterns. "A light for your candle, Miss Grace," he called. A second time he tapped, but when Grace still didn't answer, he moved on down the deck.

Grace found sleep impossible. And since she had no light, she couldn't read, either. For what seemed like hours, she lay on her cot, memories and questions crowding sleep from her head. Well into the middle watch, she got up and crept out of her cabin, but this time she didn't go to the quarter deck. No, this time she went on to the main deck and over to the railing where she had watched the burning ship. But it was far behind them, and all was dark out to sea. Just as she turned to leave, Grace heard muffled voices. They were quite nearby.

"Shush, ye! Cain't let 'em 'ear ye!"

It was Billy's voice. Grace was certain of it.

"The curse is upon us, an' that be a fact," he said. "We all knows it to be the truth, so we might as well speak it out loud. A burnin' ship close enough fer us to reach out and touch, and nary a soul on 'er deck. It be a sure sign of a curse if'n ever there be one."

"Them officers be no better sailors than we be."

This was Sam's voice, and the sound of it sent shivers down Grace's back. She pulled herself further into the shadows.

"Wot's we to do with the captain then?" asked another who Grace didn't recognize.

The answer came from Billy. "We kills 'im, is wot, same as all the others of 'em."

"But not Grace," said Sam. "Grace be mine, curse or no curse."

Six bells sounded. Three o'clock in the morning.

"Shush!" It was Billy again. "Less words we says, the better fer us all. We finishes laying the plan. After that, we only needs wait fer the right time to set it in place."

Grace heard grunts of agreement, followed by feet shuffling past her so close she could have reached her foot out and tripped them.

Long after they passed, Grace stayed crouched in her hiding place, too terrified to move. Only when seven bells sounded—half an hour, with no further sound from the plotters—did she dare slip out and hurry back to her cabin.

Grace paused at the cabin door, then she did what she had never dared do before—she tapped on the captain's door.

"Who is it, then?" the captain asked in a voice heavy with sleep.

"It is Grace, sir. I apologize for the hour. Please, sir, may I have a word with you?"

By the reflected shadows of the deck's lantern light, Captain Ross—now fully awake—stood in the doorway and shivered in his nightshirt as Grace urgently whispered everything that had happened on deck. To the best of her ability, she repeated all that Billy and Sam had said.

"The trickster, sir," Grace ended tearfully. "Surely he has come to this ship. And just look at the trouble he has brought with him!"

"Perhaps it is not about the trickster," Captain Ross replied. "Perhaps this is about you."

"Me, sir?" Grace asked in confusion. "Are you saying that even you believe I brought bad luck to the ship?"

"Not at all," said the captain. "What I am saying is that you may have saved us all."

"For such a time as this . . ." Grace whispered once again.

"Go to sleep now, and I shall do the same," said Captain Ross. "Tomorrow I will set this matter to right."

15

*W*ith a thump and a lurch, the *Golden Hawk*'s never-ending pitch and roll settled into a gentle rocking motion. Cabeto pushed himself as far up onto his elbows as he could and waited. It was true, the ship was no longer moving.

"Sunba," he called in a hoarse voice.

"I am here, Brother."

"Kome," Cabeto called.

"I am here."

"Tawnia."

"Yes, Cabeto, I am here."

"Tetteh."

"I am here."

"Hola."

"Over here, Cabeto."

"Safya."

"Yes, Cabeto. I am still here."

"Odera," Cabeto called.

No answer came from the still form behind him.

"Up! Up!" Henry Bates called as he kicked Cabeto in the side. He jerked Cabeto's arm forward, then, skipping two dead people, forced Cabeto over and locked him to the nearest living man. Henry clutched a heavy cloth over his mouth and nose, but even so he gagged and choked in the stifling stench of the ship's hold.

"Move it along!" Henry ordered as he forced Cabeto and the man shackled to him along on their hands and knees, then over to the stairs. Awkwardly, they clambered up to the deck where Lukas Fisher awaited them. Two other sailors, with serious looks on their faces, stood beside Lukas with muskets at the ready, just in case.

"The apartments of the Africans on the slave ships are fitted up with as much for their advantage as circumstances will admit," Mister Robert Norris, *representative for the Liverpool slave traders, announced. "They have several meals a day—some of their own country's food, served with the best African sauces. For variety, they have another meal cooked according to European taste. After breakfast they are able to wash themselves, whilst their apartments are perfumed with frankincense and lime juice."*

The members of the Select Committee of Parliament, smiles upon their faces, nodded approvingly to one another. Yes. Most satisfactory. Exactly as they had expected.

"Pee-ewwww, but you stink!" Lukas said as Cabeto limped up onto the deck. "Wot is it with you people? You all be just alike!" He shoved Cabeto over to the far side of the deck, where two men waited with a bucket of cold water and a bar of lye soap. In spite of his resolve, Cabeto flinched as they scrubbed at his raw ankles.

"Looky 'ere, some fool left this one's chains on whilst 'e danced," the scrubber said. "Don't matter, though. 'E's all scarred up anyways. Somethin' wrong with 'is leg an' 'e got the cat whupped acrosst 'is back, 'e did."

Dance. Yes, Cabeto knew that word. It meant jump about on the deck, and keep it up however much the rub of the leg iron cut and hurt, however much the wounds bled. He knew the word "cat" too. That was the white man's horrible whip, made from knotted leather strips that ripped open a man's flesh. They used it on anyone who didn't dance fast enough or dared to fall down from exhaustion.

Before dinner, the Africans amuse themselves after the manner of their country," Mister Norris reported. "The ship's crew encourage them to sing and dance, and to make the time even more pleasurable, the crewmen add games of chance for their enjoyment. As the men play and sing, the women and girls make frilly ornaments with beads."

Scrubbed clean and rubbed down with palm oil to make his skin gleam, given more water to drink than he'd had for days and an extra portion of meal and beans to eat in an attempt to puff him out, Cabeto stumbled in front of Henry, who led him out to join other captives, who were enduring makeovers of their own.

"Cabeto!" Tawnia screamed when she saw him. She reached out to him, but immediately Lukas struck the girl to the ground. Not so as to leave a conspicuous mark that might lower her sales value, mind you. Just a blow to her midsection, hard enough to knock the wind out of her and terrify her. Just hard enough to be a lesson to anyone else who might dare to scream.

"You!" Lukas called, pointing to Hola. "And you and you and you." That was Tetteh and Kome, and another man not from their village. "All o' you, up to be considered!"

Henry and another crewman pulled the young Africans forward and pushed each one up against a wooden wall. White men, one after another, came and ran their hands all over the young Africans' bodies. The white men forced the captives' mouths open and peered at their teeth. They checked the Africans' backs, then stretched out their arms and their legs. The white men seemed satisfied with what they saw, because after all the examining, they stood in a line with eager looks on their faces.

Then all at once they started to point and yell. One man was evidently the winner, because he looked very happy and he stayed as the others walked away. He handed a leather sack to the ship's Captain Hudson, then he tied the four Africans together with a rope around their necks. As he led them off, Hola tried to look back, but the winner lashed him back into line and yanked him forward.

Four at a time, the captives stood against the wall. Four at a time, they were taken away. Then two at a time. Then all alone. Cabeto and Sunba stood at the wall together, but the men kicked Cabeto in his lame leg and when he winced, they frowned. Then they grabbed Sunba's crooked arm and yanked it up and down, and they shook their heads and walked away. So Lukas tied Cabeto and Sunba to a tree and concentrated on trying to get someone to buy the women.

A member of the House of Commons sighed heavily and stated to the man next to him—but in a voice loud enough for many others to hear, "We have heard evidence, presented to us over and over again, that demonstrates that truth of the slave trade. There can be no question but that it actually helps the Africans by providing them safer places to live, and most certainly with better lives than they could ever hope for in their native land."

"Come, now," Captain Hudson argued. The man before him had already bought several of his lesser slaves, and Hudson was doing his best to interest him in Cabeto and Sunba, who were still tied together to the tree. "These two are not perfect, I allow you as much. Even so, they are young and strong, and I am offering them to you cheap. It's a good deal for a planter such as yourself. Work them day and night and you shall easily get your money's worth before they drop dead."

But the planter wasn't convinced. Like the men before him, he kicked at Cabeto's scarred leg and shook his head at the awkward angle of Sunba's shoulder. "I have done the calculations, Richard," he said. "The most profitable approach is to buy them young and at the top of their strength, then work them hard and give them little rest. When they are no longer useful, let them die and buy new ones to fill their places." He must have seen the disappointment on Captain Hudson's face, because he quickly added, "It is business, my good man. One must be profitable if he is to stay in business."

"I wish the cause of humanity as well as any other man," said Alderman Newnham, Lord Mayor of the City of London. "No

doubt some abuses do prevail with the slave trade, but if we simply apply wise regulations, it can be an even greater source of revenue and commercial advantage to us than it is right now. If, on the other hand, we were to abolish it completely, we would render the City of London a scene of bankruptcy and ruin!"

Here the good Alderman took his handkerchief from his waistcoat and wiped his misty eyes.

"I must suppress my own feelings," he said, "and act upon prudence. And so must each of you."

⚬

"Slave trash, that's all ye be!" Lukas said with disgust to the smattering of Africans left behind. "Nothing to do but season ye fer the final scramble and hope fer a little bit of somethin' fer me trouble."

He gave a hard shove to Safya and Tawnia, who were tied together. Tawnia stumbled forward, jerking the less agile Safya to her knees. Lukas gave Safya a vicious kick and hissed, "Git to yer feet, woman!"

Cabeto jumped to help the two, but Lukas raised his lash and brought it down hard across Cabeto's bare back—once, then again. Before he could bring the lash down a third time, Captain Hudson yelled, "Lukas! You beat his back raw and mark him as a troublemaker, and we might just as well abandon him with the rest of the refuse slaves. It's hard enough to sell lame. Impossible to sell lame trouble!"

It was with disgust that Captain Hudson looked over the remaining slaves he had to offer—a lame man, a scarred and maimed troublemaker, a woman past her prime, and the young one, hardly more than a child, who would not stop her sobbing.

"You are worth almost nothing to me now," he said with disgust. "Do not test my patience, or I will throw the lot of you to the sharks!"

⚮

"I do hope and wish to be amongst the foremost in the cause of humanity, and in opposition to every type of oppression," Mister Cruger said when he got his chance to speak. "But should the House of Commons decide to recommend abolishing the trade, then everyone who sustains loss by that decision—from merchants to planters—must needs be reimbursed for those losses." He paused to allow his hearers to comprehend the gravity of his words. "The people have been taught to associate everything cruel and oppressive with the trade," he continued, "but from my knowledge and the evidence I have seen, that has been greatly overcharged."

⚮

That night, locked in irons in a room with other "refuse"— some sick, some injured, some dying, some simply with no more will to live—Cabeto called:

"Sunba."

"I am here, brother."

"Safya."

"Yes, I am here."

"Tawnia."

Sobs.

"Tawnia, answer," Cabeto said gently.

"Yes," wept the tender child's voice. "Yes, I am here."

16

"Wake up!" Nathaniel Greenway growled. He administered a swift kick to bosun Alexander Collins, who lay sprawled in a circle of lines, his head thrown back, snoring softly. "You are supposed to be standing watch!"

Collins jumped to and pulled himself upright. "Just catching me a quick wink, is all," he said, doing his best to stifle a yawn.

"And what do you suppose Captain Ross would have to say about you over here fast asleep?" Greenway asked. "You just may find yourself on the receiving end of the cat instead of the giving end."

"This is not a warship," Collins answered, giving way to both the yawn and a full-body stretch. "Look about you and you will see that not much happens at this hour."

"And if it did, you would be the last to know!"

Nathaniel Greenway was always, and in all ways, a man of the rule book. It rubbed him raw that this rude, snappish seventeen-year-old managed to get by with such a careless approach to his duties and still retain so high a position on the ship. Everyone knew it was because he was the nephew of a major investor. The nepotism that allowed such a travesty rankled Nate Greenway no end.

"It is officers such as yourself that doom ships to the bottom of the sea," Nate snapped.

Alex laughed. "Old men worry too much," he said. Still, he went to work instead of going back to sleep, and that did bring Nate a small degree of satisfaction.

It was four in the morning, and Nate had to grudgingly admit that all was exceedingly quiet. The seas were calm under a waning moon, and the winds extraordinarily peaceful. Only the occasional sound of footfalls somewhere on deck broke the monotony of the gentle slap, slap, slap of waves against the hull. Men busy at their jobs checking the sails and making necessary adjustments. Sailors carrying on even though the officer in charge of them slept. Disgraceful! Nate Greenway would never allow himself to nap on duty. Never, no matter how calm the night or how heavy his eyes.

Actually, on this particular night Nate welcomed solitude. The whole matter of the crew's disagreeable attitude, and then of Captain Ross's refusal to address his part in what was becoming the tone of the ship, had him totally confounded. Upset him, even. To be quite honest, he was rather irritated at the whole lot of them. Greenway stretched his arms over the railing and gazed out at the tranquil sea.

And you have great experience as captain of a ship, I assume? That was what Captain Ross had said when Nate dared take the brave step of bringing the simmering troubles to his attention. And the captain had said it in a most rude way too. Insulting, actually. Even mocking.

And what was his snappish comeback when Nate had tried to explain the reasons for his concern? Oh, yes. Captain Ross had said: *"You will do well, Mister Greenway, to tend to your charts and navigational instruments and allow me to tend to the men on my ship."*

It was a quiet night filled with unrest and disquiet, with deep sleep and deeper shadows. A careless watch officer who thought nothing of sleeping on his job was followed by an exasperated watch officer who turned his back to the ship and lost himself in bitterness and angry resentments. It was the perfect night. Sam and Billy recognized it immediately, and they were quick to seize the moment.

They swiftly cobbled together the last pieces of their plan, then all they had to do was lay low until Officer Greenway's bunk mate, Officer Brandt, started out on his nightly rounds. Alex Collins was right when he said that a merchant ship was not a warship. On a warship, officers would never dare grow so complacent. Nor would they be so careless.

While the half of the crew who were not on watch duty were supposed to be asleep, peacefully swaying in their hammocks in their berth below decks, and as most of the officers did indeed sleep, two shadows—one tall and shaggy and the other stout— moved furtively through the darkened deck.

Fiddle-playing Jake wasn't the only crewman recently out of Newgate Prison. In his writings, Samuel Johnson described life in jail as worse than life at sea, but Mister Johnson obviously never had an extended stay in Newgate. For the fact was that those unfortunate enough to be thrown into the filth and disease and unbearable stench of that wretched place could be forgiven for longing for the cleansing winds of the open sea. And captains, desperate to supply their ships with a crew, were eager enough to fill the lists with any available strong backs and able bodies, few questions asked.

Sam had served even more time in prison than Jake, dodging the gallows for five years at Newgate after being found guilty of the crime of picking pockets. He made good use of his sentence by extending his craft to include picking locks. Billy would have been incarcerated at Newgate as well—and almost certainly would have hung on the gallows for his brazen acts of thievery—except that he never got caught.

Deftly, Sam popped open the lock on Jonas Brandt's and Nate Greenway's cabin door. He and Billy knew exactly what they were looking for—the officers' chest.

"There 'tis!" Sam mouthed to Billy. He pointed to a chest under the first bunk, pushed as far back as possible.

Billy pulled the chest out, and Sam popped the lock. It didn't take much rummaging for them to realize nothing was in the chest except extra clothing and an assortment of personal items. With an angry grunt, Sam slammed the lid down and snapped the locks closed, then motioned for Billy to shove it back into place.

A second chest lay under the other bunk. Billy tugged at it.

"It be heavy!" he whispered.

In the end, it took both men to force the second chest free. Sam immediately set about popping the lock.

"Whew!" Billy breathed when he opened the lid. Six new blunderbuss flintlock pistols lay on top, and beside them six leather sacks of ammunition—wrapped packets of lead balls and measured portions of gunpowder. Underneath were six curved, single-edged blade cutlasses with cupped guards at the hilt, as well as six sharp-bladed knives. Half the ship's weaponry lay at their fingertips.

Quickly, silently, the two men piled the weapons beside the door. They carefully closed the chest and snapped the lock shut, then shoved the chest back into place under the bunk. They stuffed the pistols and ammunition inside their shirts, three for each, then shouldered the cutlasses and knives. Just as silently as they had entered, the two stole out again onto the deck where they faded into the shadows.

"Pleasant morning, Nate," Jonas Brandt called out as he strode by the watch officer. Something about Mister Greenway's pensive form leaning over the deck made him stop. "Might there be something pressing on you?" he asked.

Mister Greenway gave him a curt nod and waved him on his way. When Mister Brandt did not immediately move ahead, Nate softened his stance and wished him a pleasant morning in return, then allowed as it did indeed look to be the makings of a grand day.

Jonas Brandt, growing used to Greenway's contemplative ways, hurried on. He was eager to complete his business on deck and return to his cabin. But even as Nate Greenway turned back to his uneasy contemplation, the stout shadow and the tall, shaggy one crept past him slowly . . . silently . . . and completely unnoticed.

17

Captain Ross!" Jonas Brandt shrieked as he pounded on the captain's door. "To arms, sir! To arms!"

Grace jumped up from her bunk and dashed to open her door so she could see what was going on. Doctor Wills rushed toward her, hopping as he struggled to pull his breeches on over his bare legs. The sleeves of his shirt billowed around him. Alex Collins and two other young officers were right behind him.

"Stay inside!" Doctor Wills ordered. "Shut your door and barricade it with everything at hand!"

In the cabin next to her, something crashed onto the floor, and then a commotion of voices erupted.

"Arm yourselves!" Captain Ross called out. The voices were drowned out by a stampede of running feet.

Slowly, cautiously, Grace pulled the door open, just wide enough to allow her to peek out. Now no one was on the deck. All she saw was a trail of discarded nightclothes.

"Stand down! That is a direct command!" It was the captain's voice, and it came from up ahead, midship. But the captain's order was met with hoots and jeers.

"Stand down now, and I promise you your punishment will be light!" the captain repeated.

"Yer worry is best saved fer th' punishment we metes out t' ye!" Billy shouted back. "And don't 'spect it to be light, neither!"

Billy's threat ended in the unmistakable roar of a blunderbuss pistol, followed by a bellow of fury.

Something was terribly wrong.

Grace eased out of her cabin and, pressing herself close against the bulkhead, made her way forward toward the source of the commotion. She didn't get far, however, for as she rounded the corner where the captain's cabin jutted out onto the deck, she stepped directly into the midst of battle. Grace froze in alarm as Alexander Collins leapt in front of her, brandishing a cutlass.

"Lord above, 'ave mercy on us!" screamed one of the two crewmen who danced and ducked in an effort to dodge Collins's blade.

Grace would expect as much from the brash Mister Collins, who roared out a hearty laugh with each thrust of his cutlass. But it was not him alone.

"Mister Greenway!" Jonas Brandt called as he tossed a cutlass to the navigator.

As the sword hurtled through the air, Nathaniel Greenway grabbed it by the hilt and expertly thrust his hand into the cupped guard. He jumped up onto a barrel with an amazingly agile leap for a man of his size, and from that vantage point immediately struck down two well-armed sailors. Even the stout cook grabbed up a cutlass and thrusting with his stubby arms, plunged headlong into the fray. Not only did the cook handle himself with surprising enthusiasm, he also demonstrated impressive skill with the blade.

"Watch above!" the captain yelled.

Billy had seized the cutlass diversion as an opportunity to swing unobserved up into the shrouds, and Sam and Jake followed close on his heels. Now all three hovered above the deck—Billy hard against the main mast, Sam out on the yardarm, and Jake clambering high above them all, up toward the crow's nest. Both Billy and Sam aimed fully loaded pistols down at the deck.

"Mister Brandt, take cover!" the captain ordered.

Even as the first mate dashed behind the lines and ducked down as far out of sight as possible, lead balls peppered the deck in the exact spot where he had stood mere seconds before.

But the seamen were not soldiers. Hooligans and thieves, yes, but not fighting men. Two cowering crewmen fell to Alexander Collins' cutlass. Doctor Wills's pistol felled another. After that, most of the crewmen quickly dropped to their knees and begged for mercy.

Not Billy's friend, Chester, though. He jumped up behind the surrendering crewmen and brandished a threatening knife at them. "Git up, ye snivelin' cowards!" he bellowed. "Git up afore I carve ye all to shreds!"

Before he had a chance to make good on his threat, Captain Ross blasted Chester's legs with the blunderbuss pistol's shotgun-like multiple discharge. Chester crumbled to the deck, where he lay howling.

"Now, lads, pluck those troublemakers from out of the shrouds!" Captain Ross ordered.

The winds had come up, though, and it was not an easy order to obey on the wildly pitching deck. Doctor Wills took aim at Billy with his pistol, then pulled back on the trigger. But instead of hitting Billy, the spray of lead balls simply peppered the mainsail above Billy's head with holes.

Jake let out a wicked chortle. "'Tis as I always says, old man," he gleefully called down to the captain. "We be better sailors than the whole entire lot o' ye officers!" He reared back and roared out a great guffaw. But just at that moment a wave smashed against the ship, sending sailors sprawling across the deck. The jolt knocked Jake's grip loose and flung him through the air. He splashed into the sea and disappeared in the foaming waves.

Billy, gripping the mast, and Sam, clinging to the yard, stared after Jake in shocked silence.

"That be it!" Billy roared. "That jist be it!"

Sam pointed his pistol down at the crowded deck and pulled the trigger. When the smoke cleared, Doctor Wills lay on the shot-pocked deck, bleeding and still.

For a moment, everyone gaped in disbelief. Then, his voice hard with fury, Captain Ross ordered, "Take them down . . . *now.*" Already he was taking aim at Sam with his own pistol. Jonas Brandt scrambled to toss firearms to the other officers, but there was no time to get the balls and wrapping and gunpowder passed around.

Captain Ross fired, and Sam tumbled from the yard onto the deck.

In frustrated fury, Billy pulled out his knife and stabbed it into a hole in the sail. He pulled the knife out and stabbed it into another hole, then another and another. Ripping at the sail and slashing at the rigging, he screamed, "We'll all go down to the sea! Ever' last one o' us!"

Grace scooped up Doctor Wills's pistol. She grabbed a measure of gunpowder from Mister Brandt's store and poured it down the barrel, then wrapped the lead shot in a piece of cloth and rammed the packet down the barrel.

"But he goes first!" Billy yelled. He pointed his loaded and fully cocked pistol at Captain Ross and pulled the trigger.

Grace snapped the frizzen into place, then took aim and fired at the exact moment Billy did.

When the thick cloud of gun smoke cleared, Captain Ross lay on the deck, his leg ripped up with lead shot. Billy hung upside down in the shrouds, his foot entangled in the lines.

"Miss Grace, you saved my life!" Captain Ross gasped in shocked amazement. "Can it be that you are as comfortable with a firearm as with an embroidery needle?"

"An embroidery needle?" Grace asked with mock surprise. "Why, sir, never in my life have I had occasion to use such a complicated piece of machinery!"

Plucking up his last bit of strength, the captain sighed and said with a wan smile, "Such a mysterious woman you have turned out to be, Miss Grace Winslow." Then he allowed his eyes to drift closed. His face was deathly pale. "How I will miss the good doctor," he gasped. "How I will miss . . . my dear friend."

Jonas Brandt blinked about him uncertainly. "Sir, the prisoners. What of them?" he asked the captain.

But no answer came.

Mister Brandt rose unsteadily to his feet. "I count seven seamen missing, and that number includes all the troublemakers," he reported. His voice wavered in spite of his resolve to hold steady. He plunged ahead: "This most unfortunate encounter means we have seven fewer capable seamen at our disposal. Plus, both the captain and the ship's surgeon lie injured or dying."

As Mister Brandt talked, a curious thing happened: his voice actually gained in strength. And as his voice grew stronger, so did Mister Brandt himself increase in both power and authority.

"We must lower the sails and set to the task of mending them and the rigging as well. All hands will be required to repair the damage, and it must be accomplished with all due haste."

Then Mister Brandt looked at each of the seamen on deck, all still on their knees, many quaking at the prospect of the gallows awaiting them—or worse.

"I could have every one of you shot on the spot for the crime of mutiny on the high seas," said Mister Brandt.

He paused for several seconds; long enough to let the enormity of their crime sink in.

"I could, but I shall not. This will be your punishment: no food or drink from now until morning's light, then half rations for the next two days. But with your cooperation and hard work, neither I nor anyone else shall mention again your part in this most unfortunate occurrence."

With Grace as his assistant—her graceful, thin fingers could do what his thick, clumsy ones could not—the cook removed the lead balls from the captain's leg, one by one—twelve balls in all. This was one of the few times Grace truly missed the portion of her forefinger on her left hand that had been lopped off by Tungo in the rebellion.

"I should not think it best that you be required to nurse me," Captain Ross said to Grace as she bathed his face with cool water.

"If I can bring myself to nurse Mister Hathaway, I most certainly can nurse you," she answered. For Jasper Hathaway's care had indeed once again fallen to her.

Mister Brandt called to Grace. "I need your help as well. We must sew poor Doctor Wills up in a canvas sack to prepare him for burial at sea."

The dead seamen, all sewn into their hammocks by their mates, already lay in a row alongside the deck rail.

But Grace shook her head and showed him her maimed finger. "I don't know that I can be of much help to you with a sewing needle," she said, "but I will do what I can." Then, tears filling her eyes, she cried, "Nothing about this is right."

"No," Jonas Brandt said. "None of this is right at all. But this is how it happened. And right or wrong, I am now the one in charge. Tomorrow we will all stand together on the deck, and before Mister Collins drops the doctor and the departed seamen to rest in the sea, the men will expect words of comfort from me. But I have no such words. I have not the least idea what to say."

"In the captain's book of God . . ." Grace began hesitantly. "Captain Ross . . . he read something to me, sir. Perhaps together we can find it."

And so, first for the good Doctor John Matthew Wills, then for each of the others who followed him one by one to their ocean grave, Jonas Brandt read these words from Job 19: 25-26,

> For I know that my redeemer liveth, and that he
> shall stand at the latter day upon the earth:
> And though after my skin worms destroy this body,
> yet in my flesh shall I see God.

Afterward, all the crewmen from both watch crews worked from sunup to sunup, each man napping only when he absolutely must. They took the damaged mainsail down and spread it out on the deck. With coarse sail thread and enormous needles, they sewed up the smaller tears and holes in the thick hemp fabric. Then they carefully cut patches to fit over the worst of the holes and slashes, sewing the patches in place by hand. It was rough, hard work that ripped up even the most calloused hands. Then they recut, repaired, and rewove the damaged cordage of the rigging.

For Grace, days of boredom were a thing of the past. Now each day was filled with such busy-ness that it blended into yet another weary night. Even Puss seemed to sense an urgency to get back to work, for he never again came to lounge on the floor by Grace's cot.

Grace was up early each morning. She began her day by dressing Captain Ross's wounds and changing the bandages, then she bathed his face and neck with cool water and coaxed him to eat a bit. After that she made her dreaded trip to Mister Hathaway's closed-in room, heavy with the smell of impending death, to tend to him and urge him to take the medicinal foods Doctor Wills had prescribed.

Mister Hathaway's condition had deteriorated so frightfully that his parched lips were stretched into a permanent grimace. Grace could hardly stand to see the gaping empty space where he had so proudly displayed his ridiculous gold tooth. Yet Hathaway remained as obstinate as ever, and he resolutely clamped his jaws tight against the spoonfuls of vinegar Grace urged him to swallow. As soon as she could manage to escape, Grace slipped out of his oppressive cabin and made her way back to the captain's bedside.

In the evening, when his galley duties were done, the cook came to check on Captain Ross's leg and to re-dress it. "Pray as how we don't git us into a fog," he warned as he handled the captain's wounds with his filthy hands, then wiped them on his cooking apron. "Fer it is fog wot makes infection set in, an' that's a fact."

When cook was gone, Grace said to the captain, "I am reading the second part of your God book now, sir."

"That part is rightly called the New Testament," Captain Ross told her.

"It tells about a holy man named Jesus. He could heal people with just a touch of his hand. I wish he were here to touch the fire that burns in your leg."

"Perhaps he is here," Captain Ross said.

"You mean, like the trickster?"

"No, he is not a trickster. But Jesus does belong to the spirit world. God sent him from heaven to earth to show people the way back to God."

"Oh, I think I understand," Grace said. "I know from African tales about a mediator from the Creator to mankind. One who makes a way between us and the spirit world. Is Jesus that one?"

Captain Ross sighed, and a smile creased his pained face. "Aye, lassie. That he be. You are beginning to understand."

When the sails on the *Willow* were as well put together as they were likely to ever be, acting Captain Brandt oversaw the final repair and reassembly of the intricate system of masts, yards, ropes, and pulleys that made up the rigging. With everything back in place, the crew raised the patched sails. At first they flapped listlessly in the still air. But then the sea breeze caught, and it filled first one sail and then the other. As the ship began to move smartly again, a hearty cheer arose from the men on the deck.

"It will not be long now," Jonas Brandt announced to Grace. "We should be in London in a fortnight!"

18

"Have you read this?" Lord Reginald Witherham stormed, his eyes darting accusingly from man to man. "Has any one of you taken occasion to read a word of this blasphemous writing?"

"Please, my dear Lord Reginald, do calm yourself," urged the unflappable Sir Geoffrey Philips. "It is merely words on a page and nothing more. It is but the meandering thoughts of one single man."

"No, Sir Geoffrey, *merely that* it most certainly is not!" Lord Reginald insisted. He was fairly shaking in his effort to contain his anger. "*Thoughts Upon a Slave Trade* is a book! A published book that people are actually *reading*! Even *women* are reading it! Dear sirs, prepare yourselves for a shock when I tell you that this disgraceful work has even found its way into my own house!"

The identical thought ran through the minds of all four men seated in the luxuriously appointed sitting room at Larkspur Estate: *In that case, Lord Reginald Witherham, would you not do well to take control of your own house?* Although all four men were thinking as much, none spoke his thoughts.

Still, eyebrows were lifted knowingly and glances surreptitiously exchanged.

"The rabble-rousers will be with us always," Simon Johnson allowed. "It is an irritation we have no choice but to endure."

"An irritation, you say? My dear Mister Johnson, how can you fail to grasp the singular importance of this disastrous volume?" Lord Reginald exclaimed in exasperation. "It was penned by one Reverend John Newton, who was himself once a slaver but who now claims to have seen the light and repented of his ways. His condemnation of the African slave trade, and his criticism of those who practice it, are dastardly indeed. Most damaging of all, he writes not only eloquently, but also with the poisonous power of personal experience."

"But, my most honored Lord Reginald, pray tell, why must you call all of us out once again when we should be sitting by the warmth of our own hearths? Why do you work yourself into a state that could well damage your own health?" questioned Quentin Gainesville. "That account was published a full five years ago."

"That is true," agreed Sir Geoffrey. "And for years before that, the Reverend Newton told his tales from his pulpit, as well as from many other public places. Quentin is quite right, Lord Reginald. This is nothing new."

Glaring past Sir Philips at the woolly-wigged Mister Gainesville, Lord Reginald clenched his jaw and the veins on his forehead throbbed, sure signs that his agitation was getting the best of him. Yet he managed to state with a measure of control, "What is new, my dear sirs, is that the common people have actually begun to pay attention."

Charlotte had known this day would come. She had known it ever since her husband discovered the booklet she hastily hid under the cushion of the Queen Anne chair. Her only regret was that she had not had the chance to read it herself. And, of course, now it was too late. Reginald had the volume locked away in his study—except when he pulled it out for exhibitions such as this night, when he wished to wave it around to demonstrate his indignation.

With well-honed silence—now that she had mastered the art of walking like a refined Witherham instead of clomping like a horse—Lady Charlotte eased out of her chambers and glided to the upstairs landing that happened to be conveniently located just above the sitting room. Fortunately, as her husband's irritation grew, so did the pitch of his voice. Charlotte might not hear everything the other men said, but she was not likely to miss one word that came from her husband's angry lips.

"Independence of the American colonies," he was saying. "It was right there that the breach crumbled into an open chasm. And the French, fools that they are, surrendered to the demand of the masses to grab up undue responsibility for themselves rather than to cleave to the God-given right of the monarchy to rule with unquestioned authority. From there it moves to this published declaration that has the gall to equate savages with . . . with . . . with *us*!"

Lord Reginald—quite out of breath—paused, panting, to mop the perspiration from his brow.

Quentin Gainesville took the opportunity to interject, "I pray thee, my good man, pause long enough to understand that we all agree with your concern over the present state of affairs. It truly is quite wretched. But really, we cannot be compared with America or France. We do have a Parliament in this country, and—"

"And what, pray tell?" Lord Reginald roared. "It is not in Parliament that the minds of the common people are molded and formed. It is in the public squares and the coffeehouses.

And it is in those very places that the abolitionists abound and flourish. I have private information that one coffeehouse in particular is known to house a group that is right at this very moment plotting to overthrow our nation's laws on the slave trade. Yes, our singularly fair and humane statutes, and then to force our country into an economic crisis beyond anything we have hitherto known or imagined possible!"

This time, Lord Reginald paused not only to mop his brow, but also to gasp for breath and await the shocked exclamations of his colleagues.

Augustus Jamison stared blank-faced at the flushed and panting Lord Reginald Witherham. "Indeed!" he said evenly. "I never took you for a man who frequented such haunts, my lord. Might I ask how it is that you have such personal knowledge of coffeehouses?"

Sir Geoffrey looked on with an absolutely straight face, but his eyes twinkled with uncontrollable merriment. Simon Johnson busied himself with his harrumphing, but he made his opinion clearly known by arching his bushy eyebrows and perfectly timing his sanctimonious coughs.

As for Quentin Gainesville, he simply let forth with a bark of a laugh and exclaimed, "Come now, Lord Reginald, you are amongst friends, old man. What was it that black Irish wench of yours told you?"

Lord Reginald blushed as crimson as if his face had been freshly roasted.

Ena, that was her name. The old Irish word for "fire." And a lovely little bonfire she was too. Toasted brown skin kissed with a glowing blaze, and crimson flaming through her bright auburn hair. It was that sizzling glow that had first snatched away Lord Reginald's aristocratic breath. That was what had enticed him to make her such a lucrative offer to come to Larkspur Estate to work on a day-by-day basis as a chambermaid—so good an offer that she simply could not turn it down.

Lord Reginald envisioned that ball of Irish fire to be as transfixed with him as he was with her, but whenever he positioned himself before her, and regardless of what enticements he laid in her path, she ignored him. She simply applied herself to her work as a chambermaid—albeit a most enchanting one. It drove Lord Reginald to the edge of distraction. Lady Charlotte chattered and giggled and demanded and pouted, but Ena's dark green eyes burned with passion—though not for him.

"One must foster channels of information wherever they are to be found," Lord Reginald insisted most unconvincingly. Even as he said it, he knew how ridiculously defensive he sounded.

The others gazed at Lord Reginald with impassive faces, but he knew perfectly well that in their hearts they were laughing at him. This knowledge filled him with humiliation, which in turn fueled his fury to red hot. His face and ears burned.

"The better thing would be if we all fostered channels of information which we could then share together . . ."

Well, he'd had to try.

A conquest, perhaps. That might be an explanation for Lord Reginald's attraction to the beautiful black Irish servant girl. If that were so, however, he was definitely losing the battle. Lord Reginald had determined that he needed to be more aggressive, to use his wealth and superior station in life to bolster his chances for success with Ena—even to badger her, if need be. But the result of that ploy proved disastrous. She had fled the house, vowing never to return. Still, Ena was a good cleaning maid. So, in spite of all, Lady Charlotte continued to call on her—generally when her husband was out of town and the boredom of her life got to her. Chastened by his wife—or perhaps mocked by her—Lord Reginald had followed Ena to the coffeehouse where she had found herself a position keeping fresh coffee available for customers and cleaning up after they left.

Despite Lord Reginald's wishful insistence otherwise, his quest of the Irish servant girl was no secret. Nonplused at the distressing turn the discussion had taken, he thrust upward the booklet in his hand and announced, "Reverend Newton concludes his treatise thusly:

Though unwilling to give offense to a single person: in such a case, I ought not to be afraid of offending many, by declaring the truth. If, indeed, there can be many, whom even interest can prevail upon to contradict the common sense of mankind, by pleading for a commerce, so iniquitous, so cruel, so oppressive, so destructive, as the African Slave Trade!"

In one final, dramatic action, he threw the booklet across the floor. Then, satisfied that he had made his case, he leaned back against the mantle.

For several minutes the men sat in thoughtful silence. Then Sir Geoffrey Philips said, "You say the people of London are giving their attention to this, Lord Reginald?"

"London, most certainly. But not London alone. Indeed, throughout all of England, and Scotland too," Lord Reginald replied. "And not only the commoners, but members of Parliament as well. This self-same Reverend John Newton is due to testify before a select committee of the House of Commons. Should that happen, it could well be the ruin of every one of us!"

"Come, now, Lord Reginald," Simon Johnson said with just the trace of a disdainful sniff. "I must say that your performance is worthy of the most extreme Dissenting preacher. One does not expect such shows of emotion from men of our station. I for one must insist that I cannot believe this matter to be nearly as serious as you make it out."

"Yes, yes, my good man," Augustus Jamison agreed. "The members of the House of Lords must surely share our sensibilities."

"But I am speaking of the common people. And if they should—" Lord Reginald began.

Quentin Gainesville waved him aside. "This is not the insufferable American colonies, and this is not France," he said. "This, sir, is England. And in England, in the event that you have forgotten as much, it is King George who rules, not the common people. That black wench of yours can say whatever she will, but I shall tell you the true concerns of the people of England: the price of the bread that fills their bellies and the cost of a shovelful of coal to drive out the dampness and cold. The common people's worries over their next tankard of ale are far greater than their concern over a shipload of black heathens who, I might add, are more surely better off on that fair English ship than they ever were running wild through the jungles of Africa."

Even as he was finishing his last sentence, Mister Johnson stood up and busied himself setting his coat to right. "Whilst I respect your concerns—and I truly do respect them, my lord—I must express my well-founded fear that they are somewhat misplaced. And now, I fear, I truly must take my leave."

"But I had hoped we might come to some points of action this evening," Lord Reginald protested.

"Ah, yes," Simon Johnson said as the others, making haste to follow his lead, also prepared to leave. "I do have a suggestion for the first point of action."

"Wonderful, wonderful!" said Lord Reginald. Perhaps, he hoped with all his heart, it was not too late to redeem the evening, after all.

"I would suggest that the first point might be that you keep your distance from that coffeehouse!"

Lady Charlotte hurried back to her chambers, closed the door behind her, buried her head in her feather pillow, and dissolved into peals of laughter.

19

$\mathscr{L}$ondon . . . it is on fire again!" Grace gasped as the *Willow* sailed down the Thames River, giving her the first sight of the city's hazy skyline.

"On fire?" Jonas Brandt said. "It most certainly is not!"

"But all the smoke."

"Oh, that." Mister Brandt shook his head and laughed. "It is naught but the usual pall that envelops the city. So many coal fires, you see. In every house and every trade shop. London is always thick with smoke. On some days, even in the middle of the day, a person cannot see the words on a newspaper though he holds it in front of his face."

Nothing in all her books could have prepared Grace for the sight of London. Such a vista of towering buildings. So many of them spiked with soaring spires. So many crowned by lofty steeples. All of them swallowed up in smoke billowing from a plethora of high, round chimneys.

Grace gazed out at the blanket of thick haze. "Does the sun ever shine through?" she asked.

"Now and again," Mister Brandt said. "We call those the *glorious days*."

The wide Thames, which flowed into and through London's waterfront district, was clogged with ships both great and small. Lesser vessels, such as fishing boats, could sail under the round arches of London Bridge and directly up to the docks, but the arches were not high enough to allow such tall-masted sailing ships as the *Willow* to pass through.

"Soon you will leave the ship," Mister Brandt told Grace. "A small passenger boat will take you and your baggage crate up to the dock."

"What about Mister Hathaway?" Grace asked.

Jonas Brandt shook his head. "That is not for me to say. You must ask Captain Ross that question. He desires to speak with you before you leave."

Although Clayton Ross's injury was still far from healed, he no longer burned with fever, and the wounds on his leg were somewhat less fiery and swollen.

"I am sorry, Miss Grace," Captain Ross said as she stood beside his cot. "It was my full intention to see you safely to the city. I feel as though I have failed you."

"Oh, no, sir!" Grace protested. "Thank you for all you have done for me. It is more than I ever could have hoped."

"His life and retribution for how he had lived it are in the hands of God," the captain said. "You no longer need to concern yourself with him. Whether he lives or dies, you are henceforth a free woman."

"Thank you, sir," Grace said, although she could barely choke back her terror of facing this strange, shrouded city alone. "You have been most kind, Captain Ross. I placed your holy book back on the shelf in your cabin. Thank you for allowing me to read it."

Captain Ross closed his eyes, and for a moment he did not speak. Then, looking up at Grace again, he said, "The ship cannot pass under the bridge, so I have asked Mister Greenway to see you safely onto a passenger boat. He will accompany you to the dock. Passage beneath the bridge is perilous, so ask God's protection as you near it.

"I also have provided Mister Greenway with a letter sealed with my personal seal, addressed to Mrs. Nellie Peete, a widow who lives on Bright Lane. She is a kindly woman and will provide you with a room until you are able to make other arrangements. The letter will introduce you and give her my recommendation of you. Mister Greenway will hire a coach to take you and your baggage to Mrs. Peete's house, and he will give you the letter. When you arrive there, give the letter to Mrs. Peete for her to unseal. She knows how to read. Inside are two shillings to pay her for your room."

Tears filled Grace's eyes. "Sir, you have been so kind to me. I will never be able to thank you as I ought. I have no right to ask more. But, please, sir, I must beg you one more time . . . Captain Ross, when you are well again, please take me to the United States of America. Please, sir, take me to Charleston!"

Captain Ross's face hardened. "I will not!" he said. "You do me an injustice to ask me again, Miss Grace. No, I will not!"

"Sir, I—"

"You must never go to that place, not with me or with anyone else. You must never even express a desire to do so."

"But I—"

"You have the chance to make a life for yourself in London. Do not destroy it with foolish stubbornness," Captain Ross said in a voice that left no room for more argument or tears. But when he saw the stricken look on Grace's face, he added more gently: "You cannot save Cabeto, Miss Grace. Commit him to the hands of God and let him go."

Grace said nothing more. But already she was snatching up every possible scrap of hope and tucking them all away in her heart to save for the time when she could weave together a plan. She was in London. That meant Cabeto must be somewhere in the West Indies. She had no time to waste.

"One more thing," Captain Ross said with an exhausted sigh. He reached under his blanket and pulled out a small satin purse. "Here is a bit of English money to get you started in your new life."

"Oh, sir, you have already done so much for me," Grace protested.

"Take care of it," the captain warned. "London is thick with pickpockets who will be watching for one such as you and looking to grab away your money. You must be wise and alert, and careful at all times."

Grace took the purse and stuffed it down the front of her dress. Captain Ross smiled, then he closed his eyes and drifted off.

It was with great wonderment that Grace stepped onto the passenger boat, accompanied by Nathaniel Greenway and her lidded crate of English clothes. The river was calm and the waterman adept at weaving his boat through the heavy river traffic. But as they neared the center arch of London Bridge, it seemed as though a wicked spirit suddenly grabbed hold of the boat and whirled it around and around. The waterman struggled with all his might to regain control. Grace grabbed hold of Mister Greenway's thick arm and bit into her lip.

Passage beneath the bridge is perilous, so ask God for protection. That's what the captain had told her. So Grace clamped her eyes shut and prayed with all her might as the boat rocked back and forth and dipped up and down.

Then, as suddenly as it had begun, the whirlpool released its grip. The waterman heaved a sigh of relief and rowed smoothly along on the city side of the bridge. They passed barges piled high with packages, and they passed round, leather-covered fishing boats. On every side they saw other watermen in other boats, some carrying passengers every bit as wide-eyed as Grace.

Nate Greenway helped Grace up the muddy steps of the dock, laughing out loud as she choked at the awful smell of the foul water.

"Do people actually drink this?" Grace exclaimed.

Mister Greenway assured her that they most certainly did, and what was more, she would as well unless she preferred to dry up of thirst.

People, people, people—everywhere, people! Grace had no idea so many people existed in the entire world. People walking, people riding in wagons and carriages, people pushing carts, people carrying baskets in their arms and on their heads, people selling pies and fish and vegetables and fruit and concoctions she couldn't imagine ever putting into her mouth.

"Scat!" Nate Greenway snapped as he slapped at two little boys who scratched along the riverbank.

"What did they want?" Grace asked.

"Just a couple of filthy mudlarks," Mister Greenway said. "They search the riverbank for anything they can sell. But no one wants them around, for they are only too happy to steal from a person too."

Grace looked back at the little boys.

"Come, come, Miss Grace," Nate Greenway called. Even as the stevedore unloaded her crate, Mister Greenway hailed a hackney coach, just as Captain Ross had instructed him to do. "Come along," he urged Grace. "This way, now."

Stepping over a dead dog that lay sprawled in the road, Nate Greenway hoisted Grace's crate up to the top of the carriage and fastened it with straps. He opened the door, pulled down the step and urged her into the mud-splattered coach and slammed the door shut. Only at the last moment did he remember Captain Ross's letter to Mrs. Peete. He thrust it to her through the open window. After a short argument with the driver, Mister Greenway shrugged and handed the man a shilling. The ship's navigator waved a swift farewell to Grace, then turned and loped back down the road.

At the snap of the driver's whip, the horses lurched and took off at full gallop. The coach clattered down the rough cobblestone road, shaking Grace so hard that her hat slipped off her head. Straight through a deep puddle the coach plunged, splattering muddy water through the open window and giving Grace a good dousing of street mire.

Grace was in London.

And she was all alone.

20

*A*n African mother chained to a post in the open-sided island shelter grasped her young son and crushed him to her with such intense desperation that the child gasped for breath. Even so, she could not cling tightly enough. For a white man came along and grabbed the child away from her, then shoved him outside. As the mother shrieked and wailed, her little one was bound together with other children, then all of them were pulled as one toward the auction stage.

Cabeto saw it all.

A man and his woman clung to each other, the man strong and his woman trembling against him. They entwined their fingers and dug in their nails, and it took three white men to pull them apart, but in the end the white men dragged the woman away. As her husband bellowed out his furious despair, they pulled her by her arms to the auction stage.

Cabeto saw this too.

Then Cabeto saw Tawnia sink down against Safya. "Move away, Tawnia," he rumbled softly but urgently in their tongue. "Do not be together or you will be separated forever."

A fierce blow to his side sent Cabeto sprawling and gasping for breath. He was not certain he would ever breathe again.

"No African talk allowed," the white man ordered.

As the dark cloud of pain cleared from Cabeto's eyes, and his choking gasps at last caught a bit of air for his lungs, he saw Safya push Tawnia away. Cabeto closed his eyes and concentrated on gulping air. When he opened his eyes again, almost a dozen people sat between the wise woman with the half-closed eyes and the tender young girl. Tawnia looked toward Safya, but Safya kept her eyes fastened to the floor.

"No," Cabeto whispered to Tawnia. He said it sternly in his language, and Tawnia heard him. He knew she did, for she pulled her eyes away from Safya and fixed them on her own legs.

"Rubbish," said a white worker not yet old enough to have more than a fuzzy stubble on his chin. "Best to simply toss the lot and begin anew."

"Rejects, yes," said his companion, a pale man with a straw hat pulled low over his eyes. "Women and flawed men they are. Still, it may be that we can fetch some price for them. That big one in the corner and the one sprawled on the ground, they may be worth something." He gestured toward Sunba and Cabeto.

After a moment's reflection the man in the straw hat added, "I say we take those two and a few of the others to a tavern and offer them cheap. Maybe luck will shine and someone will take the lot."

"No last scramble, then?" said the one with the fuzzy face.

"Might try. I just will not desert these on the wharf to die. They have already eaten up too much of my investment to allow such a waste. Richard Hudson is set to sail the *Golden Hawk* on to the United States with no more than half a cargo load of indigo, so we might try to get rid of the rest of the slave cargo over in America. They will take there what planters here refuse."

"Maybe," the one with the fuzzy face said doubtfully.

"Those sufficiently broken in," said the man with the straw hat. "The ones not too quick to fight. Those who don't cause us trouble. Who can walk and don't look too sick and feeble. Those are the ones they'll take on to America."

Cabeto's face registered not the slightest acknowledgment.

What did these white men know of him? Of the slave rebellion at Zulina, and Antonio the slave? What could they possibly know of his Grace, who grew up in a London house with an English father? They had no reason to suspect that a broken African they referred to as "rubbish" and "a reject," whom they saw as just an ignorant, flawed slave who babbled heathen talk, could understand words of both Spanish and English.

That night, everyone drifted away except the white men grudgingly set as guards over them, even though the captives' chains were so securely bolted to the posts that supported the building it would have taken hundreds of slaves to loosen even one captive. Cabeto watched and waited as the guards nodded their heads and one by one let their eyes drift closed. When the guards at long last snored in unison, Cabeto whispered to the slaves around him, "Do not cause trouble. Do not fight. Stay calm. Do not cling to one another. Walk upright and look well even if you are dying. Only in this way will you live to see the sun cross the sky once again."

The ones near him whispered the warnings to the ones next to them, and those slaves passed the warnings along to the ones near them, and so on, and so on.

The next day, when the man with the straw hat returned, he found quiet, compliant slaves. When he motioned them to rise, every one of them stood up, and not one revealed the extent of the effort it took to do so. The man in the straw hat smiled a self-congratulatory smile and hurried away. And all slaves remained on their feet, all supporting themselves, and all keeping their eyes to themselves.

"I told you, Richard," the man in the straw hat said as he returned with Captain Hudson and Lukas in tow. "Fully seasoned already, every one of them. What this business requires is a firm hand and a steady will."

"Back to the ship with ye, then," Lukas ordered the slaves as he cracked his whip. The tip caught Safya's ankle and jerked her down hard. At first she lay as if dead. Tawnia's hand flew to her mouth, but Cabeto shot her a warning look and she stifled her cry.

"Git up!" Lukas ordered. He gave Safya a vicious kick to her ribs.

Safya groaned and rolled over.

Sunba could not help himself. He lunged toward Safya. But Captain Hudson was carrying the cat-o-nine-tails. One lash from the cat knocked Sunba flat.

Almost immediately, Sunba got back up and stood unsteadily, glowering at the captain. Sunba's face twisted with fury, and he clenched his hands into tight fists. Then he put one foot forward.

"Not now," Cabeto ordered in his low rumble of a whisper. "Fighting will not help us. The time will come to fight. It will come, but it is not now."

For a minute, the two men stared into each other's eyes, the armed white man with all the power and the black man with nothing left to lose. Then Sunba stepped back and allowed the sadness to return to his face. He relaxed his hands and looked down at the ground.

Captain Hudson folded his arms across his chest, the cat clutched tight in his hand. His eyes never left Sunba.

"March!" Lukas ordered as he forced the slaves back onto the ship. Safya struggled to get up, but she was too slow. Two seamen grasped her by the arms and dragged her all the way across the plank, over the deck, and down the stairs to the hold. She groaned the entire way.

Back again into the horrible *Golden Hawk*.

Once again, legs were clamped into irons and chained to the bolts in the floor—although this time the slave packing was not so tight and their wrists were not chained to their neighbors' wrists.

Once again the slave ship began its endless, sickening rocking.

Once again a cloud of dread smothered out the captives' hope that they might live to see tomorrow, even as it ignited terror that they actually might have to endure yet another day.

"Sunba," Cabeto called out in a voice hoarse with despair.

"I am here, Brother," Sunba replied.

"Safya," called Cabeto.

Silence.

"Safya! Answer!"

Silence.

"Safya! A groan will do!"

Silence.

"Tawnia," Cabeto called in a choked voice.

Silence.

"Tawnia!" Cabeto demanded.

Her voice flooded with tears, Tawnia replied wearily, "From this day, I will not answer when my name is called. The call is for the living, and from this day, my soul is dead."

21

With a clatter of horse hooves, and the tooth-rattling rumble of iron wheels on loose cobblestones, the hackney coach bolted out into the mad jumble of carriages and wagons all clogged together in the street up ahead. Whipping the horses into a faster gallop, the driver easily pulled the coach past two slow-moving wagons. But a larger carriage bore down on them so fast it shook the ground as it barreled past. A small boy, unfortunate enough to step out just at that moment, would have been run down had not a quick-minded passerby grabbed him in time.

"Hot buns! Tuppence! Fresh baked hot buns!" cried a woman pushing a wooden cart.

Right behind her came another woman weaving a wagon along the crowded walk. She bellowed, "Mackerel, jist off the boat! Fresh mackerel!"

Door after door flew open in the brick houses crammed together side-by-side on either side of the street, and women with caps on their heads and aprons over their plain dresses called out to one peddler or another. Not only could they buy fish and fresh baked bread, but apples and meat pies and eggs and vegetables and flowers and herbal tonics. All this and an endless array of other things Grace couldn't make out.

In a singsong voice, a milk woman yodeled, "Fresh milk! Quick, quick! Get your fresh milk!"

Taking care not to breathe deeply, which Grace quickly learned inevitably lead to a coughing fit, she gazed in wonder at this strange world called London. So many people! So much noise!

A man drove ten cows into the street directly in front of the coach in which Grace was riding. It was all the driver could do to jerk the horses aside in time to keep from hitting them. Grace, flung against the carriage door, screamed and grabbed for some place to grip.

"Watch where ye's goin'!" the cowman yelled up at the coach driver.

"You is the one wot better watch yerself!" the driver shot back. "Else I'll slaughter 'em cows fer you, I will!"

Pay attention to the road! Grace ordered herself. *I cannot get back to the dock unless I remember the way.*

According to Captain Ross's estimate, Cabeto might already be on his way to the slave market in America. If Grace ever hoped to see him again, she would have to get there too. She would have to go to Charleston, the very place against which Captain Ross so insistently warned her.

But it was not Captain Ross's life, was it? It was Cabeto's life. And hers.

"*We cannot control what happens around us any more than we can change what happened to us in the past,*" Mama Muco had told Grace that last happy night in the village before the slavers struck. "*All we can do is decide how we will live our own lives.*"

Grace closed her eyes and whispered, "I decided, Mama. I will find a way for Cabeto and me to be together and to live free."

As Grace could see it, the only way to get to Charleston in America was by ship. Yet the coach was speeding her away from the docks, away from the ships setting their sails for the new United States. Instead of taking her toward Cabeto, it was rushing her in the opposite direction.

Grace's plan was to stay the night with Mrs. Peete, then, at first light, to walk back to the dock. She would leave the crate with her belongings behind. What did she care about those fancy frocks and hats and shoes Mister Hathaway bought for her, anyway? Once she made it to the dock, she would surely be able to find a ship going to the United States.

That was her plan. But already she was hopelessly confused. All the houses looked alike. Streets crossed other streets, then they intersected with lanes that turned into courtyards, or still more streets. And just when she thought she might start to understand the direction in which they were traveling, the coach would turn onto yet another street altogether—which looked just the same as the last street but headed in another way entirely. How could she ever hope to find her way back to the docks?

Outside her village in Africa, the single main road divided and went in two directions. Yet both paths led to the great baobab tree where the chiefs were buried and under whose gnarled branches the wise men sat. But in this city, there was no giant baobab tree. As far as Grace could see, there were no baobab trees at all. No ghariti trees, either. Or jackfruit or mangos or cashews. *Do the people in London have nothing worthwhile to eat?* Grace wondered. *How do they make healing poultices for their sick and injured?*

Grace touched her chest and felt the bulge of the purse she had hidden under her dress. Perhaps Captain Ross had given her enough money to ride back to the docks in a coach. Maybe Mrs. Peete was a kindly woman who would understand and help her. A wise person like Mama Muco, perhaps.

Oh, Mama . . . If only . . . Grace shook her head to clear away the memories, and also the sobs those memories always brought.

"Rags! Rags! Throw me yer rags!" called an old man as he slowly pushed his cart along beside the street. A gray-haired woman opened her window and tossed out something that the old man snatched up and threw into his wagon. Then he was off again: "Rags! Rags! Throw me yer rags!"

If the man wanted to pick up trash, Grace thought, his wagon could soon be filled to running over. Never in her life had she seen such piles of rotting garbage as lay open and exposed on the streets of London. Did Englishpeople not have goats to eat their refuse?

The coach made a sharp turn onto a narrow lane, then pulled to a stop in front of a small house crammed between two shops—a blacksmith on the left and a tailor on the right. The driver jumped down, unfastened Grace's crate and pulled it off the carriage top. He opened the door for her and pulled down the step.

"This be the place, miss," he said.

Then he was off.

Grace stood on the sorely misnamed Bright Lane and stared blankly at the grim house with crumbling stairs and a sagging door. A foul stench hung in the lane. Grace's first thought was to turn and run; just leave her crate in the street and run as fast as she could back toward the docks. Maybe she could still find Captain Ross and plead with him one more time. Or perhaps that kind Mister Brandt might still be around and willing to take her to America. Or even Mister Greenway. She had not even thought of begging him. Why, oh, why hadn't she thought to ask him about it when they were crossing the river?

"Is yer thinking to stand outside me 'ouse all the day long?"

Only then did Grace see the stocky woman standing at the far side of the house. Her hands were on her hips, her sleeves pushed up to her elbows, and she had a cloth tied around her hair—although a fluff of bushy gray had worked loose and hung down the side of her face.

"Mrs . . . Peete?" Grace stammered. "Mrs. Nellie Peete?"

"An' who's doin' the askin'?" the woman demanded.

"I'm Grace. Grace Winslow."

Grace pulled the sealed letter from her pocket and held it out to the woman. "To you from Captain Ross."

Mrs. Peete took the letter and tucked it into her dress without opening it. "So the cap'n sent you round, did 'e?" she said.

Without waiting for an answer, Mrs. Peete stepped over a small board-bridge beside the road, hefted up Grace's crate with surprising ease, and started for the house. Grace had no choice but to follow the determined little woman. As Grace stepped onto the narrow bridge, she suddenly understood the awful smell. Underneath flowed a river of sewage.

"A washerwoman is wot I be, though I 'spects you knows that already," Mrs. Peete was saying. "And I don't mind tellin' you, I kin use two extra hands at me washtubs."

Grace hardly heard Mrs. Peete's words, so intrigued was she at the woman's face. It seemed to be punched full of little holes.

"You don't have to start workin' today, I s'pose," Mrs. Peete said. "You kin wait 'til the mornin' when you's rested a bit."

Maybe the little holes were marks of Mrs. Peete's tribe, like the marks on Ikem's face, Grace thought. Although they didn't make her look fearsome, and they certainly were not pretty.

"Why is you starin' at me that way?" Mrs. Peete demanded. "Ain't you never seen scars from the smallpox?"

Smallpox! Grace had heard of the fearsome disease, to be sure, although she never expected to see anyone afflicted still alive and walking around. She thought everyone who got it died. Now that she saw its vestiges, however, she did recognize similar marks on the faces of some sailors. But seamen's faces were so leathered and worn, Grace took the marks to be some form of white man's wrinkles. On the streets of London, she would soon see, more faces were pitted than were smooth.

Mrs. Peete led Grace into the main room. It was piled with clothes to be washed, as well as with clean clothes waiting to be folded and placed in stacks. A kettle boiled over the fire in the fireplace.

Once the door was closed tight, the washerwoman pulled the letter from Captain Ross out from where she had stuck it in her dress and broke the wax seal. She didn't actually take the sheet of paper from the envelope, though, just the two shillings, which she dropped into her pocket.

Two doors opened off the one room. "That one be your room," Mrs. Peete said, motioning to the door on the right. "T'other be mine." She tossed Grace's baggage at the door. "Your room and one meal in trade fer your work. That's me arrangement." Then she left Grace alone.

All the windows in the house were coated in grime, but in her room the single small window was painted black. Not that it mattered much. There was precious little to see, anyway. A sagging cot almost filled the entirety of the room. No chair, no dressing table. Not even a rag rug on the floor. Grace dragged her crate into the room and crammed it between the foot of the cot and the wall.

Was it evening? Grace couldn't remember. Certainly the day had seemed endless. How could she tell time when the room was shrouded in darkness?

Grace flung herself across the cot, pulled her cloak around her, and wept.

22

$\mathcal{J}$oseph Winslow wiped sweaty palms down the sides of his new coat and stepped awkwardly into the lavishly appointed entry hall of Larkspur Estate. Whistling in awe, he dropped a farthing into Rustin's outstretched hand.

"Your hat, sir," the butler said with disdain.

Joseph laughed and exchanged his hat for the farthing.

"'Ad me own London 'ouse once upon a time," Joseph said to Sir Geoffrey Philips, in whose luxurious carriage he had arrived at Larkspur. "It were me lovely pride an' joy. But it be gone now, all gone. Burned to a crisp, is wot."

"How dreadful," Sir Geoffrey replied. "I must remind you once again, kind sir, that Lord Reginald considers Larkspur Estate far more than simply a 'London house.' This land and home have been in the Witherham family for more than two hundred years."

"Is you saying, then, that 'e be a proud man?" asked Joseph Winslow.

Sir Geoffrey did not indulge his temptation to smile. He was far too much a gentleman to cause embarrassment to another—even to such a one as this. Instead, he motioned for Winslow to follow Rustin to the parlor.

"'Oooo-eeeeee," Joseph gasped when he saw the intricate details of the richly appointed room. Mahogany furniture, constructed and carved by Europe's leading craftsmen . . . Walls covered in cut velvet . . . A lavishly hand-painted ceiling that included a sky of Prussian blue and trees of deep green, colors Joseph Winslow had sadly passed on for his own house because of their exorbitant cost. Joseph went directly to the inset bookshelves and ran his hand across the rows of leather-bound volumes, many embossed with gold leaf lettering.

"I fancies books me'self, I do," he said. "Collected a 'ole library full fer me an' me daughter to read." He made a great show of looking at the titles and pondering over each one.

"Mister Winslow, I presume?" Lord Reginald said as he strutted into the parlor.

Joseph spun around.

"That I be . . . yes, sir . . . m'lord . . . I be Joseph Winslow," he stammered. "Jist admirin' yer books, is all."

"You also enjoy the great pastime of reading, then?" responded Lord Reginald. "Tell me your favorite title, sir, and I shall be most pleased to make you a gift of it to mark the day of our meeting."

"Well, I . . . that is, I . . ." Joseph squinted at the muddle of letters and wished for all the world that he really could read.

"Another time, perhaps," Lord Reginald said. "Come, do sit." He motioned Joseph toward the Queen Anne chair.

While the maid set up tea and served it to the men, Lord Reginald and Sir Geoffrey talked casually of city events, none of which interested Joseph Winslow in the least. As a matter of fact, the talk irritated him. Seated on the best of European furniture in a stately aristocratic mansion, dressed head to foot in a new set of clothes he didn't have to pay for . . . How dare these men stir up his curiosity then speak drivel while his eagerness to know the reason for their interest fermented inside him?

From the time Sir Geoffrey Philips and Augustus Jamison had wound their way through the crowded floor to save Joseph Winslow from his humiliation at the cockfight, Sir Geoffrey had shown Joseph nothing but kindness and generosity. Besides paying his debt that night, he had bought him coffee and had even given him an extra five quid for his trouble. And all Sir Geoffrey had asked in return was that Joseph Winslow accompany him to this mansion to meet with Lord Reginald Witherham, heir to one of England's greatest family fortunes.

Ride out to the West End in a fine carriage? Well, why not?

And so, Sir Geoffrey had arrived at the appointed hour and the appointed place. Although Joseph Winslow took care to clean himself as well as a bucket of cold water would allow, Sir Geoffrey had insisted on a trip to the barbershop, then to the tailor, then to the haberdasher. The result was an entirely different Joseph Winslow.

"In Africa they called me 'Admiral,'" Joseph blurted, despite the fact that it had absolutely nothing to do with the course of the conversation.

Both Lord Reginald and Sir Geoffrey smiled, but neither replied.

As Joseph helped himself to another tea cake, Lord Reginald said, "Sir Geoffrey tells me that you were personally involved in the slave trade, Mister Winslow."

"That I was, m'lord. 'Ad me very own slave fortress, I did. Biggest one on the Slave Coast, an' that ain't no brag, neither. 'Ad the most powerful king workin' fer me too. 'Is slattees gots the slaves fer me an' I sold 'em to blokes th' like of you."

"Yes, I see," Lord Reginald answered, although he did not look as though he saw at all. "What caused you to leave so prestigious a position?"

Joseph's face darkened. "Big slave rebellion, is wot," he mumbled. Then, his voice rising with passion and a blush mottling his cheeks, he insisted, "Right there's the problem! Ye cajn't trust any of 'em. Nary a one! Not the slaves and not the African kings. And most certainly not a 'igh and mighty African princess."

Carefully, precisely, Lord Witherham picked up his teacup and took a long sip. Sir Philips did the same.

"Traitors, ever' last one of 'em!" Joseph muttered as he reached for another tea cake. Then he picked up his own cup.

"England is not what it once was," Lord Reginald Witherham said. "Refugees from the war in America have come over here. Now that war is being waged in France, more French are pouring across the channel as well. Many Irish and many Scots, all making our country theirs. Lascars from India, and Africans too—mostly living as free men—come to our fair country and work at jobs once reserved for England's own poor. No, my dear sirs, things are no longer what they once were."

Joseph looked at his host and did his best to blink back his confusion. What did he care of foreigners in England? Hadn't he had his fill of them in Africa?

"The problem, Mister Winslow—as I am certain a man as well-traveled as yourself understands—is that when outsiders come, they bring their destructive ideas along with them," said Lord Reginald.

Yes, destructive ideas. That Joseph understood only too well.

"Ideas about mob rule and the obliteration of the aristocracy. Ideas about dismantling the structure of the African slave trade and thereby no longer allowing us the wherewithal to supply workers for our vast holdings in the New World. Which would mean the destruction of the very financial foundation of London, I must say, if not of our entire country."

"'Em dirty beggars!" Joseph hissed.

"Sir Geoffrey and I, along with several other well-placed gentlemen, are determined that we shall not allow this to happen to our country. Can we count on your support and assistance . . . *Admiral* Winslow?"

Joseph puffed out his chest. "That ye kin, m'lord!" he said. "That ye most assuredly kin!"

23

*U*p with you! Up! Up!"

Grace opened her eyes to blackness, and for the life of her, she could not figure out where she was. Who was the shadowy figure shaking her?

"Up with you! The linens already be gathered in, and the cauldron be boilin' on the fire!"

Grace struggled to sit up. "Mrs. Peete? Is it morning?"

"Close enough fer the likes of us," Mrs. Peete said. "Come daylight, the first baskets of wash will be ready fer the line. Git up now, I needs your 'elp."

Fine linens trimmed in handmade lace, muslins decorated with delicate crocheted edgings, frilled shirts bedecked with ruffles, pleated bodices adorned with fine stitching—Mrs. Peete called such things the "small linen." Following Mrs. Peete's instructions, Grace set an empty bucket on the hearth, and, using the ladle that hung on the hook overhead, dipped water into it from the bubbling cauldron. When the bucket was full, she toted it to the large copper washtub assigned her, then she went back for another bucketful. She kept this up until the washtub was filled. Then she got busy washing all the small linens by hand. She washed out the general dirt, then she went to work on any spots with hard soap until each piece of clothing was clean—and her hands were rubbed raw.

"Wot 'appened to you?" Mrs. Peete asked, pointing to Grace's first finger on her left hand, where the first joint of her finger should have been.

Grace never even considered offering up the story of the slave rebellion and the mangled ransom attempt. Instead she buried her hands in the cloudy water and mumbled, "Accident at home. It was a long time ago."

Mrs. Peete shrugged and said, "Jist so's it don't slow you down." Then she turned back to her own work.

When Grace paused to straighten her aching back, Mrs. Peete said, "If you wants to stand straight fer a bit, take the basket out to the garden and throw them clothes over the dryin' line."

Outside, Grace placed the small linens over the line, piece by piece. Her dress, now soaking wet, flapped around her in the brisk wind and set her to shivering. The wind might dry the clothes, but to someone wet to the skin with wash water, it was pure misery.

By the time Grace got back in the house, Mrs. Peete had already cleaned up the washtub. "Don't use so much soap," she scolded. "I 'as to pay out me money for that, you know. Costs me two pence fer ever' pound. And don't slosh so much water around on the floor. Liked to break me back cleanin' up after you!"

Just as Grace was congratulating herself on getting her work done so quickly and so well, Mrs. Peete set out a fresh tub. "Fer the large things," she said. "Sheets and tablecloths and such." She threw down an enormous pile. "Fill the tub and start washin' these. I'll git more water from the pump up the street so I kin set the dirtiest things to boilin' over the fire."

At noon, Mrs. Peete moved the wet clothes off the table. Then she bustled about the cupboard and laid out a lunch of bread with a small dab of butter and two slices of cheese for each of them. She poured them each a cup of weak tea to wash down the bread and cheese.

"When will we be done with the washing?" Grace asked. She was so exhausted, she was close to tears.

"Not until them dirty piles be clean, dearie," Mrs. Peete said. "Maybe tonight we'll stop early and walk to a takeaway fer a meat pie."

But by the time Mrs. Peete was ready to go for the meat pie, all Grace wanted to do was get out of her wet clothes, drop down on her cot, and sleep. She was totally and thoroughly exhausted. The skin was worn off her fingers, her hands and arms were scalded and chapped, and her back felt as though it would break in two from bending over the washtub all day long.

"Do you do this every day?" Grace asked.

"Ever' day of me life," Mrs. Peete said. "And I be glad fer the work too. Pays me eight pence a day, it does. Wi' your 'elp, maybe a shilling a day. I 'as me a roof over me head and three pence to pay fer bread and cheese, and a bit of meat on Sundays. That be more than most folks on this lane kin say."

After a week of working alongside Mrs. Peete, Grace was able to move through the pile of laundry much more efficiently and with a bit less agony. Already Mrs. Peete had placed her in complete charge of the small linens. Each day, after Grace spent the morning rubbing the linens clean in the washtub, she went to the garden to hang them out to dry. The fresh air was a happy relief from the closed-in staleness of the house. Once Grace suggested opening a window, but Mrs. Peete exclaimed, "And catch the consumption and die? Air be the worst thing fer a body!"

From the washing line, Grace could watch the people of London as they walked up and down the lane. Men, women, children of all ages. Where were they all going in such a hurry? Were they working? Not a one looked to be out for a pleasant afternoon stroll.

A delightful idea popped into Grace's mind. What if she were to run out into the lane and stop each person and ask directions to the docks? Better yet, what if she were to offer a shilling to anyone who would take her there? Best idea of all: What if she offered her entire silk purse of shillings to anyone who could get her on a ship to the United States in America? To Charleston?

But she never did any of those things. Every day, after she finished hanging all the small linens on the line, she came back into the house to face a fresh tub of water and a great dirty pile of large things.

"You is a good worker, girl," Mrs. Peete said one day as she laid out the usual lunch of bread, cheese, and tea. "I's pleased to have you in me 'ouse."

"I want to leave," Grace said.

"What do you mean, you wants to leave?" Mrs. Peete demanded. "After I's so kindly shared me 'ome with you, that's what you tells me? After I's give you me own food to eat?"

"Please, Mrs. Peete, I have to get back to the dock and the sailing ships!" Grace said. Then she poured out the whole story—of the slavers who came to her village with guns flaming, of her baby Kwate, of Mister Hathaway, of Cabeto, who was even now on a slave ship.

"I must get to the place where they sell the slaves," Grace said. "I must find Cabeto before it is too late."

"If'n you gits to them colonies, girl, they will make a slave of *you*, is wot!" Mrs. Peete said.

"Then I will be a slave with my husband."

"You be a fool," said Mrs. Peete. "A fool is what you be, and I won't have no part of it."

"If I could just get back to the docks—"

"A stupid fool, that's what you be!"

For nine days, Grace had been at Mrs. Peete's house. On the tenth day, Grace arose before dawn, just as she did every day. The cauldron was already boiling over the fire, and the small linens were piled up and waiting for her. Grace spent the morning bent over the washtub and went to the garden to hang the clothes over the line and watch the people in the lane. It was her favorite part of the day.

Grace had just hung the last shirt over the line when she saw the girl walk by. A girl like her, with brown skin (though lighter than Grace's) and auburn hair. The girl was not actually African, but she was not English, either. She had one foot in each of two worlds, just like Grace!

With a gasp, Grace dropped her basket and ran through the garden gate. She lifted her skirt above her ankles and took off down the lane after the girl. At the end of the lane the girl turned onto the broad street, so Grace turned as well. The girl walked quite a way along the street, and then she turned again. Grace followed her just in time to see her disappear into a coffeehouse. Grace hesitated, but only for a moment. Then she opened the door and also slipped in.

Never had Grace seen such a place as that coffeehouse. The large room was lined with long tables where men sat bunched together in groups drinking coffee and smoking long clay pipes. The room hummed with the rhythm of excited discussion. One man stood up from a group and, after a fair bit of harrumphing, made a loud and ponderous proclamation.

Something about a politician and a speech that politician had recently made. All the others in the room quieted their talk to listen to the man, but when he finished and sat back down, everyone started up again with their own chatter.

Many of the men had hair that looked as though it had been dipped in white milled flour. It curled over their ears, each in the same way, and in the back it hung down in a tail tied with a ribbon. It was the style of rich Englishmen, not the common men Grace saw walking in the lane. Some men in the coffeehouse kept their hair covered with hats. All dressed in knee breeches, fancy shirts, and silky-looking jackets, and all had their legs covered with stockings and wore shoes with silver buckles.

At the far end of one table, an African man sat alone. Yes, certainly he was an African, and yet he dressed just like an Englishman—the same knee breeches and white stockings, the same ruffled shirt and fancy coat. No white hair, though.

Grace could not help but stare at the African man. Imagine if it were Cabeto sitting there in white man's clothes!

The coffeehouse chatter began to die down as one white head after another turned to stare at the bronze girl standing in their midst wearing a soaking wet dress.

Before Grace had a chance to wonder what she should do, the girl she had been following grabbed her from behind and pulled her rather roughly to one side. With all eyes on the two of them, the girl headed for a side door. Grace was right behind her.

Once outside, the girl turned fiery green eyes on Grace and demanded, "Who are you? And why are you following me?"

24

"Come, now, Lord Witherham, how many more times do you intend to rouse us from the comfort of our homes and insist that we come together in your sitting room only to listen to you rant?" Augustus Jamison demanded. "This really is too much to ask us to endure!"

"He is right," agreed Sir Geoffrey Philips, who seldom raised a voice of objection to anything. "We are entirely acquainted with your point of view on the growing movement to abolish the slave trade. And most assuredly, you know every man in the room is in full agreement with you. But I ask you, to what end must we listen to a repetition of the same arguments?"

"I have not called you here to listen to the same arguments repeated," Lord Witherham stated. "I have called you here to invite you to move with me from rhetoric to action."

Upstairs in her chamber, Lady Charlotte Witherham tied satin ribbons across the bodice of her new blue mantua dress so that the decorated stays would be displayed in a most alluring fashion. Then she adjusted the open blue skirt to properly show off her lacy white underskirt. As a perfect finishing touch, she fit a frilled cap on her head and gave it a jaunty tilt. If Lord Reginald thought for one moment that he could successfully command her to sit quietly in her private chambers while he stirred up trouble in the sitting room downstairs, he knew her even less well than she suspected.

"New ideas, they say?" Lord Reginald was expounding to the men downstairs. "The voice of the populace must be heard, they insist? Well, if that be so, then *let* that voice be heard! But let us make certain that the people's voice speaks *our* message and that any new ideas expressed do not stray too far from the tried and true ideas that have served us so well."

Simon Johnson sighed. "Please, Lord Reginald, do have mercy on us!" he implored. "All this talk, talk, talk! Will you not simply say what it is you have to say and be done with it?"

"I have but one word, Mister Johnson," Lord Reginald replied. He paused to fully capture the drama of the moment. "That one word, my dear sirs, is *riot*."

"Riot?" each of the three asked incredulously at the very same moment.

"Whatever do you mean?" demanded Simon Johnson.

"Six June of 1780," Lord Reginald replied.

"Yes, yes, a date we know well," said Augustus Jamison, his patience running short. "The Gordon Riots. But that was about Roman Catholics, not slavery."

"No, sir, it was not," Sir Reginald argued. "It was about the power of the people. The people attacked the aristocratic society. They attacked *us*. They demolished our houses and went so far as to attack our persons. They freed *criminals* from Newgate Prison, as you no doubt recall. Then the people joined together to burn and plunder our fair city."

"I cannot see what that has to do with—" Augustus Jamison began.

"What I am suggesting is that the same anger can be stirred up again. The difference is that this time it can be harnessed and the blame can be laid at the feet of the abolitionists. We will let the people do our job for us!"

At that moment the sitting room doors swung open and Lady Charlotte swept into the room. She smiled at each gentleman in turn, then sat down in the Queen Anne chair by the door. She carefully arranged her skirts in order to display the lacy white underskirt in all its costly beauty. Then she folded her creamy white hands in her lap, fixed her blue eyes on her husband, and waited with just the trace of a smile on her tender lips.

"Lady Charlotte, my dear," Lord Reginald said with anything but a tone of dearness emanating through his tightly clenched jaw.

It gave Charlotte special pleasure to see the fiery anger blush across her husband's delicate face. It pleased her no end to see him helpless to do anything about it.

"Please, do continue with what you were saying, Reginald dear," Lady Charlotte said in her sweetest voice. "I shan't wish to interrupt you."

"I was of the understanding that you would be occupied in your chambers this evening," Lord Reginald all but hissed.

"No," Lady Charlotte replied.

"Get on with it, Witherham!" insisted Simon Johnson. "What is it you are proposing?"

Lord Reginald looked at his wife and struggled to control his fury. "The men in this room have matters of politics and business to discuss," he said in a brittle voice. "I really must insist that you allow us to get on with it."

"By all means, do," Lady Charlotte urged. "Such things are of grave concern to both men and women. Please, do continue."

Lord Reginald, thoroughly befuddled by Lady Charlotte's passive refusal to leave them, stammered through a statement of the unrest and turmoil brought on by the new ideas of the times. Immediately, irritation and boredom crossed the faces of the men as they shifted impatiently in their seats.

Changing tactics, Lord Reginald raised his voice in a heated warning of the danger posed by the coffeehouses, but the men's eyebrows shot up. The gentlemen exchanged knowing glances, and now and then sneaked a glance at Lady Charlotte.

Again Lord Reginald altered his course, this time launching into a dramatic retelling of the devastation wrought by the Gordon Riots. Even he was bored by this performance. So in the end, he simply gave it all up, thanked the men for coming, and said he would be in contact.

"Unless something momentous transpires, I beg of you, do not bother," Simon Johnson groused. And although the others didn't say so, Lord Reginald was well aware of their hearty agreement.

After the last of the men had collected their hats and gloves, and their carriages had clattered down the driveway heading toward the street, Lady Charlotte smiled sweetly and said to Lord Reginald, "I think your meeting went quite well, dear." Then she headed up to bed.

25

"My name is Ena," said the girl with the bronze-brown skin and the auburn hair—but only after Grace had poured out her own story. At first the girl had listened with a flash of insolence in her eyes, her lips pursed tight. It was when Grace spoke of Cabeto, sailing for the slave markets in America, that Ena's fierce veneer finally cracked.

"I am not like you," Ena said. "I am not from Africa."

"You look like me."

"The black in me is from my *da*. His people were stolen from Africa and taken to the West Indies in slave ships, the same as your Cabeto. The white in me is from my mother's people. Irish, they be. My ma brought me here from the West Indies when I was very small."

"Your mother came back home!" Grace exclaimed with great excitement. "So it *is* possible!"

"No, not home," Ena replied, her voice slashed through with bitterness. "Only to England. For my ma, home is Ireland."

Ireland meant nothing to Grace, but she recognized the flash of fire in Ena's green eyes.

"Was your mother stolen from her land too?" Grace asked.

"She was, and so were many of her people. They were also forced onto ships to go to the islands of the West Indies," Ena said.

"To be slaves?"

"To breed with the Africans to make more slaves," Ena said.

Ena's simmering passion stirred up a strange new hope in Grace. Irish or English, African or West Indian, the important thing was that *someone* carried away from *somewhere* as a slave had come back alive and free. If Ena's mother could do it, so could Cabeto!

Grace grabbed Ena's arm and begged, "Your mother . . . Where is she? Will she help me?"

Ena pulled away from Grace's grasp. "My ma is dead and gone. Scarlet fever took her five years past." Before Grace could ask any more questions, Ena turned away and started back toward the coffeehouse. "I have paid employment here," she called over her shoulder. "I must attend to my work."

"Wait!" Grace cried. "Can I see you again?"

As Ena opened the coffeehouse door, she shrugged and said, "I am here every day."

Grace got back to Mrs. Peete's house to find the washer-woman boiling mad. "You run off and leave me to do all the work alone!" she scolded. "Not a word to where you be. Not a word if you be comin' back again. Could be kidnapped and layin' dead in the street for all I knew!"

With a mumbled apology, Grace hurried to ladle steaming water into the bucket for the washtub so she could start to work washing the large things that waited on the floor.

"Won't be time fer them to dry now," Mrs. Peete grumbled as she poured the last of the water from the cauldron into Grace's wash tub.

Bucket in hand, Mrs. Peete stomped out the door and headed down the road. She didn't return for a very long time. Perhaps many other women decided to go to the pump for water at the very same time. Or it could be that Mrs. Peete went first to the takeaway for a meat pie. If that was so, she didn't ask Grace to accompany her, and she brought nothing back for Grace to eat. Nor did she offer Grace any bread and cheese for lunch that day.

The old woman was right about the large things. As darkness fell and the damp fog closed in, Grace had to take them, still wet, off the drying line and lay them out over the table and chairs. Mrs. Peete stood behind her the entire time, mumbling and harrumphing.

"They best be dry by mornin'," Mrs. Peete grumbled.

"I will be away again tomorrow," Grace said.

"Away again!" Mrs. Peete exploded.

"Please, Mrs. Peete—"

"You be a good worker, Grace, and I be pleased to have you here," Mrs. Peete said. "But I needs you when I needs you. If you don't mean to work with me, jist tell me now so's I kin find other hands to lighten me load—and another body to sleep in your bed."

Grace got down on her knees and mopped the sloshed water from the floor. She wrung out the rags and spread them on the hearth to dry, just as Mrs. Peete had instructed her, then she carried the washtub outside and emptied it over the fence.

When she came back inside, she said, "Today I saw someone who looked like me, Mrs. Peete. She was both black and white, and yet not either. I followed her to a coffeehouse where she works."

"A coffeehouse, is it?" said Mrs. Peete. Her wrinkled face twisted into a frown. "Only ones go there be blokes with money to throw away and time to waste talking 'bout things no one kin change anyhow."

"I could pay you something for the room," Grace offered. She pulled the purse Captain Ross gave her out from its hiding place in the bosom of her dress. "I don't know the coins, and I must keep enough to get me back to the docks."

Grace untied the purse strings and poured fifteen silver shillings out onto the damp sheet lapped across the table.

"Whooeeee!" Mrs. Peete whistled. "'Tis your good luck I'm not of a mind to cheat you, dearie. But there be plenty about happy to take your money from you. That new girl . . . the Irish one . . . she likely be lookin' to cheat you."

"If I pay you something, could I work just until the noon church bells ring each day?" Grace asked.

Mrs. Peete plucked a shilling from the pile on the table. She turned it over and over in her hand, examining it carefully and running her calloused fingers around the edge. "Not even clipped," she said with a smile. "This will do me for now. I'll tell you when to give me more."

The next morning, by the time the sun did its best to cast a ray through the gritty windows, Grace had already folded the dry sheets, ladled steaming water to fill her washtub, and had begun rubbing spots from the small linens. By mid-morning, the small linens were all hanging on the line. Grace was ready for a fresh tub of water so she could start on the large things.

Because Grace had never seen the sun since she arrived in London, she couldn't tell time the way she always had before. But she could not miss the noon hour, because all the bells in all the steeples of all the churches on all the streets in the city of London rang out as the hour approached, then all chimed twelve in a cacophony. At the first sound of the church chimes, Grace dried her hands on her skirt, then she hurried to her room to change into a dry dress. A slice of bread and cheese, then she was off, up the street, around the corner, then on and around another.

With great anticipation, Grace stepped into the coffeehouse looking for Ena. But Ena was nowhere in sight. The only other female in the room was an older woman who sat high on a seat in a large wooden booth at the front end of the coffeehouse. She wore an elaborately pleated frock and a matching pleated hat, and she sat perched on a high stool. It was she who sold glasses of coffee to the patrons, as well as fresh candles for their candleholders. A stately man with a three-cornered hat over his coiffed natural brown hair was making a purchase. He stooped down and pulled a long clay pipe from a wooden chest, then plunked coins on the booth desk.

"Thank you, Sir Thomas," the woman in the booth said with a slight bow. "We are always pleased when you grace us with your company. Do enjoy your time with us this day."

Sir Thomas McClennon went back to his group of three other well-dressed men, all with white hair, all lost in deep discussion over some matter or other.

Everyone in the room, it seemed, was lost in deep discussion. Newspapers and pamphlets lay scattered across the tables. The man who had just bought coffee snatched up a newspaper and, to make a point Grace couldn't understand, waved the newspaper in the air.

But Ena was not in the room.

Nor was the black man Grace had seen the day before, the one wearing the suit of a rich white man. Two plump Englishmen, both with the same white curly hair, sat in his place at the back table.

Several men turned to stare at Grace. She wasn't certain what to do. Surely she would not be welcome at the tables. Anyway, if she were to sit down, what would she say? Maybe she could ask the woman in the booth about Ena . . .

And then there was Ena, coming toward her. Out of nowhere, it seemed.

"You attract far too much attention," Ena hissed. "Leave this place at once."

"But I want to talk to you," Grace pleaded.

"Then follow me!"

Grace followed Ena out the side door. Once out, Ena ran toward a field with a barn on it.

"Ena!" Grace called as she ran after her.

But Ena neither slowed her pace nor acknowledged Grace. She ran on to the barn. When she reached it, she pushed the door open, then threw herself down on a pile of hay.

"What did I do wrong?" Grace asked.

"I told you. You attract far too much attention! If I hadn't come down when I did, none of us would be safe."

Grace stared at her.

"You could get us all killed!"

26

"Come," Ena said to Grace. "Follow me. And stay quiet!"

Ena ran back toward the coffeehouse, Grace right behind her. She didn't go to the front door, though, nor did she head for the side door. Instead she hurried around to the back side. Ena glanced quickly to her left, then to her right. Seeing no one, she ran her hand down along a rough strip of wood on the back of the building. Evidently that tripped a hidden latch, because a narrow door opened a crack. Ena pushed the door wide enough to slip through, Grace followed, then Ena pulled it closed behind them.

They were behind the booth where the woman in the pleated dress sat. Grace could hear her cajoling a testy customer who was demanding that he be given a fresh pipe at no charge. Ena quickly opened another door at the corner of the coffee booth. Inside was a narrow, enclosed stairway, totally invisible to the patrons of the coffeehouse. It was so dark that it would have been impossible to see the stairs had it not been for a small opening cut high up in the coffee seller's booth that let a single small shaft of light into the passageway.

"Come, come!" Ena whispered.

Grace lifted her skirt and stepped carefully up each step. How grateful she was that Mister Hathaway had not purchased a metal skirt hoop for her! Even a broad man would have trouble on that tight staircase.

At the top of the stairs, Grace was amazed to see an entire room furnished with a long table from the coffeehouse and chairs set up all around it. Six people bunched together around the table, all engaged in urgent conversation. Like the groups downstairs, most of the men were well-dressed, with the same flowing curls affected by many of the coffeehouse's patrons. But unlike downstairs, two of the six were women—and one was the black man Grace had first seen sitting alone in the coffee shop at the back table.

The conversation stopped when Grace and Ena entered. All eyes turned to stare at them.

"So you are Miss Grace from Africa," said a man with a rolling voice and brown hair tied back in a blue ribbon.

"Grace Winslow, daughter of an English sea captain and an African princess," Grace said. "Mother of Kwate, an innocent baby killed by slavers. Wife to Cabeto, kidnapped and now in chains, on his way to the slave market in the United States of America."

"Ah, yes," the man said. "What can I say to you of the tragic injustice of the slave trade?"

"This is Mister Ethan Preston," Ena told Grace.

"My pleasure, Miss Grace," said Mister Preston. He took Grace's hand and, sliding one leg forward, performed an elegant and graceful bow. How he kept from tangling his legs together and falling on his face, Grace could not imagine. For the first time in her life, she truly did feel like an English lady.

"Mister Preston leads this group that—"

"—that spends far too much time on talk and far too little on action," interrupted the black man.

"We all agree on our goal of seeing an end brought to the African slave trade," Mister Preston said to Grace. "We do not, however, agree on the means to bringing that goal to fruition."

"Talk does nothing but waste time," the black man said. "Let those who insist that Africans are better off because of slavery be the ones to feel the weight of the chains and the burn of the lash. Let them be the ones strung up and tortured into madness. Only then will they listen to our words."

"They will say the treatment is proof that they must deal with barbarians, Jesse," a plainly dressed older woman said to the black man. To Grace she said, "My name is Mrs. Patterson. Rebekah Patterson. And this is my husband. Our hearts ache for your husband, my dear, and they also ache for you. Yet we cannot condone Jesse's idea of torturing members of parliament. Violence only begets more violence. Surely we should have learned that lesson by now."

"Do not lecture me on the subject of violence and suffering, or on the price of freedom," Jesse said bitterly.

Grace looked deep into the man's smoldering eyes and she recognized a kindred pain.

Jesse was a man born into slavery. For twenty of his thirty-two years, he had lived under his master's lash, slaving in the cotton fields of the American colonies. But Grace knew nothing of this. All she knew was that he touched a common nerve of hurt that could not be explained.

"Did you come on a slave ship?" Grace ventured with hushed caution.

"I did not! I came to England as a free man."

When rumors of war began to spread among the slaves in the American colonies, so did speculation about what independence from England could mean for them. Jesse was young and filled with hope and possibility. If the British had come to fight his masters, surely, then, they would be his liberators. So when the call came for slaves to desert their masters and fight alongside the British troops—with the promise of full protection, freedom, and land of their own when the war ended—Jesse, along with many thousands of other slaves, threw down their plows and grabbed up swords.

But the British did not win. So Jesse and the other slaves who deserted the plantations found themselves stranded on the losing side. At the signing of the Treaty of Paris, all British forces, as well as all their supporters, were ordered out of the new United States of America. Some of the slave fighters—black loyalists, they were called—fled to Canada. But remembering the British promise of land, Jesse crowded into New York with the English patriots to await a ship that would take them all to England.

It was in New York that Jesse's master found him. "He is my property and I demand he be returned to me!" Jesse's furious owner demanded.

Nor was Jesse's master alone in this claim. General George Washington himself insisted that every slave who had joined the British be returned to their owners. But Sir Guy Carleton, the new British commander-in-chief, stood face-to-face with General Washington and refused to turn them over. "We gave our promise and we intend to stand behind it," he insisted.

In the end, the Americans agreed to accept payment from the British for the slaves. Jesse Mallow was issued a Certificate of Freedom, paid for by the British government. Along with over three thousand other freed slaves, his name was duly recorded in the *Book of Negros*, and he boarded a ship for England.

"No," Jesse said again. "You do not have the right to lecture me about the price of freedom."

It was Sir Thomas McClennon who broke through the awkward moment. "We are a small group," he said, addressing himself to Grace, "but one that seeks to bring about positive change in this good land of England."

Grace recognized Sir Thomas as the same aristocratic gentleman she saw buying coffee and a clay pipe downstairs in the coffeehouse.

"Not as an excuse but as an explanation of reality, I must point out that men are being asked to consider changes to everything they were raised to believe to be true," he continued. "Furthermore, to embrace such changes puts at stake their own fortunes—yea, their very *futures*."

"Not men alone, dear sir," corrected the other woman of the group, the well-bred Lady Susanna. "The changes are no less difficult for women."

Sir Thomas bowed to Lady Susanna and corrected himself. "Men *and* women, dear lady."

Grace looked around the group, blinking from one face to another to another.

"Why are you up here?" she asked. "Why hide away in a secret room at the top of a hidden stairway? Why not sit at a table downstairs and discuss your ideas with everyone?"

"Ah, my dear, coffeehouses are wonderful places," said Ethan Preston with a deep and gracious bow. "Each one is specific to a particular interest. This one is known for its attraction to ship owners and their insurers—a group who, as you may guess, has close ties to the slave trade. Although the proprietor is sympathetic to our cause, many men who sip coffee here, smoke pipes, and bandy about their opinions, would not be so generously inclined. A goal such as ours is unexpected in this place, yet in the accepting nature of the coffeehouse, should anyone see us about, our presence would raise few questions."

"But I still don't see why you cannot discuss your ideas in the open."

"Because too many people want to see us dead is why." This was from an intense young man by the name of Oliver Meredith, who sat next to Jesse.

"Not dead, perhaps," said Mister Preston, "but they most assuredly would like to see us cease our encouragement toward the growing passions of the populace."

A sneer crossed Jesse's face. "You say no violence, but even as you speak such words, you hide up here from the violence that stalks us all down the stairs."

"Please, please . . . Can any of you help me find my husband?" Grace begged.

"Your husband is but one of many who suffer at the hands of slavers," answered Mrs. Patterson. "Our battle is to see the entire African slave trade brought to an end so that no more babies die, and no more men or women are forced onto those wretched slave ships."

"But what of my Cabeto?" Grace demanded. "His time is almost gone! At this very moment, he is on his way to the slavers' auction block!"

Lady Susanna shook her head sympathetically. "It is stories like yours that move the hearts of people," she said. "You show us the dreadfulness of what happened to your little son, and the horrors of slaving come alive to us. You show us the truth of Cabeto's wretched plight, and we understand the truth of the trade in which every one of us in some way shares complicity. You show us the toll this ordeal has taken on you, and we begin to understand the enormity of the human toll exacted by the slave trade."

"*But what of my Cabeto?*" Grace cried in exasperation. She struggled to hold back her tears. "Please! I must do something *now*! If you could get me on a ship to the United States—"

"What kind of black fool are you to talk of going there?" Jesse snapped. "You cannot save Cabeto. Your husband is a slave. All his life he will be a slave. And when he dies, he will die a slave."

"Who are you to say so, Jesse?" Ena challenged. "My mother was a slave, but she did not die a slave. I was born a slave, but I am a slave no more. And you . . . you were a slave, but you sit here a free man. Grace too. She is no longer a slave. So how can you speak with such certainty about Cabeto's life? It is in the hands of God alone."

In the silence that followed, tears ran down Grace's face.

"*Fiat justicia, ruat coelum,*" said Ethan Preston in his rolling voice. "In the words of Lord Mansfield, 'Let justice be done, though the heavens fall.'"

27

I tell you the truth, my brother, we can treat the white man as our enemy, or we can form an alliance with him and work together as friends and allies," Princess Lingongo said to King Obei.

Princess Lingongo did not respect her brother, but she did know how to control him. He wanted wealth and power, and she knew how to get both.

"As our enemy, the white man will destroy us," Princess Lingongo said. "As our friend and ally, he will make us once again the most powerful chiefdom on the coast. Our father was great and powerful, feared by African and white man alike. That is because he had the wisdom to choose which words to hear and which words to toss aside."

"I toss aside all words spoken by a white man," King Obei insisted.

"Joseph Winslow was a fool," said Lingongo. She knew perfectly well that Obei detested the white man to whom her father had given her in marriage. "Yet it was Joseph Winslow's guns and gunpowder that made our father stronger and richer than any other African chief or king. Our power and wealth came from Joseph Winslow's guns."

"Joseph Winslow is gone," King Obei said.

"Yes, but Jasper Hathaway will be more help to us than ten Joseph Winslows. Joseph Winslow knew that he was a fool. But Jasper Hathaway thinks himself to be a man of great wisdom and insight. He believes he can cheat us, yet he understands nothing of our people and our land. We can make good advantage of such an arrogant fool."

"I do not like him, and I do not trust him," declared King Obei.

"Nor do I," said Lingongo. "But what does that matter? Disliked and distrusted, he is no less useful to our people. Nor to us." She paused, then added with a bow, "That is, to you, my brother."

Five years had passed since the slave rebellion left Zulina slave fortress in ruins. Five years since Lingongo walked back to the royal palace, alone with her head held high, and—despite all—declaring victory. Five years since the elders of the kingdom pronounced the shoulders of the Great and Mighty King no longer adequate to bear the weight of ruling a kingdom of such power. Over the aging king's objection, but with Lingongo's enthusiastic encouragement, the elders passed the *sika' gua* stool on to his first son, Prince Obei.

No sooner was the new King Obei installed in the royal hut than Lingongo ordered a second golden chair to be positioned next to his. Since that day, she had sat beside him and had never failed to make her voice heard.

"When Mister Hathaway returns from England, we will increase our demands of the slave traders," Lingongo said. "We will double the price we ask for prize slaves. And we will no longer accept cloth or lead bars as payment—only guns and ammunition and gunpowder."

"He will never consent to such terms," the king said. "Jasper Hathaway will hold us to the terms of our old agreement."

"It will not be his choice," Grace assured her brother. "In no other way can he secure our cooperation. Right now he is strutting about England, making wild promises to everyone. He is showing off Grace, his personal slave, and he is bragging about how well he can handle the company's affairs in Africa. He cannot afford to see us throw our support to another."

Lingongo knew Jasper Hathaway perfectly. Bragging and strutting and showing off was precisely what he would have been doing had he been able. As it was, however, he had been carried off the ship and rushed straight to Saint Thomas Hospital for the Sick and Poor at the south end of London Bridge. Unlike most of the ill and infected who shared his ward, Mister Hathaway's illness was well known to the doctors— not only its nature but also its treatment. Mister Hathaway needed the juice of limes and lemons, and he needed it in plentiful supply whether he wanted it or not. It was not a matter for discussion.

With the proper medical remedy applied, and control completely removed from his hands, his condition improved with amazing speed. But as the bedbugs discovered the tender softness of his flabby body (the hospital was famous for them), Mister Hathaway begged the doctor assigned to his ward to take pity on him and sign his release. He would prefer to die in peace from scurvy, he insisted, than to itch and blister to death. Nor did Mister Hathaway's demands stop there. Indeed, they grew more numerous by the day. He was especially adamant in his insistence that his slave be brought in immediately to personally care for his needs.

The hospital staff ignored everything he said.

Lingongo knew Jasper Hathaway, but she knew nothing of his plight.

28

"Come!"

Ethan Preston's hand brushed against Grace's arm in an ever-so-subtle gesture as he whispered her name. Grace had lingered for some time out by the barn hoping Ena would pass by. When she did not, Grace hesitantly approached the coffeehouse. Her timing could not have been better, for Mister Preston had just stepped out the door. Grace followed him around to the back behind the seller's booth. With an expert hand, Ethan slid the panel open and ushered Grace up the hidden stairs. He was right behind her.

". . . because, as evidenced in the Magna Carta, we English are a people uniquely devoted to liberty!" proclaimed Oliver Meredith with great energy and expression. He was the youngest member of the group, and scorning such aristocratic formalities as powdered wigs and silk coats, he wore his wild hair tied back with a cord, and a simple linen shirt tucked into his breeches. "Where, then, could be a better place for the elimination of the curse of slavery to take root than right here on our glorious shores? And who better to lead that gallant fight around the world than we, the people of England?"

"Hear, hear, Mister Meredith!" Ethan Preston called out. "Well said! I should like to hear your entire speech, should you feel inclined to rehearse it again."

Heath Patterson clapped his hands. "Most appropriate, my lad. I have with me the documents collected by my Quaker brethren."

The room seemed charged with a special urgency that Grace had not felt on her first visit. Heath Patterson's wife, Rebekah, leaned forward in her chair, intent on catching every word. And Lady Susanna, who sat on the other side of Rebekah, tapped her foot impatiently.

Sir Thomas was the exception. The slender man with such an aristocratic carriage, his ever-present triangular hat on his head, leaned back in his chair. His legs crossed comfortably, he listened with his eyes half-closed.

Grace looked around the room for Jesse, but he was not there. Neither was Ena. Suddenly feeling terribly out of place, Grace wished she had not come, either.

"Ena told us your story, Miss Grace," Mister Preston began. "I do hope that does not add to your distress. But knowing our determination to see this wretched business brought to an end, she felt it best that we understand. And I must tell you, every one of us was deeply moved by what you have been forced to endure."

"The heartlessness of it all!" exclaimed Lady Susanna. "Your poor, poor little one!"

"What has become of us?" Mister Patterson asked, shaking his head. "We are a civilized, Christian people. Surely the day will come when we will all be called to an accounting by our maker."

Grace looked with wonder at the anguished, compassionate looks of the people surrounding her. People unlike her, who had never felt the softness of Kwate's face, who had never known the strength of Cabeto's arm. Yet how they cared! A whole new emotion welled up inside her.

"My father was English," Grace said with pride.

Lady Susanna motioned Grace to the chair beside her. When she was settled, Mister Preston cleared his throat. "Not too many days hence—two, perhaps three—important men will meet with us," he said, "Members of Parliament—MPs who have begun to listen to our voices with more than a bit of sympathy. Because we will have only one opportunity to address them, our presentation must of necessity depend heavily upon our careful collection of documents." He looked at Grace. "And now, at this important time, you have come to us."

"For such a time as this," Grace breathed.

"Your story has touched each of us profoundly," Mister Preston said. "Would you be willing to meet with these gentlemen from Parliament and relate your story to them? To touch the hearts of the ones who actually hold in their hands the power to change our nation's laws?"

Grace stared at Ethan Preston. "Yes," she said. "I will tell them everything. And then I will plead for my Cabeto."

Before anyone had a chance to respond, Ena topped the stairs.

"Something is about to happen!" she gasped, out of breath. "I heard it at Larkspur Estate, just after I finished cleaning the silverware!"

"Sit down, my dear," said Mister Preston. He and Heath Patterson each rushed to get her a chair. "Please, try to compose yourself."

Ena sat and gulped deeply. Then she said, "Two men came for Lord Witherham, and I listened at the door. That's when I heard them tell his Lordship that in the regrettable event that anyone from Parliament must die, they must be protected from any blame."

"Die?" Sir Thomas asked incredulously. "Why, surely those men with Witherham are not killers."

"That's not what Jesse says," Oliver Meredith countered.

Mister Preston looked at Mister Meredith with growing alarm, then back to Ena. "What else did the men say?" he asked.

"Nothing!" Ena exclaimed in exasperation. "Only for Lord Reginald to stay away from the coffeehouse so he would not be to blame."

Ethan Preston dropped down onto his chair. "We must meet with the MPs at once. Tomorrow, if possible. No one must know except us in this room."

"And Jesse," said Oliver.

"No one except us in this room!" repeated Ethan Preston.

With that, the meeting time came to an abrupt and solemn end. Rebekah Patterson gripped Grace's thin hand in her own solid ones and squeezed it tight while she and her husband said their farewells all around. They were the first to leave. Sir Thomas tipped his three-cornered hat and bowed first to Grace, then to Lady Susanna, and finally to Ena, then he was away. Lady Susanna swept soft fingertips across Grace's hand and left in silence. Oliver Meredith said to Grace, "Thank you kindly, miss," and then he, too, bid her good-bye.

"I will be in the coffeehouse," Ethan Preston said, then he also headed down the stairs.

"They are good people," Ena said to Grace.

"Yes, they are good people," Grace agreed. "But not one of them mentioned helping Cabeto. Not one of them will get me to him."

For a few moments Ena was silent. Then she said, "With all my heart, I wanted my mother back. But scarlet fever took her, and she is gone. I long to know my father, but he is lost to me in the West Indies. I am alone. I do not like it, but I accept it."

"My Kwate, who picked up bright red bissap blossoms as they blew down from the trees and brought them to me so I could make my tea, my little son who ran and never walked, who climbed and never sat still, my Kwate is lost to me forever. I can hardly bear to remember the music of his sweet voice as he called out to me," Grace said. "And my Mama Muco. Will I ever see her again? My heart tells me I will not."

"Cabeto too," Ena said gently. "He also is lost to you."

"No! Little Kwate is gone from this world. And Mama Muco stays where I cannot return. But Cabeto . . . I can still reach him. And I shall!"

"I am not saying it would be best for you to forget Cabeto, Grace. Of course he will remain with you forever in your memory. But you must let go of him. Use his story to help change laws. That way you will protect others from the fate he suffered. That's what you can do for Cabeto."

Grace shook her head. "It is not enough!" she said.

Ethan Preston topped the stairs. "A man in the coffeehouse is asking questions about you, Miss Grace."

"Me! Who is he?"

"I do not know," said Mister Preston. "An Englishman. A large man, but he does not look at all well. His hair is thin and loose, and he wears no wig. His speech seems hampered somewhat, perhaps by the great gaps of missing teeth."

"Mister Hathaway!" Grace cried in alarm. "It is Mister Hathaway. He has come to get me! He will make me his slave again!"

29

$\mathscr{S}$lap . . . slap . . . slap . . . The constant rhythm of waves hitting against the ship's hull formed a never-ending backdrop against which a boundless expanse of time stretched out in the hold of the *Golden Hawk*. The relentless beat only stopped when the ship hit seas rough enough to throw everything into confusion.

Slap . . . slap . . . slap. Against that steady cadence, accented by the rattle of chains, crooned a chorus of unbroken moans and humming cries. Every now and again it was punctuated by a soprano shriek or a baritone bellow. *The music of misery*, Cabeto called it. Day after day after day, a repeat performance of the same cruel chorus.

"Cabeto!" Sunba's scorched voice called from several rows away. "You did not call my name today."

"What does it matter?" Cabeto answered. "No one is left to answer but you and me and Tawnia, and she refuses to speak."

"We are left," Sunba answered. "We matter."

With a creak and a groan, the door cleared the hatch overhead. Two sailors struggled down the ladder, lugging a heavy cooking pot between them. Immediately the humming chorus switched to a cacophony of relentless begging and sobbed pleas.

At the beginning of the voyage, each captive cupped two hands together to capture the twice-daily meal allotment, and even then they fought the rats for every single spilled morsel. But as provisions ran low, the bean porridge was only served once a day. Now the food supplies must be really short because the once-daily portion would barely fill a single hand.

"More, more!" one person after another pleaded in a pitiful harmony of languages.

But the only reward for begging was a swift kick.

When Cabeto's helping of porridge and beans was slopped into his outstretched hand, he gulped it every bit as voraciously as everyone else. Then he licked his hand clean, slurping between his fingers and down his arms. Two more sailors followed with a water bucket—one dipper-full for each person. The woman next to Cabeto grabbed at the dipper with such desperate anticipation that she tipped it over and spilled the contents onto the floor.

"Too bad fer ye!" the sailor said as he moved along.

The woman grabbed his leg and screamed out pleas, but he kicked her away. She shrieked and begged, but he had already moved on. Straining at the chains that bound her, the woman licked frantically at the water puddled on the filthy floor. The sailor never looked back.

The white men struggled to hoist the porridge pot back up the ladder, then they passed the bucket up after it. One by one, they climbed up and disappeared through the hole.

Cabeto waited for them to pull the door shut, and the music of misery to rise up again.

But the door didn't close. What did that mean? Occasionally, the sailors left the door open, presumably to allow a bit of fresh air down into the oppressive hold. But on this day, shadows passed back and forth though the shaft of light that shone through the open hatch. Someone was doing something near the opening.

"Git on yer dancin' shoes!" a sailor called down from the top of the ladder.

Few of the Africans understood English, but every one of them knew the word "dance." Although they were glad enough to get out of their cramped positions, dancing exercise sessions meant excruciating pain. And it meant danger too. Especially now. For if provisions were indeed running low, as the cut in rations indicated, this would give the captain an opportunity to rid the ship of the weakest among them.

While two sailors stood on the stairs with guns at the ready, five others, gasping in spite of the handkerchiefs tied across their noses and mouths, climbed down and spread out among the Africans. They unlocked the chains that bolted the slaves to the ship's wooden timbers, but the manacles on their feet the sailors left in place. Then they herded the Africans up the stairs.

"Stand straight," Cabeto urged those around him. "Hold your head up high. They watch us."

As the captives emerged into the daylight, they staggered backward. It had been so long since any of them had seen light that the sun blinded their eyes. But the guards gave them no time to adjust. They pushed the slaves forward. The captives had no choice but to struggle onto the deck, where they huddled together. Once all were up on top, the guards prodded them out of their huddles.

Thump, thump, thump, thump, thump . . .

A sailor off to the side grinned broadly as he pounded out a slow beat on his drum. About a dozen other sailors gathered around to watch, many clapping in time, or stamping a foot or slapping a leg.

"When ye goin' to start the show?" one called out.

In answer, First Mate Seth Watson pushed his way up in front of the other sailors. He cradled a vicious-looking leather cat-o-nine-tails in the crook of his arm.

"Dance!" Seth ordered.

The Africans glanced uncertainly from Seth to the drummer, then around at their fellow captives.

Seth raised the cat from his arm and swung it around him ever so easily—just with enough threat to make certain his message was not lost. Many of the captives' backs already bore the marks of that cruel cat.

"*Dance!*" Seth ordered again in a voice that meant *now*!

To the sailors' delight, Cabeto jumped upward and jerked his feet out to the extent his manacles would allow. The sailors laughed and cheered, yelling for more. Excruciating pain shot though Cabeto's legs, yet he forced himself to leap again.

"Dance!" he warned the others in his own tongue.

Because he commanded it, the others obeyed. Awkwardly and painfully, through tears and pleas for mercy, they danced.

Cabeto spotted Sunba up near the front of the group, over by the door with the ladder that led down to the hold. But for a long time he could not find Tawnia. Finally he located her on the far side near the railing, but she wasn't really dancing. In fact, she was barely moving at all.

"Tawnia," Cabeto called with a note of desperation.

The girl showed no sign that she had heard him.

"Dance, Tawnia!" Cabeto warned.

The drummer picked up the pace, and the clapping, stomping sailors did the same. Seth Watson beat out the faster rhythm with his lash, and the captives did their best to keep up.

Near the front, a broad-faced man with dusky brown skin and badly swollen eyes stumbled and fell to his knees. Seth Watson grasped the lash with both hands. The man winced. He understood the threat well enough and he pulled himself up to his feet. But after only a couple of lurching dance attempts, he once again fell flat. Seth didn't even bother with the whip. He simply motioned to two sailors who grabbed up the man and lugged him toward the side. The man screamed at the sailors in a language Cabeto couldn't understand, and made a feeble attempt to struggle. But the sailors ignored him. They dragged him to the railing and threw him over.

Two women next to the railing gasped out loud and froze absolutely still. But when Seth turned toward them, they jumped to and resumed their dancing with a frantic frenzy.

Cabeto sneaked a look at Tawnia. She continued to stand absolutely still, and she paid Seth no mind whatsoever.

"Dance, Tawnia!" Cabeto yelled, although he dared not look at her for fear of calling attention to her. "Please, dance! Please!"

When Cabeto dared to steal a glance in Tawnia's direction, he saw to his dismay that instead of dancing, she was moving toward the railing. Taking care to keep his eyes from the young girl, he stopped dancing and in the most derisive tone he could muster, he screamed out African words. Sure enough, Seth Watson descended upon him and set to with his cat. He knocked Cabeto flat and laid his back open.

What Seth didn't know was that Cabeto's words were intended for only one person—Tawnia. What Cabeto said was "I beg you to stay! Please, please, for every one of us . . . stay and dance!"

As Cabeto lay on the deck, his back shredded, twelve-year-old Tawnia eased up onto the railing, leaned back, and let go.

"Dance!" Seth Watson ordered Cabeto.

Cabeto pulled himself to his feet, willing himself to embrace the blinding pain that ripped through his body. Ignoring the drummer's beat, he raised his legs as high as the manacles would permit, but in a completely different rhythm—a tormented one of haunting beauty.

When the captives were finally herded back down into the hold, one after another pleaded in English, "Wa-ter! Wa-ter!" But they got none.

Tomorrow. Maybe. For those who still lived.

Cabeto lay still in the closed-in blackness, his back seared with pain and his legs throbbing. He ordered himself to breathe in and out, in and out, in and out.

The chorus of misery took up where it had left off—steady moans and undulating cries layered one on top of the other, each in time with the breaking waves and rattling chains. How Cabeto longed to wail out his own lament above all the rest, long and loud. To scream and rail at the injustice that had swallowed them alive. But he did not. He didn't even weep, for every last tear had already been wrung from his soul.

Instead, mustering his last reserve of strength, Cabeto called out: "Sunba!"

"I am here, brother," came the answer. "I am here."

30

*T*hat man, Mister Hathaway . . . He has gone," Ena
reported.

Even so, Grace was not ready to venture from her secure
spot at the far corner of the upstairs room.

"You cannot hide up here forever," Ena pointed out.

Grace knew as much. But she also knew Jasper Hathaway.
If he was sufficiently recovered to go about the city searching for her, and if he had discovered enough concerning her
whereabouts to locate the coffeehouse, how could she dare
return to Mrs. Peete's house? Why, he might be there right
now waiting for her. Or even lurking about outside, for that
matter!

"Do as you please," Ena said with a shrug, and she started
down the stairs.

The only candle in the room that had not entirely burned
away glowed low in its candlestick. Soon the room would be
completely dark. Ena was right, of course. Grace couldn't stay
in the upstairs room forever. With a sigh of resignation, she
picked up the candlestick, lifted the hem of her dress, and followed Ena down the stairs.

As Ena had said, Jasper Hathaway was no longer in the cof-feehouse. But Jesse was there, sitting alone at the same table in the far corner. When Grace left by the side door, Jesse got up and followed her out.

"Oh!" Grace exclaimed when he came up behind her. "You gave me such a start!"

"Do you mistake me for a flabby old white man with no teeth in his head?" Jesse asked with the trace of a grin. His voice had an interesting lilt to it, not like any other voice Grace had ever heard in either Africa or England. Nor was it like Ena's manner of talk, or even Captain Ross's. It was . . . well . . . *unique*.

"What did Mister Hathaway want with me?" Grace asked.

"He wanted *you*," Jesse said. "If he could not have you, he wanted something that would lead him to you. But do not fear. His disruption so irritated the coffeehouse patrons that they closed their mouths tight and refused to part with one word of information."

"Do you think Mister Hathaway knows where I am staying?"

Jesse shook his head. "If he did, he would have gone there and waited for you instead of tracking after you asking ques-tions. It would be much easier on him, and less of a risk too."

"My father is in London," Grace said.

Jesse said nothing.

"My English father."

Jesse walked in silence.

"He loved me, my father did, at one time. He brought me lovely dresses from London. And books too. He hired a tutor to—" Suddenly remembering Captain Ross's admonition, Grace caught herself and said, "—to read to me. My father read to me, too, and showed me pictures from his books."

Jesse said nothing.

"I would not let the others at Zulina fortress kill my father, despite all he had done," Grace said.

The others had wanted to kill him. Oh, how they had wanted to. And they had good reason. Grace knew that even at the time. Why shouldn't slaves hate the man responsible for destroying their lives and selling them to the slave ships? She knew it then, but now she truly understood it. When Joseph Winslow had been allowed to sail out of Zulina harbor, with no one but her to bid him farewell, he refused to even look at her. She remembered every minute of that day. Shaking his clenched fist to heaven, he had called out a curse on her and on everyone who mattered to her.

But things can change in five years. Everything can change. As Ikem had said years before, even people can change.

Grace stopped walking and placed her fingertips against Jesse's arm. "My father is here in London," she said. "Will you help me find him?"

"Why?"

Grace struggled for words. "Because he is my father," she said. "Because he loved me once."

"And because you want his help."

"Yes," Grace said. "That too. He owes me that."

"What do you know of him?" Jesse asked.

"His name is Joseph Winslow—*Admiral* Joseph Winslow— and he longs for the feel of dice in his hands. He plays any betting game he can find. He loves the sea and sailing ships. If we can find a shipping place by the sea where men throw dice and make bets, that's where my father will be."

"I see," said Jesse. "You want me to lead you to a place where you will have a good chance of being robbed and kidnapped."

"What?" Grace exclaimed. "You are cruel to say such a thing!"

"You know nothing about London's ruffians, do you?"

"Look at me!" Grace answered. "Do you really think any-one would consider it worth taking the trouble to rob me? And were I to be kidnapped, who would pay a ransom for me? It would be a foolish criminal indeed who would prey on the likes of me!"

For once, Jesse took a good look at Grace. Her face was lovely, but streaked with grime in the manner of a poor work-ing woman. Her hair hung loose with only a small scarf tied around it. Her dress, soiled and stained, hung flat with neither petticoats nor under-shapers to round it out. Jesse knew a gal-lant response required that he energetically protest that Grace was indeed worth both robbing and kidnapping. But she was far too bright to be fooled with outright lies, however well intended. So, once again, he said nothing.

"Do you know of such a place?" Grace pressed.

"Gaming houses in London are many," Jesse answered.

"But a particularly likely one for a sailing man like my father?"

"I do know of one well concealed in an alley which is known to be a favorite sailor haunt. And it has never been raided—at least, not to my knowledge."

"Yes!" said Grace. "They will surely know Joseph Winslow. Will you take me there? Tonight?"

"You have nothing on your person to rob, you say?" Jesse mocked. "No one with money to pay a ransom should you be kidnapped? Well, then, I do not suppose you have anyone willing to claim your body after you've been stabbed to death, either, do you?"

Grace gasped.

"I am not fool enough to venture out there at night," Jesse said, "And I pray that you are not, either."

"But I—"

"Do you not have a job to do?" Jesse asked.

"Yes, but not all day long. I finish when the church bells chime the noon hour."

"Finish at the noon hour then," said Jesse. "After that, walk down Waring Street toward the square."

"But what about you?"

"I will find you."

Grace thanked Jesse and turned her steps toward Mrs. Peete's house. But Jesse called out, "Do not dress too fine, Grace. And you would do well to put away that purse you have pushed down the front of your dress."

31

"Did you leave your purse at home?" Jesse demanded when Grace caught up to him.

After the noon church bells had rung, Grace had started down Waring Street just as Jesse told her to do. She stepped aside to let a pork vendor pass, and at that very moment Jesse had climbed up from a basement stairway up ahead. Without looking back at her or waiting, he headed straightaway along the road, then turned off toward a maze of lanes and alleyways.

"Yes . . . I did," Grace answered, panting.

She almost hadn't, however. Right away, she had tucked the purse into her baggage crate among the folds of her yellow dress. But then she had a change of heart. Why should she leave her purse behind simply because Jesse told her to? So she had taken it out and dropped it back into its familiar hiding place—down the front of her dress. Still, Jesse knew London, and she most certainly did not. So, in the end, she had hesitantly taken it back out and returned it to her case and its hiding place in the folds of her yellow dress. It was not that Grace didn't trust Mrs. Peete—although at times her belongings did seem to have a rummaged-through appearance. It was that those silver shillings were all she had to get her out of London and on her way to Cabeto. She felt so much better when she had them next to her heart.

"See that small lad hanging by the street post?" Jesse said to Grace. "No, don't stare at him! Glance once, then look away."

Grace saw him. A scraggly child dressed in a man's coat, shabby and full of holes. He couldn't have been more than eight years old.

"A poor beggar child," Grace said. "If I had my purse, I would give him one of my shillings."

"Give him one and he'd have them all," Jesse said. "He's a faker, he is, placed there to watch out for someone just like you."

Grace glanced again. The boy's sharp eyes were indeed fixed on her.

"His fine hand would dip down your dress and have your purse in his hidden pocket even whilst you kissed his cheek and prayed for angels to watch over him. Then he'd eel away down the maze of streets, and you would never see him or your purse again."

"You don't know that!" Grace said.

"I *do* know that. And I am telling it to you so you will have the good sense to refrain from walking these streets alone. I don't know how it is in your village in Africa, but that's how it is in London."

Jesse stepped onto a muddy road and strode out into the slush. Grace hesitated only a moment, then she waded in after him.

With Jesse's quick pace, it was just over an hour before Grace's nose caught the smell of the Thames. But she despaired of ever being able to find the way by herself, not with the labyrinth of hidden walkways that cut behind and between the city streets.

Before they actually reached the docks, Jesse cut over to a short alley. "Down there," he said, motioning with a jerk of his head.

What Grace saw was a house with half the windows painted black and a sign above it that read *Rooms For Rent*.

"There?" she asked.

"There," Jesse said.

"Will you come with me?"

"No," he answered. "Do everything you need to do today. I won't bring you back again."

The door of the rooming house–gambling house flew open and two men dressed in the trousers and blouse of a sailor tumbled out. "And don't ye come back agin 'til ye gots a pocketful o' rhino. I ain't runnin' no charity 'ouse 'ere, is I?"

The two sailors picked themselves up, grumbling angrily.

With a confidence she didn't feel, Grace stepped up to the two and said, "Could you tell me, was there an old man with red hair in there?"

"They's plenty of old men in there," snapped the taller of the two sailors. Grace couldn't help noticing that his face was deeply pox-scarred, worse even than Mrs. Peete's. "I wasn't lookin' fer the color of no one's 'air. Ain't no money in that."

"Why ye wants to know?" the shorter one asked.

"I . . . I'm looking for my father," Grace said.

The taller one turned to go. The shorter one shrugged and shook his head, then he too walked off.

"Wait!" Grace called after them. "If you can find my father for me, I will pay you."

Both sailors stopped. Both turned to face her.

"'Ow much?" said the tall one, his eyes suddenly gleaming.

Grace shifted uneasily. "He calls himself 'The Admiral.'"

"'The Admiral,' is it then?" the short one laughed. "'E be yer father?"

"You know him?" Grace asked. "Is he in the gambling house?"

"No," said the short sailor. "'E be throwed out afore we came in. But 'e'll be back. 'E always comes back."

The tall sailor ran a grubby hand across his pox-scarred face. "Lessen the gin gits to 'im first," he said.

"Where be yer money?" the tall sailor demanded of Grace.

"Where be my father?" Grace countered. "When I see him, you'll have your shilling."

When Grace told Jesse she had left her purse in her room, she was telling him the truth. What she failed to mention was that she did not leave all the shillings in the purse.

Grace looked back toward the corner where she had left Jesse. Vendors and street women, workmen and sailors she saw aplenty, but Jesse was not there. She shivered in the damp gloom that enveloped everything like a shroud.

Had Grace been able to see the sun, she would have been better able to judge how long she paced the courtyard. Each time the house door opened, she did her best to peer in, but it was so dark and smoky inside that she could not make out a thing. Several times she plucked up the courage to stop one person or another and ask about an old man with red hair— "Admiral, he calls himself," she said—but she got little more answer than a frown and the shake of a head. More often she got an angry scowl.

A wind blew in, bringing a definite chill to the air. Grace moved across the courtyard to a bake shop and gazed in at the freshly baked loaves and buns. That's when the tall sailor with the pox-scarred face strode up to the gambling house.

"Did you find him?" Grace asked as she ran to meet the tall sailor.

"That we did," the sailor said. "If you wants to see 'im, show me yer shilling. Then I'll show ye the way."

Grace turned her back, then reached down the front of her dress and pulled out the single shilling. The tall sailor reached for it, but Grace clamped her hand tight.

"I don't see my father yet," she said. "When I see him, that's when the shilling will be yours."

The sailors led her to an open field and pointed to a man sitting alone on a tree stump. As soon as Grace saw him, she knew it was indeed her father. Not that proud, would-be English gentleman who called himself Admiral Joseph Winslow she had known as a child, but her father nevertheless. Grace handed the shilling to the tall sailor and turned her back on the two of them.

The field was not a pleasant place. It was filthy with trash and stank of old fish from the market next door. Joseph Winslow wore a nice suit of clothes, but his coat and breeches were rumpled and soiled. He tipped up his tankard of gin and drank long and hard.

"Father," Grace said.

Joseph, his hair dirty and disheveled, his face blotchy and pale, lowered the tankard with a shaking hand.

"Leave me be," he slurred.

"It has been five years, and I—"

"Who ye be, and why ye botherin' me?" Joseph demanded.

Grace took a deep breath and struggled to gather her strength. "You know me, Father. I am Grace, your daughter."

"I ain't got no daughter," Joseph said bitterly. He tipped the tankard to his lips and drank long.

"Father, I helped you when you needed me the most. I would not let the others kill you. I made it possible for you to come back home to England. Now I need your help, Father. Please!"

For the first time, Joseph looked over at Grace. He stared at her face, then he looked her up and down. "I used to have me a African for a wife, I did," he said. "Might be I could use me a good woman again . . . maybe to keep me warm tonight."

Grace jumped back. "Father! I am your daughter!"

"Ye be a liar!" Joseph yelled. He pulled himself up from the stump and, swaying unsteadily, he swung the tankard at her. "A liar is wot ye be! *I . . . 'as . . . no . . . daughter!*"

"I never should have asked you!" Grace wept. "I never should have allowed myself so foolish a hope!"

Joseph Winslow sank back down onto the stump. "It be too late," he mumbled. "Too late fer ever'one o' us."

32

"It cannot be so!" Lingongo fumed. "If Jasper Hathaway had died on the ship and never made it to England, it would not be from the mouths of foolish sailors that we heard the news!"

"Foolish sailors who themselves saw him carried away dead and toothless," King Obei reminded his sister. "Foolish sailors who watched as Grace walked away a free Englishwoman."

This was not good news for the chiefdom that sought to once again become the most powerful force on the coast of Africa. Everything Lingongo had said about the alliance with Jasper Hathaway was true, yet King Obei took special pleasure in seeing his sister's plans dashed before her eyes. It pleased him even though it meant his own kingdom would suffer. Had they not suffered before and yet endured? The very presence of the white man caused them no end of suffering.

Jasper Hathaway was dead. Of that, King Obei had no doubt. The ancestors would not allow such a man to live. The power behind the *sika'gua* stool of power was upon King Obei. It was *his* feet that rested on it.

"The ancestors have spoken," said King Obei.

He spoke nothing of Lingongo's golden chair that even now mocked him alongside his royal chair—the same size, the same height, even more grand. But already he was laying plans. If the odious Mister Hathaway was no more, that meant Lingongo's alliance with the white traders also was no more. Soon, in accordance with the will of the ancestors, his golden chair would stand by itself in the royal hut. Soon the splendor of the kings would be his alone.

Lingongo greatly desired to go up to Zulina herself, but that was no longer her right. And without Mister Hathaway, who would be there to receive her? White men from the slave ships—they did not know enough to recognize her as a princess. They looked at her as though she were just another slave to be sold. No, she could not go back to Zulina.

Reverently, Lingongo unwrapped the royal clothing from around her body, and carefully folded it as was its due. In its place, she draped a length of simple cloth around herself. With her head held high, she walked out of the royal enclave and followed the path through the sacred territory where she had spent her childhood and from which she had been ripped by her marriage to Joseph Winslow. Men along the road stopped to stare at the great Princess Lingongo who walked among them as if she were as lowly as they. Women with baskets on their heads gaped at the princess and wondered why she would stoop to wear the same working clothes they wore every day. Out of reverence and respect, each person stopped and bowed as she passed by. But Lingongo looked at none of them. She kept her eyes straight ahead.

Lingongo walked out to the boundary rocks that marked the beginning of the land of her brother's Gold Coast kingdom. Only there did she pause, and only to pay her respect to the ancestors.

When Benjamin Stevens's trustee brought him the news that Princess Lingongo was coming down the road toward his compound, Stevens laughed out loud.

"I do not think so, Jonah," he answered. "Princess Lingongo does not walk along the coast. And she certainly does not come to see me."

But Jonah was so insistent that Benjamin heaved a sigh of resignation and walked out to see.

Benjamin stared hard at the figure approaching from up the coast. An African woman, to be sure. Tall and fluid in her movements, certainly. He shaded his eyes and squinted. It could be Lingongo. But then again, it could be someone else. He couldn't tell for sure. The truth was, his eyes were not what they once were. "The African sun burns away blue eyes," a doctor once warned him. It certainly did seem so.

"Wait on the road below," Benjamin told Jonah. "Call to me as soon as she arrives."

If she arrives, he thought.

Twenty years Benjamin had lived in Africa. Twenty years in the relentless sun that burned away at his blue eyes and roasted his pale skin into aged leather. Just two years short of the entire life of his only child. Charlotte was barely toddling about the garden behind their small house in London when he left on that first slave voyage. The idea had not been to leave England for good, of course. He thought he would join a few slave crews, pocket great riches, then retire young and wealthy. Oh, the foolishness of youth!

Three unprofitable voyages in three years made it quite clear that was not going to happen. The real money, he had told Henrietta, was in running a slave house on the African coast.

"Come along to Africa and make a home there with me," he had begged.

But Henrietta would have none of it. It was not a proper place to raise an English girl, she insisted.

Well, perhaps Henrietta was right.

When his wife grew too ill to visit Africa, Benjamin wrote to her suggesting that he give up the slave trade and return to England to be with her. But Henrietta insisted it would be better if he stayed where he was—although he most certainly should give instructions to his British employer to send his pay straight to her. Maybe Henrietta was right in that too. She usually was. Certainly Charlotte no longer needed him. Henrietta had arranged a fine marriage for her. His wife was to be commended for that.

"She asks to see you, sir," Jonah announced.

"Lingongo?" Benjamin was incredulous. "Is it really her, then? Well, show her in."

To have the great and powerful Princess Lingongo in his sparse house, sitting on his own chair, to have Lingongo—who struck terror into many a heart with no more than a glare—sipping tea from his own chipped cup . . . well, it was simply more than Benjamin could fathom. Whatever could she want with him?

Lingongo spoke of her great and powerful father, and of the unforeseen fortunes of war. She spoke of the ancestors who guided her people, and of their representatives who walked on the earth. She spoke of peace, and she spoke of prosperity.

When Lingongo finally paused to sip her tea, Benjamin Steven said, "Why are you here?"

In her own time, Lingongo finished the last of her tea. Then, as no table was close by, she set the cup carefully on the floor. She leaned forward in her chair and adjusted the plain cloth draped around her. "Jasper Hathaway is dead," Lingongo said.

"That is distressing news," Benjamin replied. "But I ask you again, why are you here?"

"Mister Stevens, I have come to offer you a business proposition."

"I have seen you conduct business," Benjamin answered, "so I shall decline your offer."

"How can you decline what you have yet to hear?" Lingongo asked in a voice that flowed like honey. "I have seen your face as you watched Joseph Winslow's handling of the slaves and the slave traders. I have seen your eyes as you looked at the foolishness of his London house. I know you to be a man of moderate tastes, Mister Stevens, not given to excessive drink nor held captive by the roll of the dice."

Benjamin Stevens was indeed a moral man and a Christian. He could see no earthly reason why some white men found it necessary to add to the essential suffering of Africans. No, not even when such abuse could increase their own financial gain.

"You desire peace on the Gold Coast of Africa," Lingongo said. "I also desire peace. You want strength and prosperity for your people. I want the same for my people. Wise people work together for a common end—both men and women, both African and English."

Lingongo's buttery-smooth voice slipped into Mister Stevens's ears and into his heart, where it stirred something deep within him. Benjamin knew to be wary of her, yet the words she spoke rang true.

"It was never my choice to cast my lot with Joseph Winslow," Lingongo said. "That union was forced upon me by my father. Nor did I choose to be involved in a partnership with Mister Hathaway. That was a necessity thrust my way by my brother the king because of agreements our father signed with Mister Hathaway's English employer. But you, Mister Stevens, you are a man with a mind akin to my own. I would choose to work alongside one such as you, one wise enough to value friendship between Africans and English."

Friendship between Africans and English. Yes, Benjamin Stevens did indeed recognize this as a matter of great value. The English, like all Europeans, rarely ventured into the interior of Africa. For one thing, the perilous continent was rife with exotic diseases to which white men quickly and disastrously fell prey. For another, tribes deep in the heart of Africa fiercely opposed the white men and laid treacherous traps for them. Which was why cooperation between white and black was absolutely essential to the slave trade. Lingongo's warriors could go into the interior and conquer fresh captives, then march them out to the coast where Benjamin Stevens would be waiting to receive them in a civilized, Christian manner.

Benjamin had offered Lingongo that first cup of tea because, being a well-bred gentleman, he could not bring himself to appear rude and inhospitable. But the second cup, he offered her because he desired to do so. And then he offered a third cup after that.

"I have never seen the sense of riding through Africa in an English carriage," Benjamin said as Lingongo finished her tea, "but I would be most pleased to drive you back to your brother's kingdom in my wagon."

Lingongo found this idea most pleasing. Even though she had stayed with Mister Stevens long enough to see the heat of the day wane, she did not relish the long walk home. But the most attractive part of Mister Stevens's offer was the knowledge that her brother could not help but see that she, Princess Lingongo, had already formed a new alliance. And she had done so without his help.

33

*Y*our father is a white man," Jesse said flatly. "If you thought he would turn his back on the privileges of who he is simply to help a half-breed, you know nothing of real English life."

"What of Ethan Preston?" Grace challenged. "And the others in the group upstairs? Look at what they are doing. And they do it for people like me who are nothing to them. For people like you."

"Talk, talk, talk. That's what they do," Jesse interrupted impatiently. "Those people have it in their power to break the back of the slave trade if they only had the courage to stop their talk and move to action."

Grace blinked back her surprise. "But the men from Parliament are coming soon and—"

"—and those men will join with our group, and together they will continue to talk. Words and words and more words, and still nothing will happen. Let them meet together. It will do nothing to help us."

"You are a free man because of the English," Grace insisted. "They *bought* you your freedom."

"Their crime is not against me. It is against all of us," Jesse growled bitterly. "The pain is our pain, not theirs. The death and the suffering—those belong to us, too, not to them. The only way for us to fight back is to throw the suffering and death onto their backs. Let them feel the pain. Then they will have something about which they can talk."

"No!" said Grace. "There has been too much suffering already! And far too much death!"

"You know nothing," Jesse said.

Grace was tired of it. Tired of everything and everyone. She slowed her stride, and soon Jesse was far ahead of her. She knew where she was—on Waring Street. She could find her way back to Mrs. Peete's house by herself. What she would do after that, she had no idea.

Grace picked her way through the large things draped over Mrs. Peete's table and chairs, picked up a candlestick, and lit the stub of a candle at the fireplace.

"Ye looks a sight," Mrs. Peete said crossly.

Grace nodded but didn't answer. She knew she should help Mrs. Peete finish up the last of the wash, but she really didn't want to. She said, "I won't go out until later tomorrow. Maybe not at all. I can wash all the large things for you after I finish the small linens," and went to her room.

Grace set the candlestick on the floor next to her crate and lifted off the lid. Carefully she felt though the folds of her yellow dress until her fingers touched the smooth satin of the purse. She pulled it out, loosened the strings, and poured out the shilling coins.

One . . . two . . . three . . . four . . . five . . . six . . . seven . . . eight . . . nine . . . ten . . . eleven . . . twelve . . . thirteen.

Sighing with relief, Grace placed the coins back in the purse, one by one by one. Two were already gone, and soon Mrs. Peete would surely ask her for another. Then three of the fifteen would be gone. Still, Grace had learned an important thing today; she could walk to the docks if someone would show her the way.

The next day, Grace got up early. The fog still hung heavy and wet when she draped the small linens on the line. By the time the church bells rang out the noon hour, the large things were washed. As soon as Grace finished her lunch of bread and cheese, she set the heavily soiled pieces to boiling.

"You's workin' like a real washerwoman," Mrs. Peete said proudly.

"I *am* a real washerwoman," Grace said. "Until I go for Cabeto. Then I will be a sailing woman again."

Mrs. Peete sighed loudly and shook her woolly gray hair loose from its cap. But she didn't try to argue.

Late in the afternoon, Grace mopped the water off the floor by her washtub. "I'm going to change my dress and go out for a bit," she told Mrs. Peete.

"Don't you be walkin' the streets alone after dark," Mrs. Peete scolded.

Grace didn't answer. She ran the wet rag over her face and arms and went to her room and changed her dress.

"Cain't trust 'em link boys," Mrs. Peete said, following Grace back to her room. "They says they'll pertect you, but they'll lead you down a dark alley, like as not. Then they'll blow out their lamps and leave you at the mercy of robbers, is wot!"

Grace said nothing.

"The robbers pays 'em to do it," Mrs. Peete said.

"And just what do I have that anyone would care to steal?" Grace snapped. Regretting her brusqueness, she quickly added, "Thank you, Mrs. Peete, for worrying over me. I will take care."

With quick steps, Grace headed for the coffeehouse. After Ena's warning, she thought the men from Parliament might even come this day. She planned to tell them her story, in as complete and moving a way as possible, but she had no intention of stopping there. She fully intended to ask those important men for something in return.

According to Ena, in England men in Parliament helped the king rule the country. Something like the white partners of African kings, Grace figured. Surely partners of England's king were powerful enough to get Grace to the United States of America. Surely they could help her find Cabeto. Maybe they would even buy his freedom the way they had bought Jesse his freedom. If they would, she and Cabeto would both work for them forever. That's what she intended to say. That's what she would *plead*!

The question was, should she tell the others in the group of her plans? What if they objected? Jesse certainly would— especially the part about working in exchange for Cabeto's freedom. But what about Ethan Preston? What about Ena?

Grace was still far down the street, a long way before she would turn toward the coffeehouse, when she noticed the commotion up ahead. Confused and worried, she ran all the way to the turn in the road. And right there is where she saw him—her father, Joseph Winslow. He was running toward her, his hair flying and his eyes wild and red.

For a minute Grace thought she was having some sort of terrible nightmare. Even through the smoky haze she could make out the familiar blotchy face and straggly red hair. And then she saw the rumpled suit, and she knew for certain that it was no dream.

"Father!" Grace gasped.

At the sound of his daughter's voice, Joseph stumbled backward, as though someone had hit him in the face. Then, his red eyes darting like a trapped animal's, he lurched forward again.

"Father!" Grace cried. "What happened?"

"T'was fer ye, me darlin'," he gasped. "Fer ye!"

"But what—"

"Jist on the chance that it ain't yet too late."

Then he was gone.

Grace ran to the end of the street, but she could see nothing through the throng of people. She pushed her way forward, through the crowd and on around the corner. Up ahead, roaring flames consumed the coffeehouse.

Grace screamed and fell to her knees.

"Ena!" she shrieked. "Ena, where are you? Where is everyone?"

34

After the men manning the bucket brigades poured out their last buckets of water and counted their work complete, the gossips collected every possible detail about the coffee-house fire and hurried away to tell and retell their versions of the story. The crowds of people finally tired of gawking and drifted back home, but Grace stayed beside the pile of smoldering beams and glowing ashes and wept. Jesse would have run away, but what about the others? None of them was the kind to let threats and intimidations send them scurrying away to hide.

And Ena. What about Ena?

Grace could not bring herself to look too closely at the still-glowing pile of charred boards and red hot embers.

I should have been here! Grace sobbed. *Why was I washing sheets instead of helping my friends get ready for—for what?* The truth was, Grace didn't even know what they were doing. And "friend" was an awfully lofty term for people about whom she knew nothing but names.

The fact was, fires were a common occurrence in London. So many candles, all allowed to burn down to the very last drop of wax and wick. And in the coffeehouse, so much paper, spread out on every table. Add that to all the men with a penchant for waving newspapers around the candle flames and it was a wonder the coffeehouse had survived as long as it had. Still . . . why a fire now at this most important of times? Why just as Ethan Preston's committee finally had gathered together all the documents they needed, and sympathetic men from Parliament agreed to place it on their busy schedules to consider their arguments?

At the brush of a hand across her back, Grace screamed and jumped aside.

"Ena!" she cried when she saw who it was. So lost had Grace been in her misery and fear that she never heard her friend's footsteps come up behind her. "Oh, Ena, are you all right?"

Ena, her own eyes red and wet, nodded. Then she threw her arms around Grace and hugged her.

"Where are the others?" Grace cried. "Was anyone in the coffeehouse?"

"Almost," Ena said. "But in the end, no one was. That's what makes it all so strange."

Grace had no idea what Ena was talking about.

"The men from Parliament were to come here tonight!" Ena exclaimed. "The plans were all made, but Mister Preston didn't want anyone to know because he suspected that someone on the committee was a spy for the anti-abolitionists."

"Then how do you know?" Grace asked.

"Because I was the one who passed the word along. At the stroke of noon, each person had a private message from Mister Preston asking them to meet him upstairs in the coffeehouse. Everyone thought it was a private message. No one knew the others would also be there."

"You didn't bring me a message," Grace said.

"You always come after the noon chimes, anyway. Mister Preston said not to bother you at Mrs. Peete's house."

Grace stared at her. "He didn't trust me?"

After an uncomfortable moment, Ena said, "I knew you were not the spy. I told everyone as much. But think, Grace. Someone did know our plans. And because someone knew, someone set a horrible trap to roast the lot of us alive."

"But at noon—"

"At noon, no one was there because Mister Preston sent me running back out again with another message. 'Go back home!' I told everyone. 'Go back home and stay there!'" I caught everyone in time, before they came to the coffeehouse.

"But how did Mister Preston know?" Grace asked.

"Someone whispered the plans to him," Ena said. "Only Mister Preston knows who, and he is sworn to never tell."

Spies crept among them and informers murmured warnings, yet when suspicions erupted, the very ones who trusted her most pointed their suspicions at her.

No, Grace thought, *these people are not my friends. I don't even know these people. And these people certainly do not know me!*

The next day, while Grace was in the garden hanging shirts and petticoats and blouses on the washing line, she gazed over the fence at the people who walked up and down the lane, just as she always did. Two boys ran past, then a woman balancing a basket of pork pies on her head, calling out her wares. Then, just behind the pie woman, Grace saw Ena running down the lane toward her. Never before had Ena come to Mrs. Peete's house. Grace threw the embroidered handkerchief in her hand over the line and ran out to meet Ena.

"We'll be meeting tonight," Ena panted. "In the parlor of Sir Thomas's estate! Can you imagine? The likes of you and me, Grace, sitting in that parlor just like two ladies! Not serving anyone and not cleaning up after the others, just sitting with our idle hands in our lazy laps!"

"When?" Grace asked.

"At seven o'clock. Sir Thomas will send his carriage 'round for you."

✑❦

When Sir Thomas McClennon's carriage stopped in front of Mrs. Peete's house that evening, the washerwoman could hardly contain herself.

"A day to burn into me 'and, is wot it be!" Mrs. Peete exclaimed as she grinned and clapped her hands.

Ena was already in the carriage, and the two young women giggled and talked all the way to Sir Thomas's fine home on the West End.

As the carriage swayed and dipped gently, Grace marveled at the ease of the ride. "This carriage doesn't clatter and shake," she said in wonder.

"You must have been in a hackney coach!" Ena laughed.

But the real surprise came when Ena and Grace entered the parlor at Sir Thomas McClennon's estate. Instead of eight people plus Grace, the room was crammed with thirty or forty men and women who all talked at once.

"But to actually attempt to burn innocent men and women to death!" an angry man shouted. "I say that every person who took part in such a travesty should have his head and arms thrust through a pillory. Lay by a basket of rotten eggs and moldy vegetables, then we shall all have our say!"

"And a goodly lot of rotting fish as well," suggested a round woman in a bonnet who sat next to Lady Susanna. "Even that be too good for them, I'd say."

"Slime from the slaughterhouse floor too!" Rebekah Patterson called out, her fist pummeling the air. Her husband hastened to lay his hand on her arm and urged a degree of restraint.

Then a stranger took up the call and insisted, "Bricks, is wot! And don't tell me it ain't legal, neither. No better way to show the people's mind than to heave a good-sized brick to the rotter's head!"

"Better than a hanging," another reasoned.

Ethan Preston did his best to calm the crowd. Sir Thomas, always the picture of supreme calm and poise, flapped helplessly from one unruly group to another, pleading for composure and patience.

"Who do you think the informer was?" Grace asked Ena.

"I don't know," Ena replied. "I cannot believe it of any of them."

Grace looked around the room. "Jesse is not here," she said.

"No," said Ena. "He is not."

Mister Preston did not seem to be having much success at regaining order. An exasperated Sir Thomas ordered the front door bolted and summoned his male servants to help remove unruly persons. At one point it looked as though this might include young Oliver Meredith. He was embroiled in an argument with a lawyer who, after assessing the luxurious surroundings, suggested he be paid a goodly sum up front to prosecute the arson villains once they were apprehended.

"A vain, greedy pig," is the way Mister Meredith spat out his description of the barrister.

"Slander!" the lawyer shot back. "It is I who demonstrate a willingness to risk mob vengeance in order to champion a greater good. And, if I do dare say so, I perform my services most gallantly."

"And for a good, fat price," added Mister Meredith.

Grace whispered, "Do you think someone really intended to kill us, Ena?"

"I know someone did."

"How can you be so certain?" Grace asked.

Ena leaned close and whispered into Grace's ear. "I hear things whilst I work in the house of the woman who lived in Africa."

"Is she like us?"

"Oh, no!" said Ena. "She is all white. She looks like a ghost. She's young like us, but her hair is white and her eyes are the color of the summer sky."

Grace stared at Ena. "Like a ghost? What is her name?"

"Lady Witherham," Ena said.

"Her other name! What is her familiar name?"

"Charlotte. Her name is Lady Charlotte."

"Take me to her!" Grace demanded. "Now, Ena! Please! Take me to her right now!"

"What has gotten into you, girl? You don't want to go to her house. It is the home of the devil himself."

"Please, Ena. I *must* see Lady Charlotte. Now! Can we go in Sir Thomas's carriage?"

"No," said Ena. "I will not take you there tonight."

"Tomorrow?" Grace pleaded.

"Tomorrow," Ena conceded. "After the church bells chime noon, meet me at the barn and I will take you."

35

"What we have on our side is even tempers and rational thinking," Lord Reginald Witherham said. "Would that we could lead the march ourselves."

"Dear me, no!" exclaimed Augustus Jamison. "That would defeat our purpose, would it not? If the hope is to stir up the unstable emotionalism of the common populace, we must not appear to be involved in any way."

Lord Reginald cast a critical eye over the twelve dock-workers Joseph Winslow had rounded up with the promise of the hefty wage of a gold crown each. A motley crew they were. And yet, was this assortment of fellows not a sampling of the very populace he wanted to attract?

Lord Reginald pointed to the tallest man of the group and handed him a hand-painted placard tacked to a stick. The tall man turned the placard over and squinted at it.

"Cain't read," he said. "Wot do it say?"

Lord Reginald allowed an exasperated sigh to escape his lips. He pointed out each word as he read the sign:

AFRICA CURSED
TO SERVE US

"Civilized slave trade is what we demand," Lord Reginald stated. "And that shall be our rally cry."

"Is you incitin' a riot *fer* the slave trade or *agin'* it?" Joseph Winslow asked.

The vein in Lord Reginald's forehead began to throb. He clenched his jaw and forced himself to take a deep breath. "We are *not* inciting a riot at all, my good man," he said with exaggerated patience. "These lads here will simply march to the Houses of Parliament, as is their right as Englishmen. Those of a rational, like mind will pour from their houses to join them. What that unsettled segment of the population that inevitably allows itself to be whipped this way and that by every tearful story and emotional report will do, I know not. Nor is it my concern. Should they mob together and lose control—as they have done in the past—it shall simply prove once again how unprepared the people are to have the role of government thrust upon them."

The men stood blinking at one another.

Lord Reginald handed the placard to the tall man. "Hold it high, for all to see," he instructed. "For you, my good man, shall have the honor of leading the march."

"Leadin' 'em where?" the tall man asked.

"All the way to the House of Commons! Now, what do you think of that?"

"I don't know, sir," the tall man said hesitantly. "I do wants the money, but I doesn't want no trouble."

"Nonsense, my good fellow," said Lord Reginald in an uncommonly cheerful voice. "This group, under your leadership, shall form the heart and soul of a great populist march.

Right now coaches are waiting to deposit you in the heart of the city, and from there you shall head for The New Road and on across Westminster Bridge, then to Westminster Palace, waving your placards and chanting heartily. Along the way, men and women will rush to your side and join the march. Continue right on to the House of Commons. You shall have the great honor of presenting the people's petition against abolition. The crowd behind you will cheer you on."

"And when does we git the pay we was promised?" asked a stocky fellow with a too-tight jacket that made him look like a stuffed sausage.

"When the march is concluded and not one moment sooner," Lord Reginald snapped. "Furthermore, you will be paid the crown only if you do your job well. If you mind your promise to keep your silence and not say one word about the money or assistance to anyone, another crown will be coming for each of you. Your silence, I repeat, is of utmost importance. This is to be a spontaneous march."

"Yeah, spon— sponten'ous," echoed an unshaved fellow with a thick black mustache.

"This matters to you!" Lord Reginald insisted. "For should the slave trade come to an end, so shall your employment at the docks!"

"Remember, you know nothing of any of us," stressed Sir Geoffrey Philips nervously.

"Jist us," said the tall dockworker. "Sponten'ous."

"Who has the other placard?" Lord Reginald asked. "Come, come! Hold it high for all to see."

After a good bit of rustling about and mumbling amongst the men, a bushy-haired fellow answered, "Me, Frankie. I has it."

Frankie held up his sign:

> ## SLAVES, BE OBEDIENT
> ## TO YOUR MASTERS.
> ### Ephesians 6:5

"Using words copied directly out of the Bible was a good idea, Lord Reginald," Gus Jamison said.

Lord Reginald laughed. "Let us see the Quakers and that preacher John Wesley argue with that!"

"They only be a dozen of us," Frankie pointed out. "Nobody is likely to take us fer a riotin' mob."

Lord Reginald rubbed his head in exasperation. How many times must he explain the plan to these simpletons? The sooner he could be free of these fools, the happier he would be.

"Kindly listen attentively," Lord Reginald said as though he were addressing a roomful of dull children. "You will march from Covent Gardens, smart and confident, carrying the placards high. You will loudly chant slogans such as: *No More Abolition Talk!* and *Save African Souls* and *Slavery Keeps England Strong.* As you march forward, your rational passion will ignite others, and they will rush to join your ranks. Do not hurry. Wind through the streets, so as to give the people a chance to join your cause. Indeed, call out encouragement to them to do so. By the time you reach the House of Commons, you will be leading many hundreds, perhaps many thousands, of people who agree with your cause. But you will *not* be rioting. It is the *Dissenters* who will be the cause of any trouble, not you."

"Continue on with the march no matter what happens behind you," Gus Jamison interjected. "Keep walking. It is not for you to join in any fight. And it is not for you to involve yourselves in a riot."

"Certainly not if you expect your pay!" Lord Reginald warned.

Four hackney cabs stood ready to take the men to their starting point. Lord Reginald was most eager to have the scruffy lot on its way. Still, ruffians that they were, Lord Reginald figured that should hot-headed abolition-minded folk challenge them the result would certainly be a brawling mob—even a full-blown riot. But because it would begin as nothing but a peaceable march to deliver the people's petition as was their right, the blame would lie squarely with the reactionary abolitionists, not the peaceable marchers.

Good.

Perfect.

"Although you will not see us, we shall know with what passion and energy each of you performs his duties," Lord Reginald informed the men. "And you, my good man—" (here he nodded to the tall man) "you lead well and I will see that still another reward is included for you."

As the coaches rumbled away, Sir Geoffrey Philips said to no one in particular, "I must confess, the African trade is not a thing I personally like. I do have second thoughts about certain elements of it. Yet I recognize that we must have it. I have learned to make peace with the trade."

With the gleam in his eye of an extra shilling—perhaps even an extra crown—the tall man pulled the others together at Covent Gardens. Glancing about him in hopes of locating eyes of approval, he launched the march. And while the men's chants were admittedly lackluster, and their march was spectacularly weak in the areas of force and passion, still, they held their placards high and immediately attracted attention. More than a few people stopped to stare, although no one seemed inclined to rally around their cause. Certainly no one fell in with their march.

"*Save African Souls!*" the men chanted.

"*Remember the* Zong!" someone in the crowd shouted back.

Certainly everyone in the gathering crowd did remember that most infamous event. Who could forget such an atrocity, only ten years earlier? The *Zong*—a British ship at that!—out of Liverpool, sailing from Africa. With the ship overcrowded with slaves, crawling with disease, and running low on provisions, Captain Luke Collingwood faced the likelihood of arriving at the slave markets with a ship full of sick and dying captives, and a huge loss of money for his trouble. Too bad the slaves didn't all die at sea, he thought, for then his "cargo" insurance would pay the losses. It was that thought that inspired Collingwood with an idea. And with the encouragement of his first mate, he came up with a solution: the crew simply tossed one hundred twenty-two sick African slaves overboard to drown in the icy sea. Then they were free to give the remaining provisions to the healthiest slaves, and the insurers would have to pay for those lost. It was a business decision. A simple matter of profit and loss.

But that's not how the public saw it. Once the story became known, they were outraged.

"*Remember the* Zong!" The gathering crowd took up the chant. And unlike the dock men, they *did* have passion behind them.

"*Remember the* Zong!"

The twelve men looked around them, perplexed by the fury of the crowd.

"*Civilization to Africans!*" the stuffed-sausage fellow yelled out, desperate to change the tone. Eagerly the men with him picked up his chant.

But the crowd was already closing in around them, and someone called out: "*England—Land of Liberty!*" Soon this chant completely drowned out the men's words.

Frankie threw his placard down and darted into the gathering crowd in a desperate attempt to lose himself amongst the crush of people.

"Ye won't git yer pay!" the tall man shouted to him.

"Ye won't live to spend yers," Frankie yelled back.

On the far edge of the crowd, Joseph Winslow, fully sober, ran his hand through his red hair. He turned his back on what truly was turning out to be a mob scene, and he walked away. He neither cheered nor mourned—except for his empty pockets and the two gold crowns he would not be jingling this night.

36

 $\mathscr{L}$ ook a' this one!" a lanky sailor called to Tom Davis. He gestured to Cabeto, who could not get up on his feet. What with bad weather and a shortage of crew, the slaves had spent almost the entire voyage cramped in their chains below decks. Now Cabeto's bad leg simply would not support him.

Once again, the sailor applied his time-honored method of motivation—a kick in the stomach.

"Leave him be!" Tom ordered. "Carry him up on deck if you must."

It took two sailors, one on each side, to half-carry Cabeto up the ladder. And when they let go of him, he crumpled to the deck.

"'E don't look like much to me," the second sailor said.

The second sailor was right. Wan and boney, unable to stand on his own, Cabeto truly did not appear to be much of a slave.

"We kin dump 'im behind the post office with the rest of the refuse slaves," the second sailor suggested. "Then it be in God's hands, do 'e live or do 'e die."

Tom shook his head. "Get him water," he said. "And fattening food. Oil him down good and shiny, and give him tobacco to liven him up."

Tom looked at Cabeto's leg and frowned, but he also looked at the rest of Cabeto. "Get him moving, then clean him up. He's a good-looking one, and his arms are strong. Work the cramps out of his lame leg. We will get some profit out of him yet."

The sailors forced Cabeto's excruciatingly weak leg this way and that. To keep from screaming in pain, Cabeto focused his attention on the scraggly line of slaves as it emerged from the hold. Where was his brother?

By nightfall, Cabeto was able to stand on his own, and even to walk a bit—though with a pronounced limp.

"Is ye even tryin'?" growled the first sailor. "Ye better be, if'n ye wants to live to see tomorrow."

All night, sailors took turns walking Cabeto. They alternated the exercise with "fattnin' breaks" where they gave him porridge with cream and bread, and plenty of water to drink.

When the sun was up, the first sailor drenched Cabeto with buckets of cold water and went to work on him with a block of soap and a wash brush. He scrubbed Cabeto's feet, between his fingers, his hair—everywhere except his burn scar. Tom had warned against getting it fired up and angry looking. The second sailor dipped into a bucket of palm oil and rubbed it into Cabeto's parched, dry skin until he was dark and gleaming.

"I say!" Tom exclaimed when he saw the finished product. "He looks good, and he can walk too! With any luck, we will have English shillings in our pocket before his new owner realizes just how defective he is."

Tom Davis peered at an auction poster nailed to a tree. He hadn't scheduled an auction himself. With so much of his valuable cargo already gone, it just didn't seem worth it. Tom figured he would take whatever amount he could get for the stragglers, get his ship cleaned and stocked with tobacco and rice, then head for home.

"Well, now, I don't know 'bout that . . ." was Seth Slater's hesitant reaction when Tom asked if he could tack his slaves onto Seth's posted sale. "Why don't you put just him in the scramble?"

"In the scramble" meant that all the slaves up for sale were offered for the same price. At the sound of the drumbeat, buyers broke through the doors of the barricade in a mad scramble to grab out the "pick of the lot." Trouble was, Tom knew full well that his leftover slaves would never fetch full price. They would almost certainly be left sitting alone.

"It won't injure your sale to have my slaves in the auction," Tom said to Seth. "You have prime parcels there. All I have is damaged ones, and I plan to sell them cheap."

Seth walked over to Cabeto. "He looks good enough," Seth said.

"He most certainly is not good enough. Lame, he is. Won't go for much, that I know. That one is no competition for your fine offerings."

Finally Seth agreed—reluctantly. "At the end, though, after mine's all auctioned off," he said. Which meant Cabeto and Sunba and the others from the *Golden Hawk* had to watch as one by one people from tribes they recognized were paraded up on a block behind the post office at the foot of Broad Street, just a short walk from the wharf where the *Golden Hawk* was docked. White men in fancy clothes stood below and called out their bids—and their opinions of the offerings.

"Skin too light!" someone called out about a stony-faced man on the block who had just been pulled away from his screaming, sobbing wife. "Five hundred!"

"But good teeth," Seth called back as he forced the man's mouth open. "And a strong back that ain't been whipped, as you can see." Here Seth pushed the man around and jerked up his arms to display his smooth, well-oiled back. "He won't cause you no trouble. Seven fifty and he's yours!"

"Six hundred!" another man called out.

"Seven hundred!" Seth countered. "No less."

In the end, the man bought the light-skinned slave with the good teeth and strong, smooth back for six fifty, which meant absolutely nothing to Cabeto. But high price or low, only one thing was in Cabeto's mind: *Who has the right to put a price on a man's body and soul?*

The winning bidder claimed his prize by looping a rope over the light-skinned man's neck, pulling a pair of blue trousers on him, and tugging him away. The light-skinned man stood still and wailed out a cry in African words.

"Stop that!" roared his new owner. The white man jerked the rope hard, and the man fell on his good teeth. "Don't you never use heathen words again!" the white man ordered.

We will take our lives and meet in heaven! That's what the man with the light skin and good teeth had yelled. Cabeto looked over at the man's wife. She had heard it too. Immediately she stopped screaming. And though the white men saw nothing, Cabeto saw the man glance back at his wife.

"We have several children for sale, from about four years old to about twelve years old," the auctioneer called out. "Girls to work in the house and boys already in trainin' as overseers. Their mother is not for sale. Owners are keepin' her. But fear not, these people care nothing about family. They are more like animals in such matters and—"

"You!" Tom said as he pushed Cabeto with his foot. "You're next up."

Cabeto stood on the block, his head held high and proud. Before Tom Davis was halfway through his pitch, a stout man, sweating profusely in the noonday sun, called out irritably, "Come, come! What's wrong with him?"

"He is young and strong, and—"

"Yes, yes, and he has good teeth," snapped the stout man. "We can see all that. I want to know the problem. Don't play us for fools! You wouldn't be tacking on a good specimen like this at the end of the auction unless he was deficient in some important way!"

Before Tom could answer, another man up in front called out, "I see it! It be his leg. Burned, it is. Weak and lame, I have no doubt."

"Not lame," Tom protested. "You saw him walk up here. An old injury, yes. Scarred, yes. But think of the work you could get from a strong buck like this."

"Whipping scars on his back too," another man called out.

"But not too many, though," Tom replied.

"Two hundred dollars," called the stout man, "and only because I'm a gamblin' man."

"I only take British shillings," Tom said. "No South Carolina dollars."

"In that case, sir, you can take your damaged slaves back to England with you!" exclaimed the stout man.

"Twenty gallons of rum," called a man with a bushy mustache and unruly bristles of hair.

"British shillings, if you please," Tom repeated.

"We do not please," someone called back. "I bid twenty-five pounds of gunpowder."

"That, sir, is an insult!" Tom replied.

In the end, the man with the bushy mustache and unruly bristles of hair bought both Cabeto and Sunba together for ten gallons of rum and three hundred shillings—about half the expected price for one good slave. Even so, Tom Davis was pleased with the sale. He was in a hurry to clean and fumigate the ship, load it up, and sail for home.

As for the man with the bushy mustache, he already was thinking of the land he badly needed to clear. He had put the job off far too long. Problem was, felling full-grown trees and clearing snake-infested swamplands—those jobs were too dangerous for valuable slaves to take on. These two, though . . . why, they were just what he needed—strong yet expendable.

37

$\mathcal{G}$race gasped at the magnificence of Larkspur Estate. Imagine Charlotte Stevens living in such a castle! No, not Charlotte Stevens. It was Lady Charlotte Witherham who was mistress of this fine palace.

"Stop gawking," Ena scolded. She leaned out the window and yelled for the driver to take them around to the servants' entrance.

"Backdoor for the likes of you," Ena said to Grace.

"Aren't you coming with me?"

"Certainly not! And you must promise me you won't tell Lady Charlotte it was me what brought you here. She doesn't much fancy having me about, anyway, and if she was to know I involved myself in this business—and that I pulled you in with me, besides . . . well, she must not know."

After being let out at the back of the mansion, Grace watched the hackney coach rattle back down the drive, past the perfectly tended gardens and carefully manicured lawns, until it disappeared under a canopy of lacy willow fronds. Ena was gone. Now Grace was all alone. Once again.

Penny Owens, the maid, answered Grace's tentative knock. Expecting a delivery boy, she was quite taken aback to see a nicely dressed African woman, and then to have her ask for Lady Charlotte by name!

"My lady expects you then, does she?" Penny asked suspiciously.

"No," Grace admitted.

"Ye can't just walk in off the street and 'spect to visit with a grand lady," Penny scolded. The maid gave Grace a thorough once-over. "You is lucky t'was me what opened the door to you. Any other would have tossed you out on your ear. An' likely I should 'ave done the same meself."

"Please," Grace begged. "I know Charlotte—Lady Charlotte—from when we were girls together."

Penny's eyes narrowed, and she peered more closely at Grace. Her trained servant's eye immediately recognized the chapped hands of a washerwoman. "Is you thinkin' I'll believe a fine lady like her knew the likes of you?"

"Believe what you want to believe," Grace snapped. Then, quickly repenting of her tone, she pleaded, "Please, ask your mistress. If I am not telling you the truth, it is me that will be whipped out into the street, not you. But if I *am* telling the truth and you turn me away, then it will be you who is at fault. Then you will be the one to feel the punishment."

Penny stepped back to consider. She wiped her sweaty palms across her crisp white apron and heaved a worried sigh. She was not at all disposed toward making decisions that resulted in bringing blame and punishment down on herself. Certainly, she would not show Grace to the parlor. Nor even to the sitting room. But Penny did allow Grace to stand in the kitchen as she went to find Lady Charlotte.

"Someone to see you, my lady, in the kitchen . . . " Penny said with an apologetic curtsy.

"It be a mystery," Penny answered in response to questions concerning the visitor's identity, for she had neglected to ask a name. "Insists she knows you from the past, she does." Penny's anxiety mounted with every second. "Shall I have Rustin remove her, my lady?"

Lady Charlotte Stevens Witherham had spent her morning engulfed in boredom, and now a mystery stood in her kitchen. She had no intention of allowing such an opportunity to pass her by. Even if it was nothing but a clever beggar, it was worth a few minutes of her time.

"Grace Winslow!" Lady Charlotte gasped when she saw who was waiting for her. "Whatever are you doing here?" But before Grace could answer, Lady Charlotte took her by the arm and pulled her to the door. "Oh, Grace, you must go. You absolutely must not be found here!"

But Grace had no intention of going anywhere, and she told Lady Charlotte as much.

"Come out to the garden, then," Lady Charlotte insisted. "We can talk there. But hurry, now. Hurry!"

Lady Charlotte led her down a graveled path and through a garden door. Grace stared around her. This was nothing like Mama Muco's garden. It had no squash or calabash gourds growing, or any of the other vegetables she was used to seeing. It seemed to be completely made up of beautiful, sweet-smelling flower beds with narrow paths winding between them. Lady Charlotte led Grace to a small table and two chairs nestled under a stand of great flowering trees. The trees had vines climbing their trunks, and they gave off the sweetest fragrance.

"Honeysuckle and jasmine," Lady Charlotte said. "Magnificent, is it not?"

But Grace didn't want to talk about the garden. She told Charlotte everything, from the destruction of her village in

Africa and the death of her little Kwate, to the way the men packed Cabeto and the other villagers onto the slave ship. She told of her own ocean crossing on the *Willow*. And then she told of the charred remains of the coffeehouse.

"The important thing is that you are now safe in London," Lady Charlotte said. "Here, no one can make you a slave."

"But I don't want to be safe in London!" Grace cried in exasperation. "I want to find Cabeto! I want to live with my husband, free and in peace!"

"Oh, Grace, that's the problem with dreamers like you," Lady Charlotte said. "You just cannot accept the world the way it is."

"The way it is isn't the way it should be!" Grace insisted, a slashing edge to her voice.

"No, no. I do not pretend that it is. But you and I are never going to change the world."

"We cannot change everything," Grace said. "But you and I *can* change some things."

Lady Charlotte shook her head. "No, not I. You don't know Reginald. You do not know my husband."

Grace opened her mouth to protest, but before she could speak Lady Charlotte jumped to her feet. "Oh, Grace, I have a splendid idea! You no longer need to destroy your hands working in that horrible wash water. You can come here and live with me! You can be my personal maid!"

Grace stared at her in disbelief.

"Oh, I don't mean be a slave or anything like that," Charlotte said quickly. "We would be more like friends, except that you would wait on me and bring me my tea and draw my bath and such. It would be perfect! No one would suspect a thing. And Reginald couldn't complain about you being African, because he chases so outrageously after that black girl of his own."

Grace pulled her rough hand away from Lady Charlotte's silky smooth one. "I didn't come here to be your slave, Charlotte," she said. It shocked her to hear the icy tones of her mother Lingongo chilling her own voice.

"No, no, not my *slave*," Lady Charlotte insisted. "My *servant!*"

"Nor did I come here to be your servant. I came because one time, when I least expected it of you, you did a wonderful and generous thing for me. You didn't have to do it then, and you do not have to do anything for me now. But I came here because I thought you might help me again. Charlotte, I have to find Cabeto."

Lady Charlotte sighed and shook her head. "Really, Grace, will you stop pretending? Your Cabeto is gone. And although you may not believe it, you are the fortunate one—indeed, more fortunate than most women ever are! You once had the love of a man, even if it was for only a short while. Most of us never even have that."

Grace gazed around her at the palatial estate where Lady Charlotte lived in enormous privilege and great comfort, where she was called "my lady," and people bowed to her. Closing her eyes, Grace remembered again the mud hut, thatched with banana leaves she and Mama Muco had gathered together. An enormous spider had crawled out from the pile of leaves, and Mama had snatched it up with her fingers. Holding the squirming spider by the leg, she launched into a story about the trickster spirit Eshu and how he loved to wear the guise of a spider. Such a warm house it was, with Cabeto and Mama, and all of it swaddled in the baby delights of Kwate. A life swollen plump and round with love. A life filled with fresh hope for a new circle of life. Not like this palace—beautiful and majestic, but cold and lonely and angry and sad.

"Surely your husband is a powerful man. He could help me get to America." It was not a question, but a plea.

"He most certainly could," said Lady Charlotte. "But he will not. Stay away from Lord Reginald, Grace. He is a dangerous man. It is easy to underestimate him. Please, do not make that disastrous mistake."

Grace had no more to say to Lady Charlotte. They walked together out the garden gate and back to the house. But they did not go to the kitchen. Lady Charlotte led Grace to a side door that led into the sitting room.

"I would have our carriage driver take you to your place," Lady Charlotte was saying, "but I really do not think it appropriate to—"

At the sound of voices, Lady Charlotte grabbed Grace. "Reginald is home!" she said with an edge of terror. "He is coming this way!"

". . . and that fire only served to bring more sympathy their way!" Lord Reginald stated, bristling with disgust. "That right there is what I have been saying. Power must never lie in the hands of the common populace. The people simply are not capable of acting logically. This is particularly true of the lower classes. They react only to passion and emotion."

"Quick!" Lady Charlotte whispered. She grabbed Grace and pushed her into a small service room off to the side. "We can hide here!"

"Place the blame where you will, but the fact is, public outrage simply is not on our side," said Augustus Jamison.

"We can change that." This was Lord Reginald again.

"Please, my dear Lord Reginald," implored the ever-patient Sir Geoffrey Philips. "We have twice tried to do this according to your direction—and at great jeopardy to ourselves, I might add. No one ever accepted our insistence that the fire was started by an enraged populace weary of abolition rhetoric. I believe they suspected the truth from the beginning, but chose to ignore it out of respect for your family. You had hoped—we all had hoped—"

Lord Reginald interrupted, "That is not at all an accurate—"

"Please, my lord, I do you the endless courtesy of listening when you speak," Sir Geoffrey retorted rather sharply. "Will you not extend me the small courtesy of allowing me to make just this one point? As for the anticipated mob riot, it did indeed very nearly happen. The problem was that the mob, made up of those *supporting* the abolitionists, came off as the rational, clear-thinking ones. Those we hoped would gain support for our side did nothing but look to be the hired and paid fools they were. You want the people to speak? I dare say they are doing exactly that. The problem is, they are not speaking our message."

Lord Reginald's reply was low and angry. But Grace was no longer listening.

The coffeehouse fire! It was them!

38

I say, Lord Reginald, it would appear to me that this committee, as you insist on calling it, has outlived its usefulness," Quentin Gainesville said. "You are a man of action, and for that I give you credit. But perhaps the time has come to leave this matter of the slave trade to the politicians whose methods seem to be, shall we say, more refined than our own, and therefore have more hope of proving effective."

"The politicians think only of their careers," Lord Reginald retorted. "If it were left to them, our own well-being would matter not at all."

"I cannot agree with you on that account," said Augustus Jamison. "Why, the politicians *are* us! Landed gentry, businessmen, men of class—they stand to lose every bit as much as do we."

"Where is Simon Johnson today?" Mister Gainesville suddenly asked. "He should be here with us. It is he who is the best equipped to speak to Parliament on our behalf."

"He should be here, but he will not be," said Lord Reginald with an edge of bitterness. "As a matter of fact, he shall not be meeting with us again at all."

"Oh? Our position is too controversial for one who is himself vying for a position in Parliament, is that it?" Mister Gainesville offered with a short laugh. "One must stand by one's principles until one runs for the office of MP, eh?"

"So it is just the four of us, then," Augustus Jamison stated.

"No, no . . . Not at all!" said Lord Reginald. "In essence, we are a tremendous crowd, for we four represent the sensibilities of multitudes."

"Balderdash!" Mister Gainesville sputtered.

"In addition, I happen to have a special guest to introduce to you this very evening," Lord Reginald continued. He nodded to the butler beside the door and called out, "Now, Rustin."

The surprise guest was none other than a cleaned-up and filled-out Jasper Hathaway. It was not at all the spectacular beautiful-slave-on-the-arm presentation Mister Hathaway had hoped to make before his new employer, yet he determined to make the most of what might turn out to be his only opportunity.

"Your holdings in Africa are not only secure but are most profitable," Mister Hathaway assured Lord Reginald—although in a less-than-stately manner, what with the loss of all his teeth from scurvy and his discomfort with the artificial dentures he had just that day acquired.

Too humiliated to let the aggrieved matter of his bare mouth be any more widely known than absolutely necessary, Mister Hathaway had quietly consulted one Madame DeVrie, who advertised as the maker of gold snuffboxes but who had a thriving backdoor business making artificial teeth.

"A spectacular smile, Monsieur, that eez my promise to you," Madame had said. "And eet eez all made from healthy human teeth. They will fit your mouth as though they had grown een that very place."

And so, at a cost of three pounds, four shillings, Mister Hathaway now possessed a lower plate that stayed put solely by the force of gravity and an upper denture made from a curved strip of discarded teeth, which had the unnerving propensity to slip sideways and wobble up and down when he talked.

"And the slave fortress meets the humane standards required by a civilized people?" Lord Reginald inquired, looking Hathaway straight in the mouth.

"Most certainly," Mister Hathaway said with a bit of a mumble. "Zulina is a model slave-trading factory. It sets a high standard to which all others in the area strive to attain. A lovely castle-like fortress it is, hewn from massive rock, and fortified on all sides by cannons."

"Excellent," said Lord Reginald.

As Jasper Hathaway continued to extol the virtues of Zulina, his report heavily peppered with accounts of his own great management achievements— "I buy only the best goods, your lordship, and pay naught but beads and linen, iron bars, and, because I demand the prime, guns and gunpowder" —and his canny alliances— "The most respected and powerful of their own kings beg to engage in business alliances with me."

Lord Reginald, and occasionally one of the other men, murmured an approving "Well done!"

At the end of his recital, Mister Hathaway, most pleased with himself, ventured a smile. If only he could have made his entrance with the lovely Grace Winslow on his arm and all his teeth in his mouth!

"When will you be returning to Africa?" Quentin Gainesville inquired.

"As you can imagine, this has been a most arduous and distressing trip for me," Mister Hathaway said. "I must allow myself time to fully recover."

"Certainly," agreed Lord Reginald. "That is completely understandable."

"And how long do you anticipate you shall require, sir?" Mister Gainesville pressed.

Jasper Hathaway shifted uncomfortably. The fact was, he had given absolutely no thought at all to ever crossing that dreadful ocean again. Since he had recovered his health, his only thought was to regain possession of his property— meaning Grace. As a matter of fact, on his way to Witherham's Larkspur Estate it had entered his mind to request from his employer a position in London.

"Sir?" Lord Reginald was looking hard at Hathaway. He too, it seemed, was awaiting an answer.

"Why, I cannot rightly say at this precise moment," Mister Hathaway hedged. "No sooner than a year, certainly. Two perhaps. Or . . ."

Lord Reginald's eyebrows rose as he clenched his jaw.

"Yes, two," Jasper Hathaway said quickly.

"I pose the question," said Quentin Gainesville, "because from the reports coming to me it would seem that one Benjamin Stevens, who I hear runs a much smaller slaving business than yours, is renegotiating some of those same agreements to which you refer with the self-same tribal kings of which you spoke, Mister Hathaway. Therefore, I must wonder, sir, if your grip on the trade business in the area is as secure as you would have us believe."

"Stevens?" Mister Hathaway gasped incredulously.

"Mister Benjamin Stevens?" Lord Reginald Witherham echoed. He almost choked on the name of his wife's father.

In the crushing silence of the moments that followed, Jasper Hathaway sought desperately for a way to shift the talk into a different, more positive direction. He blurted—almost viciously, "Barely five years ago, Joseph Winslow all but destroyed Zulina fortress, and the entire trading business there as well. An infinite amount of work has been required on my part, as well as endless forbearance and the skills of an ambassador, to get the slave fortress to where it is once again productive. Were it not for me, Joseph Winslow—"

"Joseph Winslow . . ." Mister Gainesville interrupted thoughtfully. "Is that not the fellow who helped us with the fire matter?"

"Helped us, yes! Unless the rumors are true and he is more helpful to those who oppose us," Augustus Jamison said. But he laughed when he said it, and Mister Gainesville joined him.

Thinking perhaps that he had misjudged the situation as well as the man, Mister Hathaway ventured, "Mister Winslow is a friend of yours, then? And yet he is not here tonight, I see."

After a good deal of harrumphing and throat clearing all around, Lord Reginald said in cool, measured tones, "My good sir, Joseph Winslow is *not* one of us. We merely employ his services on the rare occasion that we require his . . . shall we say . . . unique skills."

Augustus Jamison looked over at Sir Geoffrey, who had taken a sudden and intense interest in an oil painting which hung on the far wall. It was a portrait of Lord Reginald as a young child posing with his elder sister Penelope, and although it had always hung in the same place in that room, Mister Jamison had never before had occasion to notice it.

"Joseph Winslow, yes," Mister Gainesville said to Jasper Hathaway. "So you know the man. That does explain much."

Lord Reginald slowly shook his head. "I had far greater hopes for you, Mister Hathaway," he said. "I most certainly did. For although you clearly are not one of us, I did believe you to be a gentleman. Indeed, I believed you to be a gentleman who, by virtue of the fact that he had risen above the horrors of that heathen land, would wholeheartedly dedicate himself to his unique position and strive to quiet the voices that seek to destroy our noble worldwide enterprises—by which I mean a gentleman who would promote a vigorous trade in slaves."

39

$\mathcal{D}$on't go out now! They will see you!" Lady Charlotte whispered to Grace. "Stay here in the service room until the men leave."

But Grace could not. It wasn't only what Sir Philips had said to Lord Reginald when the two men passed by Grace and Lady Charlotte's hiding place. Other men had followed the two into the sitting room, and Grace had heard far too much to quietly sneak away and pretend nothing had happened. Shaking with fury, she struggled to free herself from Lady Charlotte's clawing grip.

"Please!" Lady Charlotte pleaded. "You don't know them! You don't know Reginald!"

Grace answered, "You don't know me."

Lady Charlotte was weeping, pleading. "Stay with me tonight! Please. I can sneak you into my chambers, where you will be safe. Please, Grace. We can talk. If we work together, we can make up a good plan. I can call a coach for you tomorrow when Reginald is away. Please!"

Grace stared at the woman groveling before her. So fragile-looking was the pale white of her skin and her breezy-fine fair hair, she looked more like an angel than a ghost. Certainly she was otherworldly. Those soft hands that clutched at Grace knew nothing of washing small linens. Nothing of any type of work. When Charlotte used to visit Africa with her mother, she always took care to keep her distance from "the African," as she called Grace Winslow. Yet after the slave rebellion, when everyone else had turned away, it was Charlotte who had defied her own parents and provided food for Grace and the other starving survivors. What a strange person was this Lady Charlotte Stevens Witherham.

But then, Grace thought, *Who am I to make such a judgment? What a strange person am I!*

Grace got down on her knees beside Charlotte and put her arms around the thin, quivering body. "I never really said 'thank you,'" Grace whispered. "You already did so much for me. I have no right to ask more of you."

"You will stay with me, then?" Lady Charlotte asked.

"No. I cannot."

"But the men out there—"

Grace closed her eyes, and in her mind she saw the wise face of Mama Muco and once again heard her words.

"We cannot control what happens around us any more than we can change what happened to us," Grace said softly. "All we can do is decide how we will live our own lives. This is my life, Charlotte, and I cannot escape it by hiding or running. I did not hide from my father, and I will not run from Mister Hathaway. I will not be a slave. And I *will* find Cabeto."

Grace stood up and opened the service room door. She marched into the sitting room, leaving Lady Charlotte crumpled and whimpering alone on the floor.

The men, shocked into silence, stared at Grace in utter astonishment.

Quentin Gainesville demanded, "I say, Lord Reginald, is this another of your parlor games? Because if it is, I have no intention of playing—"

"It most assuredly is not," Lord Reginald answered. But for once, he found himself struggling for words.

"You talk and you talk and you talk, but you hear only yourselves," Grace said with a strength and clarity that would have made Lingongo proud. "I am well acquainted with English gentlemen, for I had two of them closely involved in my own life. One was my father, and the other almost my husband."

"Now, see here . . . you only . . . your father was no . . ." Mister Hathaway sputtered, but his own words seemed to choke him into silence.

"Do you know this woman?" Mister Gainesville asked Jasper Hathaway.

But Mister Hathaway, whose face had blanched white, was finally silenced.

"You sit in riches in your castle house and you talk of business and enterprise," Grace said. "But that enterprising business rips people's lives away from them. It tortures and murders and destroys. You call yourselves Christians, and the people of Africa you call heathens. But my Mama Muco taught me to pray to the God of all people. She taught me these words from His holy book, in the part called Micah: 'He hath shewed thee, O man, what is good; and what doth the Lord require of thee, but to do justly, and to love mercy, and to walk humbly with thy God?'"

"Now, see here—" Augustus Jamison protested. But Grace would not stop.

"If you are Christian men, where is your justice? Where is your mercy? And I ask you, with your pride as thick as the London air, how can you even see the pathway your God walks, let alone walk humbly along with him?"

Lord Reginald Witherham, at last regaining his wits, rose to his feet and pronounced indignantly, "How dare you break into my house and assume to lecture me on the subject of Christianity? There is not one thing a person such as you has to teach us!"

"Oh, do sit down, Reginald," Sir Geoffrey said wearily. "It does us no harm to listen for a change."

"I most certainly shall not sit down! A beggar wanders into my estate from off the street and—"

"Really, I hardly think her to be a beggar," said Mister Gainesville. "She dresses in silk, does she not?" Addressing Grace directly, Mister Gainesville asked, "Why did you come here, miss?"

"I am the only survivor of a family, slaughtered and sold," Grace said, her eyes fixed on Mister Hathaway. "I want to get to America to find my husband, who is right now being put up for sale on a slave auction block. I came to ask for your help. I came to *beg* for your help."

All eyes shifted to Jasper Hathaway. Flushed and sweating profusely, and struggling mightily to master his new teeth, he made a pitiful sight. In the end, he did not manage to utter one single coherent word.

"Will anyone help me?" Grace pleaded.

There was no compassion in Lord Reginald's eyes as he rose from his seat. But before he could speak, Lady Charlotte said, "A carriage waits for you, Grace." She had floated into the room completely unnoticed. "It is in *front* of the house. Go now!"

"Lady Charlotte!" Lord Reginald bellowed. "I shall not have you—!"

"Now, Grace!" Lady Charlotte repeated.

Lord Reginald lunged at Grace, but she sidestepped him and dashed through the sitting room doorway. Down the hall, Rustin himself held the front door open for her. Lady Charlotte ran for the doorway and positioned herself between the sitting room and the hall in such a way that her husband could not get around her without being most indelicate.

Sir Geoffrey Philips sank back onto the settee. He pulled a handkerchief from the pocket of his waistcoat and mopped his face and wiped his eyes. He opened his mouth, but then he closed it again and sadly shook his head. Sir Geoffrey was not a heartless man. But he was a man with great holdings in the indigo market. That was something he must not overlook.

"Watch out for Mister Hathaway," Grace called back. "He is a snake at your feet, Lord Reginald. You would do well to keep a stout stick in your hand!"

"Do not think you have seen the last of me," Lord Reginald roared at Grace, the vein in his forehead ready to pop and his clenched fists pounding the air. "Like as not, something will be found missing from my house. Greater ones than you have burned at the stake for thievery!"

40

"Why are you slowing down, Jonah?" Benjamin Stevens demanded of the trustee, who sat beside him driving the wagon.

"Respect for the ancestors, Master," Jonah replied. His face registered no emotion.

Ancestors! Benjamin wanted to yell. *It isn't the ancestors who desire the guns and gunpowder. It is the power-hungry living!* But he tugged the floppy-brimmed straw hat down further over his sun-scorched face and kept his peace.

In all his years in Africa, Benjamin Stevens had never before ventured out to the boundary rocks that marked the beginning of the land of this great kingdom of the Gold Coast. Never before had he had a reason to do so. With the tail of his shirt, he swiped at the sweaty dirt caked on his face. Benjamin had no idea of the proper greeting to call out to the African men who stared at him from the road . . . or even if any greeting would be considered proper.

The baskets women balanced on their heads—some partially filled, many almost empty—spoke of the end of market day. Boys darted out close to the wagon, chasing errant goats also on their way home at the end of the day. Benjamin had purposely waited until the sun sank low in the sky to journey across the blistering savanna. This was a dreadful season in Africa for a man with light skin and blond hair, and especially for fading blue eyes. Lingongo would not be pleased by the hour, but she would just have to wait.

When the wagon reached the royal enclave, Benjamin was amazed at the simplicity of the king's abode. Just a hut, it was. Larger than the other huts, to be sure, and more elaborately decorated. But the drabness of the hut itself disappointed Benjamin. He had imagined the king's palace to be a place of gold and jewels. At the very least, it should have enough wealth to make the venture worth the toll it exacted on his conscience.

Benjamin jumped down and started toward the royal hut. Immediately two men rushed out to stop him.

"The *okyeame*, Master," Jonah warned. "You must wait for him to speak your words to the king."

Oh, yes. The king's mouthpiece, Benjamin Stevens remembered. *The custom that absolutely must be followed. Was there no end to this day?*

When at last the *okyeame* considered the wait long enough to be sufficiently respectful, he stepped forward and said to Benjamin, "King Obei awaits you. I will make your words soft and beautiful, and then I will present them to him."

Benjamin Stevens bowed his head, removed his hat, and followed the *okyeame* into the sacred territory.

Always a temperate man, in no way pretentious, Benjamin Stevens was not prepared for the grip the royal hut would have on his heart. The gold chair, the ornately crafted pieces of solid gold jewelry that hung heavy from the king's neck and arms and ankles and adorned his brow, the cloth woven through with gold threads, golden candlesticks, golden statues. And Lingongo sitting beside the king, even more richly adorned than the high one himself.

It is not fair, a voice inside Benjamin Stevens screamed. *You are the master! You are the wise one! All this should be yours! Or at least a good part of it should be.*

King Obei sat on the royal chair, his feet resting on the *sika' gua* of power. Through his speaker he said, "You are pleased with our wealth; we are pleased with your strength. You keep us stronger than any other kingdom; we will make you more wealthy than any other white man on the coast."

Benjamin looked at Lingongo. "Keep them strong" meant trade only with guns and gunpowder, not bolts of cloth and beads and iron bars. More guns and gunpowder flowing in meant more death and destruction.

"A gift to seal our partnership," Lingongo said. She nodded to the speaker, and he took from her hands an elegantly carved gold tortoise. "The symbol of peace," she said.

Benjamin was amazed at the weight of the figure. Solid gold! He ran his roughened fingers along the satin-smooth edges and squinted to make out the details of the tortoise. Such expert craftsmanship! With what the Africans had to offer, he could go back to London and live out his days in comfort and luxury, and hold his head up in pride while his grandchildren played at his feet. And Henrietta, if she still lived, would never again have the unlimited right to brag about her great successes, for whose success could hope to measure up to his own?

"We will send our warriors deep into Africa, to distant villages four and five days' journey from the coast," Lingongo continued. "Villages not yet touched by slavers. They will bring back strong young men that you can sell for many more bars than the leftover men you can get in the coast villages. They will also bring back beautiful young girls who will raise up new slaves to your liking. Those in new villages will be easy to catch, because they will not yet know to run from us."

Africans catch Africans, Benjamin reasoned. So it had been forever, and so it would always be. If they were not slaves to the white man, they would be slaves to each other.

"Soon the ships will come once more," King Obei said through the speaker. "The trade has been slow for many months now, but if we work together, soon it will be fast and heavy once again."

It was the fortunate Africans who would be on those ships, Benjamin reasoned, for they would be going to a place of civilization. They would live in countries where preachers preached God's truth, where missionaries taught civilized living, where a heathen soul could be saved. How could giving up a few years' freedom on earth compare with life eternal?

"We choose to work with you because we know you to be a wise and temperate man, thoughtful and dependable," said the king. "We admire you for the way you conduct your life. Some white men are fools, but you are not one of them. We can work with you in trust and respect."

And so, with the gold tortoise grasped tightly in his hand and dreams of much more to come, Benjamin Stevens ordered Jonah to unload the guns and gunpowder from the wagon.

"To seal our deal," he said.

"To seal our deal," said King Obei.

"To seal our deal," said Lingongo.

As Benjamin Stevens headed for home in the empty wagon, sitting as always beside Jonah, who whipped up the horses to a fast trot, he clutched the gold tortoise and dreamed of what it would be like to lead a rich and powerful life. "I will remain honest," he vowed to Jonah. "Good and honest despite my wealth. And my power. And my great influence, which will undoubtedly stretch far and wide."

In the royal hut, King Obei raised his head high and refused to take his feet off the stool of power, even for a moment. "It is as I told you; I do possess magical powers and I do enjoy favor from the spirits. The ancestors smiled on me today."

"The ancestors smiled on *us*," said Lingongo.

41

$\mathcal{W}$here will you be goin', then?" Mrs. Peete asked in an uncharacteristically tender voice. She was not at all her usual brusque self. She anxiously pushed back locks of frizzy gray hair and wiped her face with her apron.

Instead of answering, Grace went straight to her room.

Mrs. Peete followed and called through the open door, "If'n it be the money that's troublin' you, dearie, you don't has to pay me no more. Keep your shillings for the boat, if that's what you be bound to do."

"I don't know how to explain myself," Grace said in a voice weighted down with weariness.

"Wot I be tellin' you is ye cain't just go trottin' about alone on the streets. Not in a criminal parish like this one. Not with cutthroats lurkin' about. Not a fine young girl like you, Grace. You cain't!"

It was not that Grace didn't understand the danger. And certainly not that she disbelieved it. It's just that she knew she had to leave Mrs. Peete's house immediately. How quickly she had fallen into a routine. And how easily she had found comfort in habit. From the first, it was up before dawn with twenty minutes for lunch, then work until late at night, seldom stopping before the church bells tolled nine times, or even ten, every day of the week. Mrs. Peete was a kindly woman, and she did not scrimp on the bread and cheese—she even threw a potato into the fire some nights, and they ate it hot with pickles and onions, or sometimes herring, and sometimes they even bought meat pies for supper. Later, when Grace wanted to go to the coffeehouse in the afternoons, Mrs. Peete had taken her shillings and permitted her to go.

But when Grace hid in the service room and listened to the men talking—as soon as she heard Mister Hathaway's crowing voice—she realized that the sharpness had gone from her resolve. It used to be that every night when she lay down she wept for Cabeto. Every night she traced out his picture in her mind so as not to forget a single detail of him. And every night she whispered anew her promise that she would find him. Every morning when she arose she told herself that day would be the day she would leave London for America.

But hidden away in the serving room, listening to the men talk about the slaves as though they were goats on a mountainside or fish in the sea, it suddenly struck her that many nights had passed since she had traced Cabeto's face in her mind. Days had gone by washing small linens and eating bread and cheese, and she had not yet plotted out a plan to get to America. If she stayed settled in any longer, Cabeto's face would fade away from her memory. Then she just might stay in London forever. She must not let that happen.

"But I asks you agin, girl, where is you goin'?" Mrs. Peete insisted. "You'll end up in some dark room in a cheap flophouse, is wot! They'll rent you a place on a rope strung across some damp room and you'll have to sleep with yer arms hung over it. In the mornin' they cuts the rope and you tumbles to the floor, and out you goes. Is that wot you wants?"

No. No, that was not what Grace wanted. In fact, it terrified her to even consider such a specter. But all the same, she had to leave.

Grace rummaged through her case and pulled out the plainest of her dresses—a blue and white linen. She stepped into the matching shoes, then fitted a straw hat with blue and white flowers on her head.

"You can have everything in my crate," Grace told Mrs. Peete. "My silk dresses, my hats and shoes, they are all yours. You may keep them or sell them as you wish. The crate is yours too."

Mrs. Peete gasped and dropped to her knees. Tenderly she lifted the yellow dress and pressed it to her cheek. "Oh, dearie, but they be fine! I never had a new dress, and all to meself too!"

Grace took the silk purse and dropped it down the front of her dress. Only ten shillings left. At least she didn't have to worry about the purse causing so noticeable a bulge.

"Goodbye, Mrs. Peete, and I do thank you for everything," Grace said.

"Wait jist a minute, now." Mrs. Peete opened the cupboard, and from behind the packet of tea leaves she drew out a small package wrapped in an old newspaper. She handed it to Grace. "I has no use for this dainty," she said. "Put it up yer sleeve. If'n ever you has call to wash it, think of me."

Grace unwrapped the package to find a linen handkerchief, trimmed with an elegantly handmade lace border. The handkerchief was decorated with embroidered flowers done in the most perfect stitches Grace had ever seen.

"Mrs. Peete, this is beautiful!" Grace exclaimed. "So many hours it must have taken to make it. Surely this cost very much money!"

"Yes," Mrs. Peete said proudly. "Surely it did. A fine lady brought it to me with her wash, but it fell out from the small linens and t'was left behind. The lady never came back to fetch it."

"But what if she should come looking for it?"

"Oh, I don't think so, dearie. That be years ago. Take it and remember yer Mrs. Peete."

Grace took the old woman's chapped and calloused hands in her own. "Are you a Christian woman?" Grace asked her.

"That I am, dearie, that I am," Mrs. Peete said. "I don't talk about it much, though. I jist tries to live it."

Grace brought the rough fingers to her lips and kissed them. She said, "Thank you for walking humbly with God."

Grace knew exactly where she wanted to go. What she didn't know was exactly how to get there. She started down Waring Street and watched for the basement where Jesse had emerged from the stairway when he took her to meet her father. She had been able to see the docks from there.

Grace knew she must get off the streets before dark, yet even the morning was hazy and looked as if dusk had already settled. Vendors calling out their wares pushed past her impatiently. Beggar children hung about, pleading for a farthing, their pitiful frames swallowed up in cast-off adult clothes. Men in black coats with tall hats pulled low over their eyes shuffled past, then turned to stare after her. Everyone seemed to be watching Grace Winslow.

Grace hastened her pace, then she stepped off onto a side street. Was this the way? Maybe so. Then again, maybe not. Two filthy boys scoured the gutters for rags. When they found one, sodden and foul, they snatched it up and stuffed it into a bag.

"Matches! Matches for sale," called a ragged woman sitting with her back flat against a massive brick building.

Grace hurried on. Just up ahead was a muddy cross street. She had followed Jesse across such a street, wading through the muddy water, just before she turned down a crowded lane. She waded into the muck of the street, then was almost knocked over by two men chasing rats.

"Watch yersef!" one hollered angrily.

No! This can't be the same muddy street, Grace realized with growing panic. *There is no lane here, just a courtyard!*

Grace was lost. Not only did she not know the way forward, she was not at all certain she could even find her way back to Mrs. Peete's house—should she wish to go back. Instinctively, her hand went to the hidden purse. She glanced around her, and to her alarm she saw that a boy with his back to a fence was watching her.

Buildings, divided and divided and divided again into ever smaller and smaller dwellings, squeezed as many people as possible into every available living space. Everywhere in the jumble of dark, narrow passageways were hiding places where criminals could lurk.

I must get out of these dark alleys, Grace told herself. *On a main street, that's where I should be . . .*

Grace retraced her steps back through the mud to the other side of the slop-filled street, past the building where the woman had been selling matches and the boys searching the gutters for rags. But neither the match woman nor the rag boys were anywhere to be seen. Nor could she find the main street again. All was a maze of streets and lanes and alleys.

Grace picked up her pace and walked more quickly.

When at last she came to a wider thoroughfare, she turned and hurried along the road, determined to follow wherever it went. Hackney coaches clattered by. Just above her, someone dumped a pan of garbage out an upstairs window. The rotten mess barely missed landing on Grace's head. When an unsavory-looking man headed her way, Grace edged between two peddlers' carts and hastened her steps. Could this be one of the lurking cutthroats Mrs. Peete warned her about?

What have I done? Grace fretted. *Oh, Cabeto, have I failed you?*

A plaintive cry pierced through the rumbling noise of the London street. Grace stopped to listen. It was the sound of a lash striking soft flesh—once, twice, three times. Grace knew that sound well enough. She had even felt the blows more than a few times. And then, the wail once again. A child's cry, she was sure of that. But from where?

A large brick building loomed on the corner up ahead. The cries seemed to be coming from there.

Grace walked to the front door and cautiously pushed it open. Inside, it was dark and oppressive. "What does ye want, then?" demanded a burly guard on a stool just inside the door.

"I heard a child crying," Grace explained.

"This be a workhouse! Many children cryin' in here," the man stated. "Their mothers and fathers be cryin' too."

"I . . . I wanted to come in and see the child," Grace said.

"No one wants to come in here. Ever'one wants out."

"But that poor child—"

"If it's poor children you cares 'bout, get you to the foundlin' hospital," the man snapped.

He tried to close the door, but Grace threw her determined weight against it.

"I don't know where the foundling hospital is."

"Fields north of Gray's Inn, of course. Now git away and let me be!" With that, the guard slammed the door.

Just up ahead, a man was helping an elderly woman out of a hackney coach. Grace hurried over and called to the driver,

"Excuse me, could you take me to the foundling hospital in the fields north of Gray's Inn?"

"Yup," said the driver.

"How much will it cost?"

"One shilling," the driver said.

Grace dropped her new handkerchief to the ground, and when she bent over to pick it up, she expertly retrieved the purse from its hiding place. She opened the purse strings and took out one shiny shilling, which she placed in the driver's hand.

"If you please," said the man who had helped the old lady down. His manner was most gracious. He took Grace's hand and kindly assisted her into the coach, then he pushed up the stairs and closed the door behind her.

How could Grace have known he was a professional pickpocket? Had she not had the opportunity to tuck her purse back into its hiding place rather than grasping it tightly in her hand, it would have been gone in an instant.

42

My point is that a barn is not an acceptable place to receive and entertain members of Parliament," Sir Thomas McClennon insisted.

"It seems to me a most appropriate place," remarked Jesse. "We are still talking about slavery, are we not? And not an English garden party?"

"Appropriate or not, a barn is what we have," said Ethan Preston. "And a most comfortable barn it is too, I dare say." Here he nodded to Rebekah and Heath Patterson. "Thank you, Mister Patterson, for your kindness, and you, gentle madam, for making it a comfortable meeting place."

"Where is Miss Grace?" Sir Thomas asked.

"She has gone," Ena said sadly. "She moved out of her rooming house. Gave all her lovely dresses to Mrs. Peete, she did."

"Did she provide any indication of where she planned to go?" Lady Susanna asked.

"To America," Ena said. "That's all she talked about."

Everything had changed. The friendly, comfortably passionate atmosphere of the upstairs room of the coffeehouse was gone. Although no one said as much, everyone was afraid to speak openly. For they all understood that one among them most assuredly was a traitor. And although Grace was not the only suspect, she was certainly the one who roused the most suspicions.

"Perhaps she already found someone who would make a deal to get her onto a ship," suggested Oliver Meredith. "If that were so, well . . . it might be an explanation for what happened."

"No!" said Ena. "I saw Grace right after that fire. I can tell you, it was a horrible thing for her!"

"I'm certain it was," Oliver Meredith said with a hint of sarcasm.

"Come, come! We shall not set about accusing Miss Grace," Mister Preston said. "She is not even here to speak up for herself."

"No, let us not accuse Miss Grace," said Mister Meredith. "Too many others among us also need to give an accounting for ourselves."

"Such as you, Ena," said Rebekah Patterson. "It's true that you have done us a great service by relaying messages through the coffeehouse, your job being conducive to that effort. It is also true that you alerted us to matters as they came to your attention at the Larkspur Estate. Yet rumor has it that you were exceedingly friendly with the master of the estate—the self-same Lord Reginald Witherham who heads the movement that seems dedicated to eliminating us in any way possible. That accomplished, it would conveniently leave the slave trade wide open, would it not?"

Lady Susanna fixed her eyes on Ena. "And you are the one who brought Grace to us," she pointed out. "Everything we know about her, we know through you."

Fire flashed in Ena's eyes. "Although my experience is not as painful as Grace's horror, I too know what it is to be born a slave, the daughter of slaves. Again and again, I risked my back for this group. Did any of you do as much?"

"We shall not continue this—" But Ethan Preston's attempt at protestations was useless. The accusations had taken on a life of their own.

"What of you, Jesse?" demanded Heath Patterson. "Kill and destroy—it is what you longed to do from the start."

"Did you hear nothing I said?" Jesse shot back with contempt. "Harm the *enemy*. Those were my words. Make *the enemy* feel the grip of pain and death. Not destroy ourselves."

"And how, pray tell, are we to know who the enemy truly is?" Mister Patterson pressed.

Jesse jumped from his seat. Seething with anger, he demanded, "Are you making an accusation against me?"

"Stop it! Stop it now!" Ethan Preston demanded. "Ena was not a traitor, nor was Jesse. Miss Grace was not either. The traitor was all of us."

In the pandemonium of "No!" and "Not I!" and "Ridiculous!" that followed, Mister Preston pleaded for calm. "If you will all listen, I will tell you the truth of our folly."

The group had begun meeting in the coffeehouse after Sir Thomas McClennon and Ethan Preston—already regular coffeehouse patrons—gravitated to each other during a few open discussions on the issue of slavery. In one another, they quickly recognized kindred spirits, each dedicated to more than mere banter over a one-penny glass of coffee.

It was through Heath Patterson that the offer came to use the hidden upper room in the coffeehouse, for the owner was a fellow member of the Society of Friends—a Quaker like the Pattersons. Mister Patterson brought along his wife, Rebekah, who in turn recommended the wealthy Lady Susanna. Oliver

Meredith was invited to join the group after his passionate arguments for the abolition of the slave trade were duly noted on several occasions. Somewhat later, Jesse Mallow made the acquaintance of Mister Preston, and, despite the ex-slave's simmering emotions and volatile ideas, he added a great deal to the group's understanding of the drawbacks of the greatly touted Sierra Leone solution to the problem of England's left-over slave population.

"Build a utopia?" Jesse had challenged. "You can gather up the black people and ship them back to Africa, but you can never pretend nothing happened to them. We are still black, but we no longer speak the tongues of the land, and we can't remember the old ways. You may call your plans for a new country a 'province of freedom,' but in truth it will be nothing more than a way to rid your land and your consciences of people who no longer serve your purpose."

As for Ena, she was a maid of mixed African-Irish heritage with a slave background who worked in the coffeehouse. It was a turn of fortune that her passions burned hot and lay with the cause of abolition. Ethan Preston and Sir Thomas recruited her to act as messenger for the group. She never gave anyone reason to question her loyalty, despite the pressure she suffered from Lord Reginald Witherham.

"When I went to get coffee on our last day before the fire, I heard you and your wife talking in the coffeehouse, Mister Patterson," Ethan began.

"It is a crime for a man to talk to his wife, then, is it?" Heath Patterson challenged.

"You asked her how one properly acts when in the presence of members of Parliament, and your wife allowed as how if you didn't know by now you had no time to learn."

"Well, that hardly gives away a country's secrets, now," Mister Patterson bristled.

"Except that not ten minutes later Oliver Meredith stood beside the coffee booth and offered to buy coffee for Lady Susanna," Mister Preston continued.

"And now you would have that be a crime as well?" asked Mister Meredith.

"Certainly not. You are indeed a gentleman, sir. And Lady Susanna responded most graciously by offering to have her carriage collect you for the 'special occasion,' as she called it. You thanked her kindly and requested that she come around one o'clock in the afternoon. All would be in place by two, you said."

As everyone eyed everyone else, Mister Preston continued: "And you, my dear Sir Thomas. One can always trust you to keep yourself to yourself. Yet this one time you stopped at the tables in the coffeehouse to urge all the men in attendance to make their voices known on the abolition matter."

"A general suggestion, I assure you," said Sir Thomas.

"But to one listening carefully, neither the timing of your prodding nor the urgency with which it was delivered would be considered general," Mister Preston replied. "Certainly not to a coffee maid sitting all day in her booth—a woman placed in that position with specific instructions to listen for anything the least bit informative, perhaps? She, of course, heard everything, being well aware of our existence since she alone heard our footfalls coming and going behind her booth. She also overheard our passionate intent when we were careless on the stairs, or when we let our voices rise too loud in the room. So it was not difficult for her to pass along pieces of conversation to others who could fit them together into a whole."

Ethan Preston looked at Jesse. "You heard all that I heard at the coffee booth, did you not? For all your talk about making the MPs pay, you rode out to warn those representatives from Parliament of possible danger. Unfortunately, your warning was intercepted, and you, Ena, when Lord Reginald Witherham asked for your help in preparing for a party at his house, gave him the entire schedule of when you would be occupied. You told me as much yourself."

"Hmph!" growled Heath Patterson. "It sounds as though you are implying that every one of us was at fault except you, Mister Preston."

"Not at all. I am more at fault than anyone. For I heard the rest of you speak, yet instead of having the wits to grasp the risks we were all taking and the damage being done, I, like you, accepted it all as normal. We are all equally to blame."

Silence filled the barn.

"My wife and I," said Heath Patterson, "will not quit the fight!"

"Hear, hear!" said Sir Thomas. "Nor will I!"

"Nor I!" agreed both Lady Susanna and Ethan Preston.

"I shall stand with the rest of you," said Oliver Meredith.

Jesse said, "And I. I will fight to the end."

"Me also," said Ena softly. "I just wish Grace was here."

"She is," Ethan Preston said. "She left us her story, did she not? And the passion that burns within her. Of us all, Grace best understood that silence is the most dangerous course. She left us her resolve to speak out loud."

"And her determination to act," said Jesse.

43

"It be for me to teach you," Job said to Cabeto. Only, Cabeto wasn't Cabeto anymore. His new master, Silas Leyland, had renamed him Caleb. "You do good, we both gets our food and our rest. You do bad, we both gets whupped and we goes hungry."

Cabeto-now-Caleb said nothing.

Job chopped at the hard-packed ground alongside Cabeto, hacking with a rusty hoe at the root of an ancient, gnarled oak tree.

"When a white man comes, keep your eyes down. Always keep your eyes down. Learn to talk their talk and obey their rules. You'll never again walk free. You'll never again see your home in Africa. That's how it be."

"Then I will die," said Cabeto.

Job shrugged. "Don't matter to me if'n you die. Don't matter to me if'n I die. My heart already be ripped away when my woman was sold away from me."

"They sold your wife?"

"Soon as our baby come, that's when they put my woman on the auction block. Don't know what become of the little one. Gone to heaven, I hopes."

Cabeto jammed the hoe into the ground. Ever since that awful day, he'd done his best to block all thoughts of little Kwate out of his mind. He could not bear the horror of that day. Yet he could not escape it, either. When he closed his eyes at night, Grace's shrieks pierced his dreams, and the sight of his child, broken and limp in Mama Muco's arms, haunted him and left him gasping for breath.

"They got yours too."

Job knew.

Months had passed since Cabeto had wept for his son, months since he had fanned the faint flame of hope that he might one day see Grace again. His arms moved in rhythm with Job's arms as they chopped together at the baked-hard ground, but inside, Cabeto was dead. All that remained was the shell called Caleb.

"Death be natural," Job said. "Not this. This not be natural even for dogs or for sick cows. It surely not be natural for human menfolks and womenfolks."

"None of this is natural," Caleb said.

"A body can lay aside his hunger," Job said in cadence to his chop, chop, chopping. "He can lay aside the forced work, so hard it breaks his back. He can lay aside the lash of the whip. But he can't never lay aside the tearin' away of the ones he loves."

Caleb slammed the hoe into the ground with such vengeance it startled Job into silence.

The day had started with the first splinters of morning light, even though no sun was yet visible in the windowless slave cabin packed with twenty or so men, women, and children. Only a few were fortunate enough to have wooden shelves on which to sleep. Caleb and Sunba—his name now was Samson—lay on the rough wood floor. Master Silas came in with the dawn, his fancy black overseer, Albo, in tow. Master Silas held up a lantern and pointed to the new slaves.

"Caleb is to dig out the old trees, and Samson is to drain the swamp," he told Albo.

With nothing all day but bread to eat and water to drink, Caleb worked until evening stars blinked in the sky.

Back at the cabin, Caleb took the bowl of stew and crust of bread the old slave woman handed him, then he slumped down in front of the cabin. Only then, in the fading light, did he see his brother sprawled on the ground over to one side, raw and bleeding. Dropping the stew, Caleb started toward him.

"Sunba!" Caleb cried. "Sunba, what happened to you!"

Immediately, what felt like fire-hot knives sliced into his back and laid Caleb flat. Albo stood over him, his lash poised for another strike. "No African names! He is *Samson*."

Caleb pulled himself up and crawled on his hands and knees to his brother. He ran his hand over his brother's raw back, but he did not speak, for he refused to call the one he knew to be Sunba by the name of Samson.

When Albo moved on, Caleb went back and picked up his half-spilled bowl of stew and brought it to his brother. Carefully he fed him a few spoonfuls. Only when Sunba shook his head that he could eat no more did Caleb sit beside him and finish the rest.

"The light will come early," a woman urged in a husky voice. "You best move on in and git yersef some sleep."

Caleb stood up and did his best to lift his brother. "Come, Sunba," he risked in a whisper.

"Sunba could keep up the work and not be lashed as a lazy man," Cabeto's brother said. "Sunba could walk by himself and help others. But I could do none of that. Do not call me his name. Sunba is no more. I am the white man's Samson."

"We will find a way to get out of here," Caleb whispered. "You and me together."

"I do not know, my brother," said Samson. "Two men in the swamp with me did not come back tonight. A snake bit one man, and he died screaming. The other sank into the mud and disappeared. I work hard, but I can only lift with one shoulder."

"When I finish digging out the old trees, I will help you," Caleb said.

"How many trees did you dig today?"

Caleb didn't answer, so Samson repeated his question: "How many trees did you dig today, my brother?"

"Not even one," Caleb admitted.

Almost before they got to sleep, morning light splintered the blackness of the night sky.

"Up! Up!" Albo called.

Caleb struggled to his feet to face another day. When he saw how Samson struggled, he helped his brother up. But Albo pushed Samson aside. "Not you," he said. "You stay in the cabin." When Caleb hesitated, Albo raised his whip. "Go!" he ordered. "You work with Job. Get that tree out before the sun sets, or you will get no supper tonight!"

When the slaves had all gone to their appointed jobs, Samson stood uncertainly in the slave cabin, alone. He could hear Master Silas outside calling to Albo, "Where is the useless one?"

"In the cabin, Master."

"Take him to the field and shoot him," Silas Leland said. "Then dig a hole and bury him."

When Albo came into the cabin, Samson tried to fight him, but Albo had the whip. "You can go easy or you can go hard," Albo said. "You looks smart to me. Go easy."

Samson struggled, but it did him no good. Albo tied his hands behind him and led him out and down the road. As they walked along—Samson bound and the gun barrel jammed into his back, and Albo, holding the gun, forcing him along—slaves paused over the cotton bolls, over the fence building, over the swamp clearing, over the garden tending, each one shedding a tear and breathing a prayer. Caleb, on the other side of the plantation, was spared the sight.

A dashing young white man riding from the other direction saw the two and pulled his horse to a stop. He brushed back the black locks of hair that fell over his forehead and called out in a tongue even stranger to Samson's ear than Master Leland's, "*Arrêt!* Where are you going with that *slav?*"

"Takin' him to the field to shoot him for my master, Master Dulcet," said Albo, taking care to keep his eyes averted from the white man.

"*Ne presser pas,*" said Monsieur Dulcet. Albo looked at the ground and shook his head uncomprehendingly. Dulcet repeated with a touch of impatience, "Do not hurry, I say." He climbed down off his horse and walked over to inspect the bound man. "*Nom?*"

"Samson, sir," Albo answered.

"Does he talk?" the Frenchman asked.

"Only just a little," Albo said. "He be fresh from the ship."

Monsieur Dulcet took in Samson's wretched condition. "*Mon Dieu!*" he exclaimed. "He is not much, is he?"

"No, Master," Albo said. He shifted uncomfortably. "My master said to shoot him and bury him in the field."

"I propose to save you the effort, and to reward you for your trouble as well," said Monsieur Dulcet. He reached up to his saddle, unbuckled a small bottle of homemade whiskey and handed it to Albo. "You take this and give me the slave. No word to your master."

Albo's face brightened. "Yes, Master Dulcet."

"Off with you, now!" said the Frenchman.

Albo took the whiskey and was off at a run.

Monsieur Pierre Dulcet looped a rope over the back of his saddle, strung it down, and tied it tightly around Samson's bound wrists. Then he mounted his horse and headed back up the road in the direction he had come. Because he prided himself in his kindness to all creatures, Pierre Dulcet kept the horse at a steady trot and would not allow it to gallop.

✒

When the stars lit the sky, Caleb waited for his brother to return from the swamp, but he did not come. As the moon rose, Caleb waited, but still Samson did not come. Only when Albo ordered Caleb inside the cabin did he find his place on the rough floor, alone.

"Sunba!" he whispered.

But this time there was not one person left to answer.

Caleb wept long into the night—for his brother, for his son, and for his Grace. Perhaps, if the ancestors could find him so far from home, he would see them all in the next life.

44

"You will scrub the floors, then?" the stiff nurse demanded of Grace.

"Floors, yes. Sheets and dishes and clothing too," Grace said. "Anything that needs scrubbing I will scrub."

The nurse noted the rough, cracked skin of Grace's hands and smiled her approval. The sure mark of an experienced workwoman. She did, however, look most disapprovingly at the fussy slippers on Grace's feet, stained and slopped with mud though they were.

"Get yourself a pair of sturdy shoes and the work is yours," she said. "You will be provided with your room and two meals each day, same as the children, and one shilling each week pay."

"I don't know where to get sturdy shoes," Grace said doubt-fully. "Or how much they cost."

"Six shillings and I will get them for you," the nurse said.

Grace gasped. "Six shillings!"

"Five shillings and your first week's pay, then."

Had she had anywhere else to go, Grace would have walked out of the Foundling Hospital on her fussy muck-splattered slippers and been gone. But she had no other place, and a safe bed and warm meal were worth more than all the shillings she had left in her silk purse.

"This institution is a hospital for the maintenance and education of deserted children—commonly called the Foundling Hospital," the nurse said. "I am Nurse Hunter."

"Pleased to make your acquaintance," Grace said.

Without bothering to respond, Nurse Hunter strode down the hallway, and Grace hurried to follow. "We give babies a name—Lamb is the most common surname, though we do try for variety—then we dispatch the babies to the country to be breastfed. They are returned to us at the age of three. Once back, we see that they are inoculated against smallpox. You will not see children with scarred faces here."

Five small girls in a line, all dressed alike in brown serge dresses with crisp, starched tops, walked past Grace.

"Our girls are well-trained," said Nurse Hunter. "From the age of six they take part in the housework. It prepares them for positions as useful servants to any what might show a willingness to employ them."

Nurse Hunter pointed out a large room with two rows of boys sitting in chairs, all reading out loud. They looked to be about nine or ten years old. Outside the window Grace saw tiny lads—dressed just like the older ones, in brown breeches and jackets, each with a cheerful touch of red on his shirt— chasing each other or tossing balls or squatting on the ground spinning tops.

Even without the sturdy shoes, Grace managed to scrub the kitchen floor, as well as the floor of the room where the children ate. She also parted with five shillings for the shoes, which meant she had only four left in her silk purse.

When her work was finally done for the night and Grace had finished her supper of homemade brown bread and a bowl of pease porridge, she stretched out on the cot in her pantry-sized room. Cold and loneliness overtook her, and she wept for Cabeto. That was when she heard the muffled cry. Not a wail like the child under the lash at the workhouse, this was a cry that sounded the way her heart felt: Broken. Discouraged. Abandoned of all hope.

As Grace lay still and listened, an unfamiliar emotion swept over her. If she felt so lost and alone, how must these little ones feel? Her baby Kwate was no more and Mama Muco was lost to her, but she still had Cabeto. It was true that an ocean separated them, and many obstacles loomed between them. But he was in America waiting for her, and she could still cling to her hope of finding him. These little ones, though, they had no one anywhere. What hope did they have?

Grace got up off her cot and tiptoed to the hallway. She stepped out and paused to listen. Ah, yes, farther down the hallway the cry came through a door that stood ajar.

Grace went down the hall, then eased the door open just enough to press herself through. She blinked as her eyes adjusted to the light. It was a large room filled with rows of small cots, each with a child under a blanket. Many of the little ones were restless, several sniffling, but one little girl, no older than five, lay on her back, wailing. Grace moved to the weeping child and gently laid her hand on the little face.

"You're burning with fever!" Grace exclaimed.

"That's Jane Lamb," said the girl in the next bed. "She's bad sick. Doctor came already, but he said he can't do nothing for her."

"There, there, little one," Grace said gently as she caressed Jane's head. "You are not alone."

Jane shook violently under the unexpected touch, and the rest of the room fell silent.

"Did you know, Jane Lamb, that there is a tender shepherd who knows the name of every one of his little lambs? He surely does. And He carries each one on his shoulders to a place of safety."

"Even me?" Jane asked in a gasping whisper.

"Yes," said Grace. "Especially you."

"Who is in here?" The door flew open wide, and Nurse Hunter stood in the doorway holding a flaming candle high. When she saw Grace bending over Jane's bed, she demanded, "What are you doing in the children's room?"

"This little one was crying," Grace explained.

"All children cry until they are taught to do otherwise. It is none of your affair. You are a cleaning maid, not a nursery maid. Return to your quarters at once."

"But Jane is sick, and I—"

"At once!" Nurse Hunter ordered.

Grace brushed her hand across the small fevered brow. "Remember the shepherd," she whispered.

The next morning, while keeping an anxious eye on the activity around her, Grace took her cleaning cloth and worked her way toward the children's room. Every time someone approached, she made a great show of wiping the handrails or dusting a picture frame or scrubbing at an invisible stain. No one paid her any mind until Nurse Hunter happened to pass by in the company of her superior, Nurse Cunningham.

"Cleaning maid!" Nurse Hunter ordered. "I instructed you to stay away from the children's room, yet here you are again."

"Please," Grace pleaded, dropping all pretense of work. "Is little Jane any better this morning?"

"I cannot see how the state of a child's health has the slightest bearing on your ability to scrub the entry hall floor!" Nurse Hunter exclaimed.

"Little Jane died last night," Nurse Cunningham said quietly. "Thank you for caring."

Grace wept through the rest of her chores. After she finished in the entry hall and moved on down the general hallway to start work on that floor, she looked up to see two solemn little girls standing in the doorway looking at her.

Grace wiped her face, sat back on her heels, and smiled at the girls.

"Hello," she said.

"Hello," said the taller girl, who looked to be about seven. "I'm not a Lamb, miss. Will the shepherd carry me too?"

"What?" Grace asked.

"The shepherd what took Jane away on his shoulders. Robert and Peter say no. They say because they also have the name Lamb that the shepherd will care for them. But not for us, because I am Hannah Rose and she is Phoebe Rose. If we're Rose and not Lamb, will the shepherd watch over us too?"

"Of course He will!" Grace said.

"Will you tell us a stowy about a wose?" Phoebe lisped.

"I would like to very much," Grace said, laughing. "Perhaps sometime I will be able to do that."

Nurse Hunter called out, "Girls! Get back to your chores, and do not distract the help!"

But Nurse Cunningham was also watching and listening. And what she saw was someone who at times might prove more useful with the children than in scrubbing and polishing floors. Any chambermaid could perform such a task, and chambermaids were cheap and plentiful. Why, half the Foundling Hospital was filled with a ready supply! But someone who could give hope to cast-off children—now, that was a rare find indeed.

Before the week was out, Grace told the children at the Foundling Hospital stories she had read in God's book, the

Holy Bible. She told them about Noah and all the amazing animals he squeezed into the great boat; of Joseph, who was betrayed by his own brothers and sold as a slave but who ended up forgiving them and saving their lives; of Moses, who made the ocean divide in half so his people could walk to the other side without getting their feet wet; of Daniel, who slept with the lions and never even got nipped. She told them about Esther, the orphan slave girl who became a queen "for such a time as this."

And then one day she told the children about Cabeto.

"But how will you find him?" Hannah Rose asked.

"I'll ask the shepherd," Grace said. "The one who saved the animals, and brought Joseph out of the well, and divided the ocean into two parts with a dry path down the middle, and closed the lions' mouths, and put an orphan slave girl on a queen's throne."

"And is taking cawe of Janie," lisped Phoebe.

"The shepherd can carry Cabeto on his shoulders until you get to him," Robert Lamb said.

Grace swallowed hard. "Yes. The shepherd will do that," she said. "Until I get there."

Discussion Questions

1. The horrendous inhumanity of the African slave trade engulfs *The Voyage of Promise*, yet we also see shadows of other types of enslavement. In what way was Charlotte "in prison"? How about Ena? What types of enslavement did Grace endure?

2. In an unimaginably desperate situation, hope survived. What do you think keeps hope alive in even the most hopeless of situations? What allowed Grace to persevere despite all she suffered? What kept Cabeto going? What was different for Tawnia?

3. It is impossible to imagine the terrified confusion that comes from being ripped away from everything familiar and being thrust into a strange and hostile world. What seemed to be the most difficult element of this cultural upheaval for Grace? For Cabeto? What do you think have been the long-term effects of this aspect of the African slave trade for our world today?

4. Some people insist that it is never appropriate to interrupt a work of fiction with nonfiction. In your opinion, did it strengthen the story to know that the italicized sections in Chapter 15 (defending and extolling the slave trade) were actual quotes from people in positions of power? Why or why not?

5. Everyone has a reason for doing what they do. What motivated Lingongo? How about Joseph Winslow? Jasper Hathaway? Jesse Mallow, the ex-slave member of the abolition group? Lord Reginald Witherham? Captain Ross? What was Grace's motivation?

6. Captain Ross told Grace: "It is not only terrible people who are capable of doing terrible things." Do you agree with this statement? Can you cite examples of when it has been proven true? The captain also said: "Not everyone acts out of malice and greed." How did

Grace demonstrate the truth of this statement? How did others: Cabeto? Captain Ross? Mrs. Peete? Mama Muco?

7. Mama Muco told Grace: "We cannot control what happens around us any more than we can change what happened in the past. All we can do is decide how we will live our own lives." Do you agree with this? How did this principle affect Grace? Were you to apply it to your life, what might it mean to you personally?

8. At the end of Book 1, *The Call of Zulina*, Ikem insisted that people can change. Twice in *The Voyage of Promise*, Grace harkens back to this statement. In what way did each of these characters change by the end of the book: Grace? Charlotte? Joseph Winslow? Cabeto? Benjamin Stevens? Did you see changes in any other characters?

9. It is always tricky to look into the past and make judgments from the comfortable wisdom of the present. But certain things never seem to change. For instance, we human beings seem to have an insatiable ability to temper the hard truth with our own self-interest. In the days of the African slave trade, this tempering extended to insisting that God was on the side of the slavers. How might this ability toward self-interest have prevented good people from seeing the slave trade for what it was? In what ways does self-interest fog our sight today and prevent us from doing the right thing?

10. Captain Ross tells Grace that "good comes from bad. From the worst comes the best." Mama Muco reminds her of the verses from Isaiah 61: "The Lord hath anointed me . . . to give unto them beauty for ashes." Have you ever experienced this in your own life? Would you be willing to share that experience? We'd love to hear from you at www.GraceInAfrica.com!

Bonus chapters from Book 3
in The Grace in Africa series

The Triumph of Grace

1

London 1793

*W*ho is it? Who is out there?" Nurse Hunter demanded. She rushed down the hall of the Foundling Hospital. "Must you knock the door completely off its hinges?"

Even in the best of times, Nurse Hunter was not a patient woman. And now, with her nerves already inundated by two weeks of unrelenting rain, the persistent pounding on the front door pushed her to the point of exasperation. Her characteristic staccato steps clicked through the halls with even more haste than usual.

Grace Winslow paid Nurse Hunter no mind. She extracted another bedsheet from the bundle young Hannah held in her outstretched arms. With an expert hand, Grace stuffed the sheet alongside the soggy heap already jammed into the corner where the dining hall floor connected to the entry hallway. Then she dropped to her knees and forced the padding firmly into place.

As Nurse Hunter tugged the water-swollen door open, Grace straightened her back. She sighed and brushed a stray auburn-tinged lock of black curls from her dark face, now glossy with sweat. "Whoever you are, do not trail mud over my freshly scrubbed floor," she murmured . . . but not loud enough for either Nurse Hunter or the newcomer to hear.

A worthy concern it was too. With the road outside an absolute torrent of muck, first one person and then the next tracked the mess inside and down the hallway faster than Grace and the girls could clean it up. Even courteous people carried the foul outside into the building. And whoever it was raising such a row at the door was obviously no courteous person.

Through the open front door, a rough voice demanded, "We's come fer Grace Winslow!"

"And just where do you fancy yourself taking our help in the middle of the day?" Nurse Hunter demanded. "The children sweat in their beds with the fever, and every corner of this building has sprung a new leak. I'd be a fool to hand our best worker over to you, wouldn't I now?"

"Takin' her to Newgate Prison, is wot," came the sharp reply. "On orders of Lord Reginald Witherham hisself."

Grace stiffened. Lord Reginald Witherham? Charlotte's husband? An entire year had passed since she had escaped that dreadful man's house! Oh, Lord Reginald had been frightfully angry with her back then. But a year ago. Surely by this time—

"And what right does this Lord Witherham have to remove our help from this charitable establishment?" Nurse Hunter insisted, her long, thin arms akimbo on her spare body.

"Grace Winslow be a thief, is wot," the irritated voice replied. "Now, kindly step aside. Elsewise, we be taking you along with her."

A thief! Grace could not believe what she had heard. She was no such thing! Charlotte would tell them as much. Yes, Lady Charlotte, Lord Reginald's wife. She knew everything that had happened in that house. The entire time Grace was there, Charlotte had never been away from her side.

A tall, burly man in a shabby greatcoat pushed past Nurse Hunter and forced his way into the entry hall. Right behind him was a short man with bushy eyebrows and an overgrown mustache.

"Hannah!" Nurse Hunter ordered. "Run and find Nurse Cunningham and bid her come immediately. Hurry, now!"

The child dropped the bedsheets. She looked uncertainly from Nurse Hunter to Grace to little Phoebe, whose arms were still piled high with folded cloth.

"Go!" Nurse Hunter commanded.

As Hannah bolted down the center hall, the burly man spied Grace. "That be her!" he called. Both men lunged for her.

"Wun, Gwace!" Phoebe screamed. "Wun away fast!"

But before Grace could get her wits about her, the men were upon her. The tall, burly man held her firmly in his grasp, and the bushy-faced one bound her wrists with a rope.

"It is all a mistake!" Grace protested. "I never stole anything!"

Without bothering to respond, the men shoved her toward the door. Phoebe shrieked and Nurse Hunter scolded, but the men paid no mind. They hustled Grace out into the rain, then over toward a waiting carriage with doors that bore the gold leaf letters **WL** — the unmistakable monogram of Witherham Larkspur, Lord Reginald's estate.

"Here, now!" Nurse Cunningham panted as she ran up after Hannah. "What is the meaning of this?" When she saw

Grace in the grip of the two ruffians, she ordered, "Loosen our servant this instant! I insist!"

Nurse Cunningham might as well have been speaking to the trees.

"We are a charitable house for orphans, sirs!" she exclaimed. "Have you no concern for the welfare of poor children?"

The burly man shoved Grace through the open carriage door and hefted himself in beside her. The bushy-faced man scurried up after them and settled himself across from Grace and the large man, then he yanked the door shut. Not one word was spoken. Not one word was needed. The driver whipped the horse. The carriage jerked forward and rattled onto the cobblestone street.

Grace tugged herself around in time to see the two women and a clutch of children staring after her. Wide-eyed, they huddled together in the driving rain.

"I am no thief," Grace said.

"Save it fer the magistrate," the burly man told her. "It's him wot will hear yer plea."

Grace started to object, but the bushy-faced man glared hard at her and growled through his mustache in such a terrifying way that she closed her mouth and sank back in miserable silence.

A year of schemes and plans. A year of saving every shilling of her pay from the Foundling Hospital. Months of gathering bits and pieces of men's clothes.

"When may I go back to the Foundling Hospital?" Grace ventured.

The burly man barked a sharp guffaw. "The Foundling Hospital, is it, then? Be there a graveyard out back? One with a poor hole, perchance? 'Tis the only way you will be seein' the likes of that place again."

"Should've said yer good-bye's afore the door closed on this carriage," said the small man with the bushy face. His deep, growly voice unnerved Grace. "You won't be seeing them children again. Not in this life."

Grace shivered in her drenched dress and sank further into the seat. Each clomp, clomp, clomp of the horse's hooves was like a hammer driving a spike of despair deeper into her heart. Why now, after all this time? Surely, with his powerful con-nections, Lord Reginald Witherham could have found her at any time during the year she had worked at the Foundling Hospital. Why now, just when everything was almost ready?

For the past year, at the end of every long day, Grace took off her only dress, laid it over the single chair in her room, and slipped into the loose cotton garment Nurse Hunter gave her for sleep. Then she lay on her cot and did the same thing every night: regardless of how weary she might be, she would not allow her eyes to close until she had first traced Cabeto's face in her mind. She recalled its every curve— the laughing tilt of his mouth, the broad shape of his nose, the spark of assurance in his eyes. With Cabeto firmly fixed in her mind, Grace whispered again the promise she had called out to him on that awful day in Africa: "*I will see you again. I promise!*"

Cabeto, in chains. Cabeto, forced onto the slave ship. Cabeto, the slave. Oh, but Cabeto, in America waiting for her!

Unless . . . unless she couldn't get to him in time. One year, Captain Ross had told her. Maybe two. That's how long it would be before Cabeto's master would likely work him to death.

One year, maybe two.

"Don't you worry yerself about Newgate Prison," the burly man taunted. "Lord Witherham, he be in such a state, I guar'ntee that you won't be there fer long."

Mistakes happen. Grace understood that. Misunderstandings occur. If she were in her village in Africa, she and her accuser would simply sit down under the baobab tree—the spirit tree—with the wise old man in the village and they would all talk together. The wisdom of the ancestors would rise from the spirit tree and fill the mind of the old man, and he would guide the disagreeing sides to a place of understanding. In Africa, the two would walk away in harmony. But this was not Africa. It was London, where no baobab trees grew. Even if a spirit tree did exist in London, it would be lost among the crush of tall buildings and chimneys that clogged the city and church spires that reached to the sky. Nor could the wisdom of the ancestors hope to pierce the unyielding shroud of thick, smoky fog that held London in its relentless grasp.

"Lady Charlotte—I must speak to her!" Grace said.

The burly man burst out laughing. "You? And what would the likes o' you say to so fine a lady?"

"I know her, you see, and—"

"If you knows anything at all, you knows to shut yer mouth while you still can."

"Exceptin' to beg fer mercy," interrupted the man with the bushy face. "Surely you knows that. Elsewise you be about to gift all London with the pleasure of watchin' you dance at the end of a hangman's rope."

2

The charge?" asked Magistrate Francis Warren.

Attired in a long black robe and with a white powdered wig on his head, the magistrate looked frighteningly official, even though he sat at his own desk in the parlor of his own home and rubbed his hands warm before the fire of his own hearth.

"What charge do you bring against this woman, Lord Reginald?"

Magistrate Warren peered over the wire-rimmed spectacles perched on the bridge of his nose and squinted with filmy eyes at Lord Reginald Witherham, who sat stiffly on the opposite side of the fireplace. With great show, Lord Reginald set aside the teacup he so expertly balanced on his knee. Then he rose to his full, unimposing height and bowed low to the magistrate. Lord Reginald artfully posed himself to one side of the opulent marble mantel—head high, left hand behind his back for a touch of elegance, right hand left free for gesturing. For an entire year, he had bided his time. After so great a display of discipline, this moment was far too sweet to allow to it to pass without indulgence.

Slowly, deliberately, Lord Reginald turned his attention to Grace Winslow. Miserable, wet, and shivering, she stood some distance from the fire, flanked by the same two men who had brought her from the Foundling Hospital.

"Your Lordship," Lord Reginald began with a most dramatic flair, "this African woman who stands before you—" here he paused to look at her with disgusted pity—". . . is naught but a wanton thief!"

"I see."

The magistrate heaved a wearied sigh.

Grace caught her breath.

An air of victory settled over Lord Reginald's pale face. He lifted his narrow jaw and fixed Grace in as searing a glare as his soft features could manage.

"Sir," Grace said, but not to Lord Reginald. She searched the magistrate's craggy face for understanding. "Are you the wisest man of this town? Are you the one who hears disagreements and leads your people to a way of healing?"

"Your Lordship!" Lord Reginald interrupted with a great show of indignation. "I really must protest this display of insolence!"

Ignoring Lord Reginald's incensed huffs, and allowing the trace of a smile to push at the corners of his mouth, Magistrate Warren answered Grace.

"I should be most pleased to think of myself in such lofty terms," he said. "But, to my great misfortune, I fear that such a calling is not mine. You stand before me today for one purpose alone: to make it possible for me to determine the quality of the case brought against you. With that single intention in mind, I am required by my office to insist that you remain silent as I hear Lord Reginald Witherham state his charges against you. Afterwards, I shall determine whether or not you shall be bound over for trial."

With a sigh of impatience, Lord Reginald abandoned his carefully orchestrated pose and stepped up to the magistrate.

"I took pity on the wretch," he informed Lord Warren. "That was my downfall, Your Lordship. Out of naught but kindness, I allowed her to enter my house, and she repaid my benevolence with blatant thievery. She took my goodwill as an opportunity to remove from my estate as many items as she could secret under her skirts. Of that I have not the least doubt."

Grace gasped in disbelief. She had been inside Lord Witherham's house, that much was true. But she was only there one time, and then she had never been left alone. No, not for one minute.

"Sir, that is not true!" Grace protested. "I never—"

"Madam, you have no right to speak," the magistrate cautioned. His voice was kind, yet firm. "This is an official hearing."

"If you just ask Lady Charlotte, she could tell you—"

"Hold your peace, madame! If you do not, I shall have no choice but to have you removed forthwith straight to Newgate Prison!"

Lord Reginald allowed himself the indulgence of a satisfied smile. Yes, yes, all was proceeding precisely as he had planned. Justice wrought would surely be worth the year's wait.

"Your Lordship," Lord Reginald continued. "I ask permission to submit for your excellent consideration one particular piece of evidence."

Here Lord Reginald reached into his pocket and pulled out a fine linen handkerchief, sewn with the daintiest of hands and most delicately trimmed in an elegant lace border.

Grace cried out in spite of herself.

"Surely you see the quality of this piece of finery," Lord Reginald continued unabated. "Embroidered flowers throughout, all done in the most perfect of stitches. This piece is easily worth six shillings. Perhaps as much as eight."

"Missus Peete gave me that handkerchief!" Grace cried. "Where did you get it?"

"Silence!" Magistrate Warren ordered.

"It was in my room, sir! I kept it always under the pillow on my cot!" Grace insisted.

"I shall not repeat my injunction," insisted Magistrate Warren. The kindly creases in his face hardened into angry resolve.

"The handkerchief was indeed retrieved from the cell where the accused has lived for the past year," said Lord Reginald, "but not under the cot pillow where she lays her head at night. No, no. It was hidden away behind a loose stone in the wall." Lord Reginald paused dramatically. "I ask Your Lordship, does that not provide ample proof that Grace Winslow is nothing but a common thief? That she is only using the Foundling Hospital as a convenient place to hide herself, cloaked in the guise of a nurse caring for homeless children?"

Magistrate Warren ran his hand over his face and heaved a weary sigh. "A six-shilling handkerchief, then. Have you evidence of further thievery, Lord Reginald?"

"Even such a one as she is not fool enough to keep stolen goods lying about," Lord Reginald answered. "Undoubtedly she visits the rag fair regularly and offers for sale whatever she has pilfered. This particular piece, however, she evidently determined to keep for herself." Here he held the handkerchief high, as though it were a great trophy. "Perhaps such a dainty allows her to believe that she truly is a lady . . . and not merely an escaped slave."

"None of that is true!" Grace cried in exasperation.

"Silence!" ordered the magistrate.

"And I am not a slave!"

Merely an indictment to decide whether or not the evidence was sufficient to try the case before a trial jury; that was all Magistrate Francis Warren was called upon to render. It was not his place to pass judgment, and certainly not to set a penalty for the accused. A blessing, that.

"Have you any witnesses to call, Lord Reginald?"

"No, Your Lordship," replied Lord Reginald with a deep bow. "Taking into consideration the obvious circumstances of this case, I did not deem it necessary to inconvenience such witnesses."

Since Magistrate Warren would not permit Grace to speak in her defense, he most certainly did not extend her a like invitation to call witnesses.

"I am certain you will find that I have set before you a case most worthy of trial," Lord Reginald continued.

Magistrate Warren knew perfectly well what he had before him: a black woman—a mere cleaning maid—one of a multitude of her kind in London. She faced a charge brought by an exceedingly wealthy lord, an aristocratic gentleman of great power and influence. A servant of foreign extraction could disappear into the depths of Newgate Prison—or worse—and never be missed. On the other hand, Lord Reginald Witherham had it in his power to do much to propel a cooperative magistrate forward politically, or he could wield equal influence to destroy an uncooperative one. Magistrate Francis Warren could ill afford to subject himself to such a risk. And, really, why should he? There was, after all, that expensive handkerchief to consider. What further evidence did he require?

Magistrate Warren pounded his gavel down on his desk and pronounced, "Grace Winslow, I commit you to Newgate Prison to await trial on the charge of thievery."

Forgetting himself, Lord Reginald Witherham actually allowed a whoop to escape his thin lips. He looked triumphantly at Grace and repeated his words of a year earlier: "*You have not seen the last of me*." Then he added, "Is it not as I told you, Grace Winslow? If you thought you could hide from me, you were indeed the greatest of fools!"

Magistrate Warren's shoulders slumped. He swiped at the sweat that glistened in the crevices of his weary face.

Grace looked neither at the uneasy magistrate nor at the gloating Lord Reginald. She shut her eyes tight and desperately tried to trace Cabeto's face in her mind. His mouth . . . his eyes . . . his brow . . . But this time she could not.

After all Grace had endured, after all she had survived, it had finally happened—Cabeto had slipped away from her.

Do you have questions or comments?
Would you like to learn more about author
Kay Marshall Strom?

Visit her at her website www.kaystrom.com
and on www.GraceInAfrica.com

You are also welcome to join in the discussions on her blog:
http://kaystrom.wordpress.com

Abingdon Press has many great fiction books and authors
you are sure to enjoy.

Sign up for their fiction newsletter at
www.AbingdonPress.com
You will see what's new on the horizon, and much more—
interviews with authors, tips for starting a reading group,
ways to connect with other fiction readers . . .
even the opportunity to comment on this book!

What they're saying about...

Gone to Green, by Judy Christie
"...Refreshingly realistic religious fiction, this novel is unafraid to address the injustices of sexism, racism, and corruption as well as the spiritual devastation that often accompanies the loss of loved ones. Yet these darker narrative tones beautifully highlight the novel's message of friendship, community, and God's reassuring and transformative love." —*Publishers Weekly* **starred review**

The Call of Zulina, by Kay Marshall Strom
"This compelling drama will challenge readers to remember slavery's brutal history, and its heroic characters will inspire them. Highly recommended."
—*Library Journal* starred review

Surrender the Wind, by Rita Gerlach
"I am purely a romance reader, and yet you hooked me in with a war scene, of all things! I would have never believed it. You set the mood beautifully and have a clean, strong, lyrical way with words. You have done your research well enough to transport me back to the war-torn period of colonial times."
—Julie Lessman, author of *The Daughters of Boston* series

One Imperfect Christmas, by Myra Johnson
"Debut novelist Myra Johnson ushers us into the Christmas season with a fresh and exciting story that will give you a chuckle and a special warmth."
—DiAnn Mills, author of *Awaken My Heart* and *Breach of Trust*

The Prayers of Agnes Sparrow, by Joyce Magnin
"Beware of *The Prayers of Agnes Sparrow*. Just when you have become fully enchanted by its marvelous quirky zaniness, you will suddenly be taken to your knees by its poignant truth-telling about what it means to be divinely human. I'm convinced that 'on our knees' is exactly where Joyce Magnin planned for us to land all along." —Nancy Rue, co-author of *Healing Waters* (*Sullivan Crisp* Series)
          2009 Novel of the Year

The Fence My Father Built, by Linda S. Clare
"...Linda Clare reminds us with her writing that is wise, funny, and heartbreaking, that what matters most in life are the people we love and the One who gave them to us."—Gina Ochsner, Dark Horse Literary, winner of the Oregon Book Award
          and the Flannery O'Connor Award for Short Fiction

eye of the god, by Ariel Allison
"Filled with action on three continents, *eye of the god* is a riveting fast-paced thriller, but it is Abby—who, in spite of another letdown by a man, remains filled with hope—who makes Ariel Allison's tale a super read."—Harriet Klausner

www.AbingdonPress.com/fiction

What Others Are Saying About the Grace in Africa Series

"I've been a fan of Kay Marshall Strom's work since reading *Once Blind*, her novelization of John Newton's life from slave trader to abolitionist. Regardless of whether you read Strom's works of fiction or nonfiction, her heart for freedom, justice, and the respect of persons from all nations shines through. In the Grace in Africa series, Strom transports us to Africa in the late 1700s. The blending of diverse African cultures lends authenticity and additional depth to this series, which is passionately written and keeps high interest from start to finish!"
—*Jennifer Bogart, blogger and fiction reviewer*

"I always love it when a writer can step out of the norm and surprise and engage me, and Kay Strom did that. I'm looking forward to reading the next books in the series."
—*Tredessa C. Rhoade, fiction reviewer*

"Few books call so poignantly to that deep place within us as those in the Grace in Africa series by Kay Marshall Strom. Even as the Scriptures tell us that "deep calls to deep," so do the convicting words of this epic tale call to the God-given conscience within us, that part of us that is stamped with the very image of God and that forbids us to love with anything less than our very lives. From the moment we first meet the lovely but naive Grace Winslow to the instant when we see the noble and selfless image of God rise up from deep within her, we find ourselves challenged to that same depth of commitment. This is more than an entertaining story, though it is that; it is also a call to arms, a challenge to "fight the good

fight" without compromise or lukewarm faith. Grace in Africa is a call to believers everywhere to remember that there is no greater love than to lay down our life for our friends and, if need be, our enemies as well."
—*Kathi Macias, bestselling author*

"Strom writes so graciously and passionately that one feels informed and edified by the message of redemption that weaves throughout the storyline as her characters show us hope in the midst of hopelessness—and virtue that can rise above evil."
—*Jeannette Morris, blogger and fiction reviewer*

"Strom perfectly renders the utter hopelessness of the slaves in Africa. There is no way out and no place to go if they could escape. There's an unflinching depiction of slavery and the characters' fight for hope. I can't wait to read the next book in this series!"
—*Christy Lockstein, fiction reviewer*

SISTERS IN SERVICE

New Life for Abused and Exploited Women and Girls

Sisters In Service, a Christian not-for-profit established in 2002, works to restore the lives of abused and exploited girls and women in high-risk places around the globe, equipping them to live in freedom and faith for a strong future.

The SIS Strategy: Identify and Strengthen Best Practice Local Initiatives

Overseas SIS intervenes through practical grassroots programs of rescue, education, economic empowerment and spiritual life from West Africa across the Middle East and throughout Asia.

We strengthen local projects that utilize holistic interventions to strengthen women and girls to combat the risks and ravages of abuse and exploitation. We create long-term "sister" relationships with the best implementers we can find to make God's love known in practical ways to those in abject poverty.

Share Research, Raise Awareness, Equip Advocates

We research injustices that women and girls face and best practice solutions, set measurable, agreed upon goals, provide learning exchanges for implementers, evaluate, report on, resource and foster programs for maximum effectiveness.

In the U.S., through our Advocacy Program, we compile research, publish and organize to educate people about the hard-hitting issues least reached women and girls face: child marriage, malnutrition, illiteracy, sexual abuse, and exploitation. SIS's advocacy program trains and deploys volunteers as passionate spokespersons and intercessors for our best practice interventions.

The latest summary evaluation of our labors shows that in one year 37,000 individual women and girls were given the good news of God's love along with practical help for an area of suffering: rescue and restoration from sex slavery, training in health and nutrition, literacy, discipleship, vocational and leadership training.

Could it be that God is calling *you* to be part of His story to restore and redeem abused and exploited girls and women now and forever?

Please contact us at info@SistersInService.org
11095 Houze Rd., Suite 200 • Roswell, GA 30076
Toll-free (877)552-1402